Knot Guilty

Knot Guilty

BETTY HECHTMAN

BERKLEY PRIME CRIME, NEW YORK

THE BERKLEY PUBLISHING GROUP
Published by the Penguin Group
Penguin Group (USA) LLC
375 Hudson Street, New York, New York 10014

USA • Canada • UK • Ireland • Australia • New Zealand • India • South Africa • China

penguin.com

A Penguin Random House Company

KNOT GUILTY

This book is an original publication of The Berkley Publishing Group.

Berkley Prime Crime Books are published by The Berkley Publishing Group.
BERKLEY® PRIME CRIME and the PRIME CRIME logo are trademarks of
Penguin Group (USA) LLC.

Berkley Prime Crime hardcover ISBN: 978-0-425-25297-0

An application to register this book for cataloging has been submitted
to the Library of Congress.

FIRST EDITION: November 2014

PRINTED IN THE UNITED STATES OF AMERICA

10 9 8 7 6 5 4 3 2 1

Cover illustration by Cathy Gendron.
Cover design by Rita Frangie.
Interior text design by Kristin del Rosario.

Acknowledgments

Thanks to my editor, Sandy Harding, for once again suggesting just the right changes. Molly would have never lived if it hadn't been for my agent, Jessica Faust.

Amy Shelton of Crochetville.com shared her booth with me at Stitches Midwest. It gave me a whole other view of a yarn show. I loved Amy's crocheted crown. It's something Adele would definitely appreciate. Thanks to Delma Myers for all her help with the Knit and Crochet Show. Thanks to Stacy of Bee-Lighted Fiber and Gifts for sharing her booth at the Vogue Knitting Live Show and showing me the knitting needles made out of shovel handles. Gwen Blakley Kinsler gave me a new perspective on the yarn world and the inside information on why crochet is the underdog.

A special thank-you to Linda Hopkins for her gracious help with the patterns. I don't know what I would do without her eagle eyes.

The Thursday Knit and Crochet Group of Rene Biedermann, Alice Chiredjian, Terry Cohen, Tricia Culkin, Clara Feeney, Sonia Flaum, Lily Gillis, Winnie Hineson, Linda Hopkins, Debbie Kratofil, Elayne Moschin, Paula Tesler, and Blanche Tutt offer warm friendship and lots of yarn info.

Roberta Martia has been a supporter and cheerleader since the first book. It's been a long time since my days at Roosevelt, but I'd like to thank Professor Dominic Martia for all that I learned from him. Though our group dispersed years ago, I am still grateful to Jan Gonder for her comma aid. And my family, Burl, Max, and Samantha, are essential recipe tasters. If they don't give me a thumbs-up, it's back to the drawing board.

Knot Guilty

CHAPTER 1

YOU KNOW THAT SAYING ABOUT BEING CAREFUL what you wish for? My name is Molly Pink, and I can tell you it's one hundred percent true. Ever since my husband, Charlie, died, I've been saying that I want to try flying solo. To live without having to answer to anyone. You know, I could wear sweatpants with a hole in them and eat ice cream for dinner. I'd be the captain of my own ship.

I thought I was headed right to that lifestyle. I'd gotten past my grief and had started a new chapter in my life by getting the job at Shedd & Royal Books and More as the event coordinator/community relations person. But then I met Barry Greenberg and we had a relationship. Okay, maybe he was my boyfriend. It's hard for me to say that word, even in my mind. It just sounds so ridiculous since Barry is a homicide detective in his fifties.

You might notice I said *had* a relationship. Really it was

off and on again and off again and on again. You get the picture. But now it was finally off forever.

Let me offer a little catch-up on that. During all the off and on again of our relationship, there had been the complication of my friendship with Mason Fields. Mason had always wanted it to be something more, but I had wanted it to stay the same.

Then, when Barry and I had yet another hiccup, we decided we would be better off as friends. Barry had seemed to accept it, but then he showed up and said he was walking away from the whole situation. He said the friendship thing was all a sham and I was the only one who didn't know it. Then he suggested I go out with Mason because I deserved better than what he, Barry, could offer.

It reminded me of the whole King Solomon story when two women were fighting over a baby and the king offered to cut it in half. One of the women stepped forward, relinquishing her claim rather than seeing the baby injured. The king knew that meant she loved the baby more and gave it to her. So, it seemed Barry was saying he cared more because he was so concerned with my happiness. But that didn't mean I was ready to resume our relationship.

I had never told Mason about Barry's gallant act. Actually, I had barely talked to Mason after that. It was all on my part and I'm not even sure why. He left messages and I didn't return them. Then the holidays hit and I got lost in work. Mason stopped trying to contact me. I can only imagine what he thought. In the end, I had let my social life go dark.

Assorted people had been staying with me for various reasons, but that had all ended as well.

The final step came when my son Samuel moved out— well, in—with his girlfriend. Though he didn't take his cats.

And suddenly there I was alone. At least almost alone. I had the two cats and two dogs: my terrier mix, Blondie, and Cosmo, a little black dog that was supposed to be Barry and his son's dog, but that's another story. So here at last was my chance to soar on my own wings. Do whatever I wanted. Answer to no one.

At first I was so busy with the holidays and everything at the bookstore, I didn't think much about being on my own. But it was January now, and as I once again looked around my cavernous living room, it all began to get to me. I made a tour of the three bedrooms on the other side of the house from mine. Only the one I used to keep all my yarn and crochet stuff in showed any signs of life. The other two were uncomfortably neat. My footsteps echoed as I walked into the kitchen. It was just as I'd left it when I went to bed. Just like yesterday and a lot of yesterdays before, there were no dishes in the sink, no ravaged refrigerator. No one had come knocking at my door in the middle of the night looking for comfort after a bad night with suspects. No one had called and suggested a fun outing. All the peace started to overwhelm me.

I made coffee for myself quickly. Did I want to sit around and revel in all this quiet and independence? No. I couldn't wait to get to work and the problems, the confusion, and most of all the people. I'd heard the statement that silence is deafening, and now I understood it. I needed some noise. I needed some upheaval in my life. Yes, I had learned my lesson about being careful what I wished for. I'd gotten it in spades and absolutely hated it. I knew what I had to do to stir up the pot of my life.

I didn't even drink the coffee in my kitchen. I filled a commuter cup and made sure the dry cat food bowl was full and located where the dogs couldn't help themselves. And I left.

It took a bit of doing to zip up my jacket while holding the coffee mug as I crossed the backyard. Even here in Southern California, January days are short and chilly. I probably seemed like a wimp for bringing it up when it was icy and snowy back east, but the dew had frozen on the grass.

The sun had already melted the thin layer of frost on the greenmobile, as I called my vintage blue green Mercedes. *Vintage* sounded so much better than *old*. I ran the windshield wipers for a moment, and they got rid of the residue of moisture. One negative about my car: no cup holder, which meant I had to hold the commuter mug between my legs. I looked down at my usual khaki slacks and hoped I'd make it to work without any coffee stains.

A few minutes later, I pulled the car into the parking lot behind Shedd & Royal Books and More. Once I was inside, I inhaled deeply, noting the familiar fragrance of the paper in thousands of books, mixed with freshly brewed coffee coming in from the café, and nodded a greeting at Rayaad, our chief cashier.

The last of the holiday merchandise was gathered on a front table with a sale sign. Even after all these years it still seemed odd how the same merchandise looked so exciting before the holiday and irrelevant after. I mean, a chocolate Santa was still, at the heart, chocolate.

Any day we'd start putting up Valentine's Day decorations and sell the same type of chocolate the Santa was made out of shaped like hearts wrapped in red foil.

As I made my way through the store, I saw the playwrights' group gathered in a tight circle around their facilitator. The yarn department was in the back corner of the store, and along with handling events and community relations, it was my baby. I always liked walking in and seeing the feast of color from the cubbies of yarn. Ever since we'd put up a permanent worktable in the middle of the area, it was never empty.

I recognized a few faces of my fellow Hookers. That's hookers as in crochet. The Tarzana Hookers had been meeting at the bookstore since even before the yarn department had been added.

We exchanged a flurry of greetings just as Dinah Lyons caught up with me. She's my best friend, a fellow Hooker and an English instructor at the local community college. She slipped off her loden green boiled wool jacket and dropped it on a chair.

"I need to talk to you," I said as we hugged each other. "I've decided to change my life." Dinah's eyes snapped to attention as she got ready to listen. Then my voice dropped. "It'll have to wait." Mrs. Shedd had just joined us. She was the "Shedd" in Shedd & Royal and my boss. This wasn't a usual gathering of the crochet group to work on projects. This was a meeting.

"Give me an update," Mrs. Shedd said quickly. She never seemed to change. Her blond hair didn't have a hint of gray even though she was well into her sixties. She'd been wearing a soft pageboy style for so long, I bet her hair naturally fell into place when she washed it.

She didn't sit and seemed a little nervous, but that seemed to be her default emotion lately. Keeping a bookstore afloat these days wasn't easy. We were surviving, but only by broadening our horizons. Thanks to my efforts, the bookstore had become almost a community center. Besides the playwright group, I'd added other writing and book groups. We'd recently taken on hosting crochet-themed parties, which was turning into a nice success. And, of course, we had author events.

But what we were attempting this time was really a stretch and required an outlay of cash. "Tell me again why we're doing this," my boss said, looking for reassurance.

Adele Abrams joined us as Mrs. Shedd was speaking. Adele was still dressed in her outfit from story time. Just guessing, but I bet she'd read *Good Morning, June*. It was a children's classic written in a different time when girls wore pinafores like the pink one Adele wore over a puffy-sleeved dress. She'd completed the look by forcing her brown hair into tiny little braids. Adele would have stood out even without the outfit. She was tallish and amply built, and her voice naturally went toward loud.

Before I could say anything, Adele began. "This is the chance of a lifetime. We are carrying the torch of crochet into the world of knitters." Mrs. Shedd didn't look impressed. Who could blame her? She wasn't interested in us being pioneers as much as doing something that would make a profit and help the bookstore. I was relieved when CeeCee Collins slipped into the chair at the head of the table and took the floor away from Adele.

"I feel responsible for encouraging you to have the booth at the yarn show. I'm sure it's going to be a big success," CeeCee said to my boss.

CeeCee was the real head of our crochet group, though Adele never quite accepted it. She was also a well-known actress who, after a long history of TV and film appearances, had started a whole new chapter in her career when she began hosting a reality show. Then she nabbed the part of Ophelia in the movie based on the super-hit series of books about a vampire who crocheted. We'd been hearing there was Oscar buzz about her performance since the movie had come out, but rumor is different from fact, and the actual Oscar nominations were going to be announced in the next couple of weeks. Needless to say, CeeCee was a little edgy.

As always, CeeCee was dressed to be photographed. She said she'd seen enough celebrities snapped in jeans and T-shirts with their hair sticking up to learn her lesson. But, she claimed it was a fine art, not to look too done. Kind of like her reality show. It was supposed to look real, but a lot of editing and planning went into what the audience ended up seeing.

CeeCee noticed the two women at the other end of the table who were not part of the group. They appeared to have no idea what was going on. CeeCee, in her typical gracious manner, explained that we were talking about the bookstore's upcoming booth at the Southern California Knit Style Show.

"This is a very big deal because it's the first year they're including crochet in the show. Before, everything was just about knitting. You know, knitting classes, fashion shows of knitted garments, design competitions for knitted pieces. There probably wasn't even a lonely crochet hook for sale in any of the vendors' booths in the marketplace."

CeeCee made a slight bow with her head. "I'd like to think I had something to do with K.D.'s change of heart." She explained to the women that K.D. Kirby put on the show along with being the publisher of a number of knitting magazines. "I was the only crocheter included in an article in *Knit Style* magazine about celebrity yarn crafters. I think hearing about how popular the craft is and seeing what wonderful things you can make made her realize what a mistake it was not to bring crochet into the show."

The women nodded their heads in unison to show they

were listening, though I noticed knitting needles sticking out of their tote bags. "So, this year there is going to be a crochet category in the design competition with yours truly as the judge." CeeCee did another little nodding bow before adding that she was also going to be acting as the celebrity face of the show.

One of the women finally spoke. "So you mean you can do more with crochet than just make edging on something or use up scraps of yarn to make one of those afghans full of squares?"

Adele was squirming in her seat at their words. All of the Hookers thought that crochet was the more interesting yarn craft, but Adele took it even further. She thought crochet was superior to knitting, and she wasn't afraid to say it.

CeeCee put her hand on Adele's shoulder. It looked like it was just for reassurance, but I knew it was to hold her in her seat. "Why yes, crochet has become quite a fashion statement. Designers have taken intricate lace patterns that had been used to make doilies and are blowing them out into shrugs." CeeCee had taken her hand off Adele's shoulder, and my bookstore coworker took the opportunity to pop out of her chair and start talking.

"I'm going to be teaching one of the crochet classes," Adele said, doing an imitation of CeeCee's bow. "A stash buster wrap." The women didn't seem to know what to make of Adele's statement and looked back to CeeCee for some kind of reassurance.

CeeCee dropped her voice and spoke directly to Adele. "We need to talk about that."

Since the booth was sort of my baby, I jumped in and told Mrs. Shedd how we'd come up with a plan to bring shoppers to our booth. "We're going to teach people how to make a little granny square pin with some beads for decoration." I was glad I had brought a sample and showed it to my boss and the women.

"That's wonderful," one of them said. "I bet a lot of people will want to make one of those."

It was like music to Mrs. Shedd's ears, and she looked a little less tense. "Bob wants to have us offer some of his treats," I added. Bob was the barista at the bookstore café. He also made fresh baked goods. "The wonderful smell alone would act like a magnet."

Mr. Royal arrived carrying a piece of poster board with a miniature version of the booth he'd constructed. He laid it on the table in front of us all, as more of our group arrived. We all leaned over and admired it. The two newcomers got up and walked to the head of the table to get a better view.

"It's wonderful," I said. It looked like a little store. There was even a sign across the front announcing the name of the bookstore in big letters. "There's just one thing missing," Adele said as she scribbled something on a piece of paper and tore off a strip. She attached it to the bookstore sign. It said: "Crochet Spoken Here."

Mrs. Shedd seemed a little less worried when she saw the name of the bookstore prominently displayed. "A lot of the people coming to this show are local. We want to make them aware of us. Perhaps you can add something that mentions all the groups we have meeting here."

I reassured Mrs. Shedd that with the Hookers helping we'd make sure the bookstore was well presented.

"I'm depending on you two," Mrs. Shedd said, referring to me and Adele, but looking squarely at me. We were the bookstore employees, and no matter what help the others offered, the buck stopped with us, or actually, me.

I'd been hired as the event coordinator and community

relations person, and Adele had been given the kids' department as sort of a consolation prize, since she thought
my job should have been hers. But somehow with one thing
and another we'd ended up working as a team, putting on
the crochet parties and now this booth. Adele balked at
being left out of running the yarn department, but she'd
cooked her own goose with her strong feelings about knitters. She didn't even think we should have knitted swatches
of the yarn we sold.

Yes, I knew how to knit. The basics, anyway. All those
knitted swatches had been done by me. There was no way
we could have a yarn department and shut out knitters,
even if some yarn stores weren't so happy with crocheters.

"No problem," I said with a smile. "We've got it covered."
Mrs. Shedd muttered something about hoping so, because
if this booth turned out to be a disaster she wasn't sure
what she would do. Then my boss left the area, saying there
were things she had to take care of.

"I didn't get a chance to tell her about the kits I'm going
to sell," Elise Belmont said. She'd extracted one from her bag
and put it on the table. "If Mrs. Shedd had seen these, she
wouldn't have been so worried. We're going a sell a million of
them." Then Elise caught herself. "Or at least the whole
stock. Do you want to see all the different kinds?" she asked.

Elise was a small woman with wispy brown hair. She
seemed a little vague until you knew her, and then it was
obvious she had a steel core even if she did look like a good
gust of wind could carry her off. The group shook their
heads at her offer. We didn't need to see the kits; we knew
what they were.

I sometimes wondered what Elise's husband, Logan Belmont, must have thought about her love affair with Anthony,

the crocheting vampire. She'd read all the books, had seen the movie made from the first one countless times, and had even convinced CeeCee to get the film's star to sign a life-size cutout. What did Logan Belmont think of having a full-size figure of Hugh Jackman staring at them as they slept?

The kit on the table was the first one she'd made for her vampire scarf. It had black-and-white stripes with a red tassel, or what she called traditional vampire colors. Get it? The white was for their pale, colorless skin, the black for their clothing choice, and the red—I'm guessing you can figure that one out. Her stitch of choice was the half double crochet, which she insisted looked like a fang.

Rhoda Klein rolled her eyes. She was a matter-of-fact sort of person with short brown hair and sensible clothes who couldn't understand an imaginary affair with a literary bloodsucker. "I think Mrs. Shedd would be more interested in the free crochet lessons we're going to offer."

"Did I miss something?" Eduardo Linnares said as he joined us at the table. He was holding a garment bag and laid it on the chair next to him. "I brought what you asked for," he said. Dinah suggested he show it to us. Eduardo had been a cover model until recently. He'd been on countless covers of romance novels dressed as pirates, wealthy tycoons, cowboys and assorted other hero types. The one thing all the pictures had in common was that his shirt always seemed to be unbuttoned down the front. When he started being cast as the pirate's father and pushed into the background on the cover, he'd decided it was time to move on, and he'd bought an upscale drugstore in Encino. We were asking him to go back to the old days for the weekend.

He opened the garment bag and laid a pair of leather pants and a billowing white shirt on the table. We figured dressed in that outfit, he'd attract a lot of people—well, women—to our booth.

"Anything to help out," he said. Like all of the Hookers, he was grateful to the bookstore for giving us a place to meet. He'd been a lonely crocheter until he'd found us. The plan was that he would teach his specialty. It was hard to believe, with his big hands, but he was a master with a small steel hook and thread. He'd learned Irish crochet, which was really lace, from his grandmother on his mother's side.

Sheila Altman came in at the end. When she realized she'd missed everything, her brows immediately knit together and she started to go into panic mode. Somebody yelled to get her a hook and some yarn. Sheila was actually much better at managing her anxiety than she had been, but she still had relapses, and nothing calmed her better or faster than some crocheting. Adele made a length of chain stitches before handing it to Sheila, who immediately began to make single crochets across. She didn't even look at the stitches or care that they were uneven; the point was just to do them and take some deep breaths. After a few minutes she sank into a chair. "That's what I'm going to teach at the booth," she said with a relieved sigh. "How to relax."

We talked over our plan of action for a few minutes. Who was going to be in the booth when and what they were going to be doing. Sheila put down the crochet hook and took out a zippered plastic bag with a supply of yarn in greens, blues and lavender. "I thought I could sell kits, too, if it's all right." She showed off one of the kits, which included directions for a scarf.

Sheila was known for making shawls, blankets and scarves using combinations of those colors. Her pieces came out looking like Impressionist paintings. I told her it was fine, and it was agreed that the kits would be sold only when the two women were there to oversee them.

With everything settled, we all started working on our projects. The two new women asked if it was okay if they stayed, and we all agreed. Adele sucked in her breath when they took out knitting needles and began to cast on stitches with the yarn they'd just bought.

"Calm down," I said to her. "None of us like the way knitters treat us like we're the stepsisters of yarn craft. But we'd be just as bad if we treated knitters the same way."

Adele started to protest but finally gave in and went back to working on a scarf made out of squares with different motifs.

Dinah moved closer to me. "You said there was something you wanted to talk about?"

I was hoping for a more private situation. Not that I had secrets from the rest of the group. One of the beauties about our group was that we shared our lives with each other. Good, bad, happy and sad. Still, I wasn't quite ready to share my decision with all of them. Not until I saw how it worked out.

Before I could say this wasn't the best place to talk, CeeCee interrupted. "We need to talk now." She looked around and saw that Mrs. Shedd had gotten all the way to the front of the store. CeeCee moved in closer, making it clear what she was about to say was just between us and probably some sort of problem. "When K.D. decided to bring crochet into the show, she asked my advice about who might teach classes, and I suggested Adele. All the knitting classes are taught by elite knitters who have written pattern books and traveled around doing workshops. She called them the knitterati." CeeCee turned toward Adele. "She's now found some master knitters who know how to crochet, and, to get to the point, K.D. has her doubts about having you teaching a class. And to be honest, there haven't been a lot of people signing up to take the class."

I watched the whole group suck in their breath and prepare for Adele's reaction. As predicted, Adele seemed shocked and huffed and puffed that she was more qualified to teach the class than all the famous yarn people. CeeCee put up her hand to stop Adele. "The point is, K.D. would like you to give her a personal demonstration." Before Adele could object, CeeCee added that it wasn't a request, it was a command, and that K.D. would just get someone else to teach the class otherwise.

Adele absorbed the information and begrudgingly said she would do it. There was no way I was going to let Adele meet K.D. alone. Who knew what she would do? Adele actually seemed relieved when I suggested accompanying her.

"I'm going, too," CeeCee said. "My reputation is at stake since I'm the crochet liaison for the show." She looked from Adele to me. "Did I mention she's expecting Adele tomorrow morning?"

Adele began to sputter about having to audition and the fact that she hadn't been consulted about the meeting time, but CeeCee made it clear she had no choice, and we agreed to meet at the bookstore and go together. I was grateful there were a few minutes of peaceful yarn work before the group broke up.

As I got up from the table, Dinah linked arms with me. "Now we can talk."

CHAPTER 2

DINAH AND I TOOK OUR CONVERSATION INTO THE café. It was cozy with the scent of freshly brewed coffee mixed with the buttery sweetness of freshly baked cookie bars. Most of the tables were full, but we found one by the window that was far enough from the others to afford some privacy.

There was a slight delay in placing our order while the barista, Bob, talked to me about what he was going to make for the yarn show. He offered several alternatives, and I finally left it up to his judgment. His lips lifted into a satisfied smile that made the dot of beard below more prominent. I know it was called a soul patch, but to me it looked like a mistake in shaving.

"I'll pick up the treats on the way," I said, and he assured me they would be packed up and ready to go.

Once we had our drinks—For me, a red eye and for Dinah,

a café au lait—we settled in and Dinah looked me in the eye. "Well?"

Actually, this was the first time we'd had to really talk in a while. We'd both been busy, and we'd either been on the run or there'd been other people around.

Before the holidays, Dinah had been giving her students their final exams and grading their final projects. Her ex's kids with his latest ex had come for the holidays. I knew it sounded crazy, but she'd gotten attached to the kids, and since neither of their parents were doing much of a job at being parents, the kids adored her. And then there was Dinah's relationship with Commander Blaine. She was so used to guys who turned out to be jerks that she kept waiting for him to start acting like one. Only recently had she finally accepted that he was the nice guy he appeared to be.

After the holidays, she'd begun a new term and was teaching an additional class. It had gotten so that we'd only seen each other at the Hooker meet-ups at the bookstore, and those had been less frequent because of the holidays, too. Dinah had no idea of the turn my life had taken.

Before I told her my solution, I had to explain the problem. "My personal life has become flat, dull, quiet and boring. With everything going on with the bookstore, I didn't notice at first. Do you know that we now have even more adult writers' groups, a junior writers' group, reading groups and even a cookbook lovers' group. Then there are the crochet parties that we've been putting on almost every weekend, and finally the kids' crochet group. I was so busy putting all those things together, and putting in all the extra time at the bookstore during the holidays, that it wasn't until Samuel moved out that I noticed I was living the life I'd claimed I wanted."

"Samuel moved out?" Dinah seemed surprised. "Molly,

you should have called me," she said. "I could have easily added some noise to your life."

I quickly explained that Samuel had moved in with his girlfriend about a month ago. "It doesn't matter now. Maybe it's even a good thing because I have realized what I want, and more important, what I don't want. All that stuff about wanting to try flying solo turned out to be nonsense. More than the commotion, I miss being with someone. When Barry and Mason were both around vying to be the man in my life, I took it for granted."

Dinah leaned in closer, her eyes bright. "I sense that you're going to do something," she said.

"I've thought it over, and I definitely want a man in my life. What's more, I know who now. I've decided to be pro-active," I said. "Of course, there is always the possibility that I'm too late."

"Who is it? Who are you choosing?" Dinah asked, ignoring her drink. She knew that Barry had stepped away saying I'd be better off with Mason. Barry's reasons for stepping back had been that his job was more than a job to him and that he'd always be off chasing leads and could never promise any kind of normal lifestyle. It had really touched my heart when he said that I deserved more than that. Barry's lifestyle had been hard for me to deal with, but I also knew he needed me, and there was that chemistry between us.

"No matter what Barry said, I'm sure he'd forget it all if you called him and said you wanted to work something out," Dinah said.

I shook my head. "No. I think Barry is right, that I would be happier with Mason," I said.

Dinah's eyes widened and she said, "Wow."

"Mason is a great guy. How many times has he come

through for me? I know he'd be there for a whole meal, not running out after the salad saying he had to track down a suspect. And he's fun to be with. There aren't always issues and he's never let me down. We're both looking for the same no-strings kind of relationship," I said. "Or we were."

"Then he doesn't know that he won the Molly lottery yet?" Dinah said.

"It's been months since I talked to him. Who knows where his head is—or his heart." All my self-assurance drained out and I slumped. "What was I thinking?"

Dinah saw me wavering. "Just do it. Don't think. Call him now." Dinah pushed my cell phone toward me.

I picked up my BlackBerry reluctantly. "Okay, I'll do it, but I'm calling his office. That way he'll know it's me." I didn't add that he could act accordingly, which meant he could choose to not take my call. I felt my heart thud a few times as I hit the call button and heard the phone begin to ring.

The receptionist answered with the law firm name. Mason was a partner, and I felt my breath catch when she got to his name in the title. I was really doing this.

When she finished, I asked to speak to Mason and she put me on hold. I was trying to think of something clever to say to Mason when she came back on the line.

"I'm sorry, Mrs. Pink, Mr. Fields is out of town." Then she offered to connect me to his voice mail. I mumbled a no and hung up.

I told Dinah the gist of the call. "Is he really out of town or is that just a polite way of saying he doesn't want to talk to me?" I said. Dinah tried to reassure me, but I was sure she knew it could have been a brush-off. Mason was definitely a catch and probably had met someone else. Someone with more sense than I had who would grab him up.

Dinah had to get to class and I had to get back to work. I put my phone away and headed back into the bookstore.

"Pink," Adele called out in a stage whisper as I went past the entrance to the children's area. She waved to me to come, while looking around the bookstore in a furtive manner. I had gotten so used to her calling me by my last name I didn't even notice anymore.

"What's up?" I asked, grateful to have my mind taken away from the call to Mason.

"You can't tell Mrs. Shedd that K.D. Kirby is making me audition. Please," she said with a worried look. "This is so embarrassing. It's just another incident of knitters trying to put us crocheters in a corner."

I didn't agree that was the motivation. It made perfect sense that K.D. might have doubts about Adele's teaching abilities. There were only a few crochet classes offered, and the other ones were all taught by people K.D. knew. The only thing Adele had going for her was CeeCee's recommendation.

I assured Adele I wouldn't tell our boss and said that I'd make up an excuse why we had to meet with the woman putting on the show.

After that, I spent the rest of my workday doing my regular work, like straightening up the yarn department and dealing with some hurt feelings in the poetry group. As had become my habit, I didn't leave the bookstore until we closed.

I appreciated the greeting I got from Cosmo and the cats when I got home. The three of them were the welcoming committee waiting by the door. Blondie was asleep in her chair in my room and as usual had to be coaxed to go outside.

Everything was almost as I'd left it, except Cosmo had knocked over the trash and spread it all around. I cleaned it up and considered dinner. Now that I could have ice cream for dinner without anyone looking askance, I didn't want it. Instead I pulled out one of the dinners for one I'd made up. I had taken to cooking a big pot of something and then dividing it into neat little portions that could be heated quickly. At the last minute I changed my mind and made some steamed broccoli, mashed a potato and microwaved a vegetarian sausage I'd gotten to like when Mason's daughter was staying with me. She was a vegetarian and had introduced me to a bunch of new foods.

I even set up a place in the dining room. But eating alone didn't take long, and there was no reason to linger at the table. I cleaned up and grabbed a crochet project. I had a whole array of half-done projects that I cycled through. This time I picked the tote bag I was making out of red cotton with navy blue accents.

I had my smartphone sitting next to me, and my eye kept going back to it as I thought over my call to Mason's office. It might have been true that he was out of town. It was stupid of me not to leave a message. If he really was out of town, he might have called when he got his messages. This way I'd never know for sure.

I fiddled with the BlackBerry until the list of contacts came on the screen. I had the opposite of a magic touch with the cell phone. It turned itself to silent, never told me I had messages and screens appeared on it when I wasn't even touching it. This time when the contact list showed up, it went right to Mason's name all by itself.

His cell number was staring me in the face. Was this some kind of sign?

In a moment of bravado, I hit the little green receiver icon and the phone began to dial. There was still time to hit the red icon, but instead I let it ring.

After about the fourth ring, I started expecting his voice mail. This time I would leave a message. Though nothing that would show my cards. I was thinking of something benign to say when I heard his voice come on. It took a moment for me to realize it wasn't a canned recording asking me to leave a message, but a sleepy-sounding voice, a live voice.

"Mason?" I said tentatively.

"In the flesh," he joked. I heard him suck in his breath. "Am I dreaming or is that really you, Molly?"

I said something about being sorry—that it seemed I'd awakened him. "Where are you?" I asked, realizing the receptionist might have been telling the truth.

"East Coast," he said. After a pause he continued, "It's 2 A.M. here." But when I apologized again, he shrugged it off. "What's up?"

It was the moment of truth. My opportunity to be proactive had arrived, and suddenly I had cold feet. There were a few moments of dead air, and he actually asked if I was still there. Then the Mason I knew and loved kicked in, and he realized I had something to say that was difficult.

"I'm guessing you have something on your mind," he began. "You're having a hard time with it, aren't you, Sunshine?"

I mumbled a yes and wanted to kick myself for being so wishy-washy. Just say it, I told myself, and then it came out in a stream. "Mason, I realize I was wrong about what I thought I wanted and I'm sorry that I didn't return your calls but now I know that I want to have a relationship with you."

All I heard was breathing, and my heart sank. A multitude of thoughts went through my head. He wasn't alone. He was trying to think of a nice way to turn me down. He'd fallen back asleep during my run-on sentence. But then I heard him chuckle. "Whew," he said finally. "I thought you were going to tell me you and the detective got married."

Mason didn't know what Barry had said when he stepped out of the picture, so I told him. Mason chuckled again. "He gave you the noble speech. Most women would have melted for that." I didn't want to tell Mason that I had thought about it. Didn't the "noble speech," as Mason called it, mean that Barry really loved me more? He was more concerned with my happiness than his own.

But this was about what I wanted, and that was Mason.

"So?" I said, finally. "What do you think about what I said?"

"Hallelujah, you finally saw the light." It seemed like it was taking a moment for it all to sink in. "I wish I were home. I'd come over and we could toast the beginning of us."

He started figuring when he'd be back in town. "I'm going to be tied up with a client when I get back," he said. He gave no details about who, and I didn't ask, knowing he couldn't say. The whole lawyer privilege thing. I knew it was probably somebody I'd heard of. Mason's specialty was dealing with celebrities who had gotten into trouble. They required a lot of care along with his legal expertise.

"It's just as well. I am going to be tied up with work all weekend."

He was wide awake now and sounding very happy. "We've waited this long, what's a few more days. We can work something out."

All the tension had left my body, and I felt myself smiling. "Yes, we can," I said. Neither of us wanted to get off the phone, but finally I said he ought to get some sleep, and he agreed.

"Love you," he said just before he clicked off.

He was already gone before I could react.

CHAPTER 3

I WAS STILL SMILING ABOUT THE PHONE CALL THE next morning. I kept thinking about what it would be like spending time with Mason again, this time as a couple. It might have been a bit teenagerish, but I was kind of floating a little above ground. However, I had to force my feet back to earth. There was too much going on for me to be wandering around in a romantic fog.

When I walked outside and felt the cold morning, it was the slap of reality that I needed. I was glad I had a warm jacket on, but the chilly air went right through my cotton khaki work pants. The thermometer in my car confirmed that it was cold. Forty-four degrees. There was still even a thin coating of frost on the windshield of the greenmobile. Not that it was going to last. Already the rays of sunlight were working on turning the ice into droplets of water.

The ride was so short, the heat had barely started to

warm the interior of the car by the time I pulled into the parking lot of Shedd & Royal. CeeCee pulled her electric car next to mine, and we were both getting out at the same time. She looked at her royal blue car, clucking her tongue.

"Being green gets tiresome. Sometimes I wish I had my gas-guzzling Caddie back." She sighed. "But can you imagine the flak I'd get. We celebs are supposed to be an example and all. If we drive electric cars, other people will want to emulate us and give up their inefficient cars, blah, blah, blah." CeeCee looked down at her deep brown fur jacket. "This fake fur looks almost too good. I hope none of those animal rights people start harassing me. I feel like I need to wear a sign that says it's not real."

While we stood there talking, Adele zoomed into the parking lot in her gray Matrix. She flounced out of the car and over to us. "You two don't have to go with. I can handle K.D. Kirby all on my own."

CeeCee and I said, "No," in unison, and Adele rocked her head at what she considered a waste of our time.

"If you insist," she said. "Let's get going." She looked at my vintage car and CeeCee's little electric number. "I'm driving."

Adele led the way back to her car. She had dressed for the occasion. She was wearing an example of her stash buster wrap. She'd focused on yarn in shades of red with just enough deep blue to throw in some contrast. The wrap wasn't really warm enough for the cold morning, but Adele wasn't about to hide it under a coat. Underneath she wore slacks and a top in a bluish shade of lavender, which made the color of the wrap pop even more.

She hadn't spared the makeup, either. Adele had the habit of going to extremes. When her boyfriend suggested she tone things down when she met his mother, she went so far, his mother thought she was too dull for him. And then when she had another chance to try to impress Mother Humphries, as she called Eric's mother, she went too far the other way, wearing clothes that were too bright and turning the drama up to a fever pitch.

Was it any surprise that Adele was a wild driver? I heard CeeCee letting out gasps from the backseat as she reached over the passenger seat grabbing my shoulder. Adele took one of the canyon roads through the mountains. She zoomed past Sunset Boulevard, through the residential streets of Beverly Hills and onto Wilshire Boulevard. I think we both let out a sigh of relief when we turned off Wilshire and into the parking lot for the Knit Style head-quarters. It was one of the classic old buildings along the major thoroughfare. Just two stories tall, it was white stucco and had been built in the days when time was spent adding decorative details to the facade.

We walked around to the front, and I looked through the large ground-floor windows into a yarn store. CeeCee saw me instinctively heading for the door.

"The Knit Style Yarn Studio is part of K.D.'s empire, but we're meeting her upstairs in her office," CeeCee said, taking my arm and steering me to a glass door that had "Knit Style Publishing" written in gold paint. Inside there was a small alcove with a bunch of plants and a door to an elevator. Ahead of us a marble staircase led to the second floor. Was there really a red carpet going up the center of the stairs? Yarn studio, red carpet, I thought, shaking my head. Maybe just a little pretentious.

This was going to be the first time I met K.D. Kirby in person. All the dealing for the booth had been done by phone and email with her staff. We followed the red carpet up the stairs and ended up in a reception area.

"Let me handle this," CeeCee said, turning to Adele and me, but mostly to Adele. I got it. Her reputation was at stake. I had the feeling she was sorry she'd suggested we have a booth at the show and that Adele teach one of the classes. CeeCee pulled ahead and approached the receptionist, who seemed to know her. It made sense. CeeCee had been there for the photo shoot to go along with the magazine article.

I glanced at the framed covers of the knitting magazines that graced the white walls. It was fun to see how the style of the magazine and the style of the knitted garments featured in it had changed over the years.

A man came into the reception area and looked over the three of us. He recognized CeeCee and greeted her with a hug and an air kiss, before turning to us.

"Delvin Whittingham, I work with K.D.," he said in a clipped tone. "And you must be Molly Pink." He held out his hand for me to shake it. He let go and moved on to Adele.

"Adele Abrams, crochet expert," she said, putting out her hand before he had a chance to offer his. I tried not to stare at him, though it wasn't his self-important expression that got my attention. It was his clothes. His outfit was the kind of thing that could look totally stupid or very hip, depending on the style at the time. He reminded me of a mismatched puzzle with all kinds of pieces that really didn't belong together. The skinny jeans gathered at his ankles, spotlighting the red pointy shoes. On top, he wore a black T-shirt, layered with an unbuttoned white dress shirt and a red brocade vest over that. He accessorized with a knitted tie done in some kind of variegated yarn that made it looked striped and a gray fedora-style hat. Oh, and there seemed to be a lot of chains going between his belt and pants pocket.

"K.D. is expecting you," he said, taking us down a corridor to the knitting mogul's office. It took up a corner with lots of windows that looked out into the foliage of elegantly trimmed trees. The furniture was all beautifully refinished antiques, including the large desk that K.D. Kirby was sitting behind. I'd seen a photo of K.D. before, but seeing her in person was quite different. Let's just say the photo had perfect lighting and some nice Photoshop touches to remove imperfections. Not that the magazine head looked bad. She just looked real. She was one of those people whose hair turned grayish white early, and instead of making her appear old, because of the texture and abundance, it made her stand out.

I guessed she was somewhere in her fifties, but who could tell anymore. Maybe it was true that fifty was the new thirty. Her features had the look of someone who knew who she was and was used to being in charge. I couldn't put my finger on what exactly it was. Maybe the almost defiant set of her mouth. Of course, she was stylishly attired. It wasn't so much the clothes, exactly, but how she wore them. K.D. seemed to use the basic black dress as a backdrop to show off the lacy mohair shawl in shades of yellows and gold tied at just the right angle around her shoulders.

We'd barely gotten past introductions when Adele began to model her wrap. She did a few turns and then let it slip from her shoulders and flung it on K.D.'s antique desk. I noticed K.D.'s eyebrows go up, but other than that she didn't respond.

"Why don't you sit down." She indicated the two chairs in front of the desk, just as another chair was brought in. "Delvin, show her where to put it," K.D. said with a dismissive wave.

When the three of us were seated, she began. "I'm very hands-on with my magazines, the yarn studio and this show. We are the most elite of the yarn shows, and people come from all over the world to take our classes." She looked directly at Adele. "We charge a lot for our classes, and our teachers are all world-class. When I decided to add some crochet classes and CeeCee suggested you as a teacher, I thought she understood our criteria." She looked even more directly at Adele. "The point is, I ran a Google search on you and nothing came up."

I suddenly got it. She was asking Adele for her pedigree. "Most of our teachers have published numerous pattern books, have design credits and have done workshops at shows and retreats. What about you?"

Adele squirmed in her seat and mumbled she was more into practical aspects of crochet. "Well, then do you have some kind of certificate showing that you are a master teacher?" K.D. pressed. Adele looked to us for help.

CeeCee stepped in and tried to smooth things over, explaining that Adele's passion for crochet was going to make her class memorable.

Delvin had remained standing. He picked up the wrap and looked it over. "It looks pretty simple. Why not just let her give us a demonstration of her teaching method," he said. K.D. reluctantly nodded, and he turned to Adele. "What Ms. Kirby would really like to see is a snippet of how you plan to conduct the class."

I thought it interesting that while he was trying to give

the appearance that he and K.D. were equals, when he was in her presence he called her by her last name. She was the power.

"No problem," Adele said, reaching into the tote bag she'd brought along. She took out several small balls of yarn in shades of red and an unusual crochet hook, which got K.D.'s attention right away.

"Let me look at that hook. Where did it come from?" she said, holding out her hand.

Adele seized the moment. "You won't find another hook just like that anywhere." Adele went on about how it had come from an author who'd come to the bookstore. A doctor who had written a book on alternative healing methods and suggested crochet as a means of relaxation. He'd carved the hook himself. Adele started to talk about the immediate connection they'd had but CeeCee saw K.D.'s eyes begin to glaze over and stepped in.

"Dear, why don't you just go right into a demonstration on how to start the wrap." She picked up one of the small balls of yarn and pressed it into Adele's hand. I think we both let out a breath of relief when Adele dropped her story and showed off how to make the foundation chain for the wrap. Adele might be over the top on a lot of things, but she was an excellent teacher. Just to make sure K.D. got that, I explained the crochet parties the bookstore put on and how Adele handled the lessons. I went on about what a passionate teacher she was. K.D. only had to watch for a few minutes before she seemed satisfied.

"That's enough, Adele." K.D. put up her hand like a stop sign. "I think you will do. Your class is so basic and we are charging less for it. Actually we're discounting all the crochet classes since they're new." I watched as Adele paused and cocked her head. She wasn't very good at picking up the subtext in things, but this time Adele seemed to infer that what K.D. said wasn't a compliment.

It was an awkward moment, and I was afraid of what Adele might say, so I stepped in and made a big deal about admiring a Lucite box on a pedestal with an oversize pair of gold knitting needles crisscrossed in it. The light caught on the tops of the needles and reflected back. "Are those diamonds?" I said.

K.D.'s manner changed and she smiled at me. "Those needles are the company's logo. We use them for everything including the Knit Style Show. And yes, the stones at the end are diamonds."

Adele's face clouded over, and she peered closely at the box. "Logo, huh? We ought to have one for crocheting."

CeeCee and I looked at each other and nodded. Our mission had been accomplished. K.D. was okay with Adele's class. We ought to get going before Adele messed things up.

CeeCee and I stood up and prepared to each hook one of Adele's arms and make an exit, but before we could, K.D. turned to CeeCee.

"Have you considered what I said?" the woman with the shoulder-length fabulous whitish gray hair asked. CeeCee suddenly looked uncomfortable. "You are a celebrity. Your role in that vampire movie has generated an Oscar buzz. Why not hang out in an environment that suits your status? Join our group at the yarn studio."

I didn't dare look at Adele. I was afraid there might be flames coming out of her eyes after that comment. Actually, I wasn't that pleased with it, either. K.D. had stopped just short of demeaning the bookstore and our group, but I wasn't about to show it. I felt bad for CeeCee, who had been put on the spot. No matter what she said, somebody was going to be upset.

"I caught a glimpse of your store before we came up here. It looks wonderful," I said, hoping to distract the magazine head. I was relieved when it worked, and after correcting me that it was a studio and not a shop, K.D. offered to show it off. I was pretty sure it was another play to win over CeeCee, but I acted thrilled at getting a personal tour from her.

"We shoot a lot of photographs for our magazines here," K.D. said as she led us into the store through a private entrance. Delvin was by her side, opening doors and then holding them for the group.

When we walked inside the retail area, I stopped and glanced around in awe. It was so perfect that it looked like a yarn store in a movie set. The back wall was covered with cubbies of different sizes and shapes filled with yarn in luscious colors and textures. Sweaters, scarves and shawls made from the yarn were artfully displayed. At one end of the store there was an antique library table with refinished wooden kitchen chairs. Each had a bright-colored seat cushion and all were uninhabited for the moment. Not so for the grouping of wing chairs around a large coffee table strewn with designer tote bags and balls of yarn. The comfortable chairs were all filled with knitters.

"K.D., can I do something for you?" a woman said. She turned to the rest of us and introduced herself as Thea Scott, the manager of the store.

While K.D. pointed out CeeCee and admitted that she was trying to get her to join their regular circle, I checked out the store manager. She had the contemporary look down: black jeans, black shirt not tucked in and a knitted men's tie that she wore with the knot pulled loose. Her short brown hair seemed to have some kind of color added to make it such a velvety shade, and it was styled in the mussed-up, asymmetrical cut that seemed so popular. It made me glad to work in the Valley. We always got the rap for being suburban and nowhere near as hip or trendy as the city side of the Santa Monica Mountains. I looked down at my khaki pants and tucked in my shirt, which was practically my uniform. I didn't need a mirror to know that my shoulder-length naturally brown hair was hardly a contemporary style. The chilly weather was the reason I was wearing a purple and blue cowl, more than style. And the black sweater I had on over my white shirt wasn't even cashmere.

Thea dropped the ball of yarn she was holding, and when she bent over to pick it up, her shirt rode up exposing the brand name of her jeans. She must have realized it and reached back to pull down the shirt. In this crowd, the lowly brand just wouldn't cut it.

Adele and CeeCee had separated themselves and were looking at yarn. Delvin had left. K.D. turned her attention to the group of women around the coffee table, zeroing in on one of them. Her stare sharpened and her eyes narrowed before she leaned close and conferred about something with Thea. K.D. shook her head and didn't seem happy with whatever the manager had said and marched over to the group. There was a sameness to the women's appearance. They had almost identically styled hair in the glossy shade of mink that seemed to be in now, and they all wore layered tops with lots of accessories and soft leather boots. K.D. singled out one of them who stood out because she had a tiny tattoo of a butterfly on her hand. It was obvious there was some kind of altercation going on. I'm afraid I'm like a moth to a flame when it comes to trouble, so without even consciously doing it, I edged closer until I could hear what was going on.

"You know the rules, Julie," K.D. said as she picked up the yarn sitting in the woman's lap. "Did you really think taking off the label would fool me? You can only hang out here if you buy the yarn here. All our yarns are made of fibers like silk, wool and cotton. This . . ." she said, holding out the forest green peanut-shaped skein as if it had cooties, "is acrylic."

Julie's humiliation was too uncomfortable to watch. I backed away and pretended to look at the glass case on the checkout counter. When I looked up, the woman with the tattoo abruptly got up from the table and stuffed the yarn in her fancy tote bag before storming out. The other women kept their gazes on their yarn work, but I had no doubt they heard every word.

"Sometimes K.D. gets carried away," the store manager said. I'd been so busy being nosy I hadn't noticed that she was behind the counter. "I said I'd talk to Julie privately, but K.D. takes everything so personally. There was no reason to embarrass Julie that way." I quickly learned that the woman with the acrylic yarn was going through a difficult time. Her husband had lost his executive-level job, and she had four small kids, two of which had special needs.

I didn't want to get into the middle of something, and instead of commenting on what Thea had just said, I asked about the contents of the case, noting there was a whole selection of silver knitting needles. They had different colored stones inlaid in the top. At the end, there was a complete set of different-size needles in a satin roll. The clear stones at the top twinkled in the reflected light.

"Can I see those?" I asked, indicating the set of needles in assorted sizes. I explained I was in charge of the yarn

department at the bookstore and that we were having a
booth at the upcoming show. "I'm afraid all we carry are
plain metal and wood needles, none with ornaments. Those
seem like the ones in the Lucite box that K.D. Kirby
showed us."

"Except those are made out of gold plate and these are
sterling silver. Both have diamonds." Thea took out the
rose-colored fabric holder that had slots for all the needles
and laid it on the counter. She left me to examine them
when one of the women in the group waved her over. I
didn't do a lot of knitting. Most of it was just swatches to
serve as samples of our yarn, but I was still curious about
the elegant needles. Even the case they came in was elegant,
made out of a satiny material. Then I noticed the price
sticker, $3,500, and I almost choked.

Thea rejoined me, carrying some knitting, and laughed
at my expression. "I know where you're coming from, but
our customers don't care about price. Those women have
money to burn, as the cliché goes. If anything, they like it
when things cost more." She pointed to the pairs of needles
with colored stones on them. "Those are cheaper because
the stones are just semiprecious. Would you believe we sell
more of the ones with the diamonds?"

Adele had joined me at the counter. She looked aghast at
the satin roll with the silver needles. "Those are like the
publishing company logo," my coworker pointed out. "We've
got to make a logo for crochet. And I have a great idea."

I shuddered at the thought.

CHAPTER 4

WHEN THURSDAY ROLLED AROUND, I WAS TOO wound up to even notice the deadly quiet in my house. Mason was on my mind. He'd gotten back in town late the night before and called on the way back from the airport. He wanted to come over. But I could hear the exhaustion in his voice, and I was concerned about the yarn show starting the next day. It was not the time for a big reunion.

"You're not going to change your mind on me, are you?" he teased before I heard him yawn. I had been a bit elusive in the past, and I could see his concern.

"And you're not going to take off because it was really just all about the chase, are you?" I countered. I sounded like I was joking, but there was still a bit of concern in the back of my mind. I was facing the big 5-0 and had been around long enough to know how relationships went. Nothing made someone seem more desirable than when they were out of reach. But if they suddenly turned around and waited with open arms, it was a whole other story.

"If it was just about the chase, I would have given up a long time ago. I'm just glad you finally realized what everyone else has known all along. We belong together. And I can't wait to start showing you how right they all are."

I might have been facing the half-century mark, but his words sent a shiver of excitement down my body. And I knew he was right about us belonging together. He was always easy to be with. There were no issues. It was all just about having fun. We were on the same page about a relationship, too. He was divorced and not interested in getting married again. I wasn't, either. We both wanted something with no strings.

I was still thinking of our good-bye as I fussed around the kitchen. He'd ended the call with a "love you" again. The first time he'd said it, I'd melted. The second time I'd begun to wonder if he really meant it. And now, I was beginning to think it might just be an automatic sign-off to whoever he was involved with, like the way people automatically say bless you when someone sneezes.

I pushed it to the back of my mind; I'd deal with it when we finally got together. Right now I needed to focus on what was directly in front of me. Today was it. The day we set up the booth and the show opened. Maybe if we'd just decided to have a small booth, I wouldn't have been so keyed up. But somehow between Adele's insistence that we were going to be the champions of crochet at the show, Mrs. Shedd's idea that it was a chance to sell our wares and advertise all the things the bookstore had going, and my willingness to be responsible for it, we ended up getting a triple-size booth at the very front of the show in a prime spot, for a pricey cost.

I had a long day ahead of me, and without the backup of my son or the assorted people who'd stayed at my house to take care of the animals, I had to make sure they had everything they needed.

I filled the cat bowls, which were well out of reach of the dogs. I gave Blondie and Cosmo a breakfast of dry food followed by a long stint in the yard before I packed up my stuff and headed to the car.

It was just a short drive to the heart of Tarzana. I pulled into the parking lot behind the bookstore. I had things to pick up for the show, but first I was meeting my friend Dinah for breakfast.

I walked past the bookstore and down the block to Le Grande Fromage. The French café was busy and smelled of buttery croissants and fresh-brewed coffee. Dinah waved from one of the round tables.

"I wish I could help you with the setup," Dinah said when I joined her. "But at least I can make sure you have a good breakfast." She'd become downright motherly after all the time she's spent taking care of her ex's kids and had food waiting for me. I half expected her to start feeding me the scrambled eggs.

"You must be a mind reader. I have a nervous stomach and some eggs are about all I can manage right now."

Dinah smiled. "I'm not a mind reader. I just know you very well." She pushed the covered cup of coffee toward me. "It's a red eye."

She waited until I had started on the food and coffee. "So, give me a Mason update." Of course, I'd already told her about my first call to him right after it happened, but that was all she knew.

"He called me Tuesday morning," I said with a laugh. "He wanted to make sure he hadn't dreamt my call. He called again that night and last night when he got back in town." I must have gotten a dreamy look on my face because Dinah nudged me and asked for more details.

"He wanted to come over, but it was late and he was yawning and I was worried about today. I told him I was going to be tied up all weekend, and he's stuck with a client." I explained to Dinah that being stuck with a client didn't just end at five for Mason. "His celebrity clients demand a lot of attention."

My late husband, Charlie, had worked in public relations. In Southern California that meant dealing with assorted entertainment types, so I was familiar with the drill. Whoever it was would need a chaperone to make sure they didn't say the wrong thing. It didn't matter if the chaperone was an attorney, agent or publicist, they'd also get stuck doing menial stuff like sending back their client's lunch at some pricey restaurant because their soup wasn't hot enough. Celebs in trouble had to be guarded even more so these days. Before, it seemed celebrity types always got off, the worst punishment being a slap on the wrist. But these days, they were getting jail time.

"Of course, he couldn't tell me who or what they were accused of having done," I said. I hesitated and brought up the love-yous at the end of his calls and my concerns.

"I hate to say it, but he does come from the world of fake hugs and air kisses," Dinah said, then reconsidered when my face fell. "Don't worry, I'm sure he really means *something* by it." Then she reminded me how I kept saying all I wanted was a casual relationship with him anyway. "So, it doesn't really matter if it's real or just his catchphrase way of saying good-bye to his woman friend."

"I suppose you're right," I said, trying to sound like I meant it. Everything Dinah said was correct, and I shouldn't really be concerned, and yet . . . "Enough about that," I said, closing the subject. "What we really should be talking about is how we're going to schedule the granny square project."

We were looking for ways to attract people to our booth, and we'd decided that letting people make something at no charge would definitely be a draw. Dinah had come up with the idea of granny square pins with some beads added and even designed the pattern. Since it was her design, I wanted to have the pin-making sessions when Dinah was there so she could supervise.

We were just hashing out a schedule when the door to the small café opened and Adele came in. Actually, *came in* was too mild a term. Adele always made an entrance. It was partly the clothes. There could be no doubt which side of the yarn fence she was on. She was crochet all the way. I'd never seen the black jacket before, but it was a definite showstopper. Actually, the jacket was merely a backdrop for the embellishments. Flowers in different sizes, patterns and colors adorned it. She did her best catwalk impression as she crossed the café, making eye contact with the other diners as she did. I did hear a few oohs and aahs.

"I thought I'd find you here," she said, dropping her tote bag on one of the chairs before going to the counter to order her breakfast.

When she came back, she focused on me. "This is our chance, Pink. Crochet is going to have its chance to shine." Adele pulled out an empty chair and sat down. "That Kirby woman isn't going to keep us in the yarn world shadow. They have a logo, and now so do we." She reached into the oversize tote and took out a pair of the biggest crochet hooks I'd ever seen. "They're size X," she said with a smile. The tiny steel crochet hooks were numbered, starting with 14 being the smallest and going to double zero. The larger hooks came in assorted materials, and their size notations were alphabetical. The biggest I'd used was a P. I didn't even know an X existed. It turned out it didn't, exactly. Adele had made it by cutting a plunger handle in half and then shaping the tops of each into hooks.

"I wouldn't want to try to crochet with them, but they're sure to stand out."

"That's an understatement," Dinah said as Adele laid them on the table. She'd bound them together in a criss-cross fashion like the gold knitting needles K.D. had on her desk and then painted them with gold paint that seemed to have some glitter mixed in. There was a line of dots stuck to the front of both hooks.

"I couldn't do jewels," Adele said, fiddling with the pair. "So I did this." The dots on the front of the hooks came to life, and I realized they were LED lights in red, yellow and blue. Adele touched the hooks again and the lights began to flicker on and off. "Aren't they great? We can put them right at the front of the booth, along with this." She unfurled a banner made out of shelf paper that said "Crochet Spoken Here" in large letters.

Adele lost her look of excitement for a moment, and she looked almost panicky. "Mother Humphries is coming to the show this weekend." Adele put the heel of her hand to her forehead in a melodramatic gesture. "I have to shine to impress her."

She was being so overly dramatic in her tone and manner that it was hard not to laugh. But both Dinah and I knew she was serious. Leonora Humphries was the mother of her boyfriend, Motor Officer Eric Humphries. Adele had already tried to win her over twice and failed. I wasn't sure the third time was going to be the charm.

It seemed like the first move to make if she wanted to win Leonora over was to stop referring to her as Mother Humphries. Somehow Adele had missed that the woman cringed every time she called her that.

When her breakfast arrived, she insisted they pack it to go. "Pink, we have to get there. We're the champions of crochet." She waved the crossed crochet hooks over her head like they were some kind of magic wand. She was on her way to the door, saying she had to pick something up at the bookstore.

"It looks like destiny is calling you," Dinah said with a laugh. When I made a face, she tried to reassure me. "Don't worry, I'm sure the setup will be fine. I'm coming later to help out, and so are the rest of the Hookers. You'll see. Adele's flamboyance will be a benefit." She looked at her watch. "I've got to go, anyway." Dinah started to gather up her things as I did. "A student asked for a meeting about his grade on a paper." She rolled her eyes skyward. "These freshmen are trying to make up their own language." Dinah had a thing about words. She liked whole ones. It was bad enough when her students tried turning in papers written in text talk, as she called it. Instead of *you are*, they wrote *u r*. But now they'd begun speaking and writing in half words. *Amazing* had become *amaz*, *excellent* had become *excel*. "I wonder what the short version of *flunk* is." Then she laughed. "Of course, how very old school. I could just say he was going to *f*—it if he didn't do the paper over and use real words."

"And someday, he'll thank you for it," I said. Dinah had a gift for turning clueless freshmen into real college students. I was sure this kid would be no different. We walked down the street together.

"I have to pick up some things at the bookstore," I said, opening the door to go inside. "I want to catch up with Adele."

Dinah gave me a fast hug. "See you later," she said as I went into Shedd & Royal and she continued on to her car.

Bob caught me as I went past the café. "I have everything all ready," he said. I was confused for a moment, and then he reminded me that he was sending over some baked goods to represent the bookstore café in the booth.

"I tried something new. I'm calling them Oatmeal Power Squares." He opened up a large tin and showed me how he had placed each of the squares in a paper baking cup. He waited while I tasted one.

"Bob, you've outdone yourself. These are delicious." I put the lid on and took the sign he'd handed me that featured the café menu. While we were discussing whether to sell them or offer them as free samples, Adele made her way to the front door. She was gone before I could tell her not to do anything before I got there.

Oatmeal Power Squares and Adele's crochet hook logo made out of plunger handles. It was pretty clear our booth wasn't going to be boring.

CHAPTER 5

THE BUENA VISTA HOTEL AND EVENT CENTER WAS on Ventura Boulevard in Encino. It was a relic from the old days and for a lot of years had been *the* spot to hold a trade show or wedding. Recently, it had gotten new owners and a complete makeover and was now a boutique hotel and event center. The low building used for events was small by the current standards but just the right size for a yarn show.

I was surprised that K.D. held the Knit Style Show in the San Fernando Valley. She had snob written all over her, and I was sure she was the kind who thought the civilized world ended with Beverly Hills and the Westside of L.A. But then I realized there was one benefit that this side of the Santa Monica Mountains offered that had probably trumped her snobbery. Free parking. Like so many other places in the Valley, the Buena Vista offered a huge courtesy parking lot.

If I hadn't known the Buena Vista was there, I could have driven right past it. It was surrounded by bushes that had been coaxed and trimmed into a green wall. I didn't go in the curved driveway in the front but turned off onto the side street and went into the driveway that led to the big parking lot at the back of the complex.

Adele's Matrix was already there when I pulled in. There were a lot of vans with their doors open, being unloaded. A parade of people wheeling assorted carts were walking toward the event center, but Adele wasn't among them. I'd only stopped at the bookstore for a few moments, so I wondered how she'd gotten so far ahead of me. It worried me to think of what she was up to.

The five-story hotel faced sideways with a long two-story building attached to it that featured the lobby and several restaurants. The event center was really a continuation of that low building and went toward the back of the property.

I didn't stop to admire the lovely grounds. I rushed past the pond, barely noticing the floating lily pads and the regal swans. Many a Valleyite had gotten married in the lovely rose garden, but to me it was just a blur of color as I headed toward the entrance.

Adele must have driven there with a lead foot. As I moved down the inner corridor there wasn't even a glimpse of her in the distance. The marketplace, as the vendor area was called, was being held in one of the larger spaces, and the double doors were open for easier access.

Just before I went in, I checked the escalator that led to the second floor. The classes were being held in the meeting rooms up there, and I wondered if Adele had gone to check hers out. Actually, I hoped she had, as she was less likely to cause any trouble in an empty room. But the moving stairs were going up without any passengers. A registration booth had been set up in the outer corridor. I stopped and got my badge and the ones for the Hookers who would be coming later. Adele's had already been picked up.

The exhibit hall was a cavernous space bustling with activity as all the vendors were busy setting up their booths. Aisles had been created with the use of curtain-covered panels. I did a quick survey of the area around the entrance as I came in. A table with administration stuff flanked one side of the door, and a rather elaborate booth was being erected on the other side. I was surprised to see a sign that said "Cline Yarn International" across the front. I was familiar with the company. Their headquarters were in the San Fernando Valley, and we bought a lot of the yarn for the yarn department in the bookstore from them. But I'd never seen them selling direct to the consumer before.

I glanced to see if our contact with the company, Paxton Cline, was in the booth, but there was only an older woman who seemed to be directing things. The business was founded and run by Paxton's grandmother, Ruby Cline, and I guessed that was her. She was sharply dressed in fashionable jeans, leather cowboy boots and a long red sweater no doubt knitted from their yarn. So much for the image of some gray-haired granny in a rocking chair, I thought with a laugh.

I had no trouble finding the Shedd & Royal booth. It was in the first space in the first row. Actually, we had the first three spaces. I had no trouble finding Adele, either. As Mr. Royal was putting the finishing touches on the storefront he'd created out of wood, she was on a ladder hanging the "Crochet Spoken Here" banner she'd made right below the "Shedd & Royal Books and More" sign.

"Pink, check it out," she said, gesturing toward the long

table set up at the front of the booth. Her crochet logo was sitting on a black velvet–covered pedestal. She'd turned the thing on and the LED lights blinked on one at a time. Nobody was going to miss that.

Mr. Royal came around to where I was standing. He was about the same age as Mrs. Shedd, which I guessed was in the sixty-something category, but they wore their age so differently. It just wasn't fair the way men aged so much better than women. With his agile build and shaggy dark hair with a few wiry gray strands, he looked a decade younger than his partner.

"I think you can add builder to your multitude of professions," I said, admiring the job he'd done. Joshua Royal had traveled all over and done everything, leaving Mrs. Shedd to run the bookstore. When I'd first started working there, he was such a silent partner, I had wondered if he really existed.

He led the way to the back of the booth and showed off the wire cubbies for the yarn, tables for assorted yarn-related supplies, freestanding racks and shelves for the books. "All that's left to do is to put out our wares," he said, showing me the plastic bins of yarn and the boxes of books. The yarn placement was strictly up to me, but he thought we ought to put the craft books together and set the craft-related fiction and mysteries in their own section. "Be sure to put this in a prominent position." He held up a poster that detailed everything the bookstore had to offer besides books. This was a chance to remind local people of the various groups that met at the bookstore and our yarn services and crochet parties. I read it over and laughed when I saw the last item—our world-famous café.

"Says who?" I asked, pointing it out. Mr. Royal looked a little sheepish. "Pamela talked me into putting that in. She said I'd been all over the world and might have mentioned our barista Bob's cookie bars and coffee drinks."

I laughed at Mrs. Shedd's marketing strategy and set the tin of Oatmeal Power Squares on the table, along with the menu.

Mr. Royal chuckled at the idea of giving out samples. "They'll be gone in half an hour."

Adele had finished with her sign hanging and joined us. "Pink, look who we have for neighbors," she said with a dismissive wave toward the booth across the aisle. A slightly more discreet sign than ours read "Knit Style Yarn Studio." Thea Scott was helping another woman unload bins of yarn and arrange them. It made sense that the yarn store K.D. owned would have a prominent location and that the store manager would be running it. Thea was wearing a sample of her yarn expertise: a multicolored triangle shawl worn like a neck adornment with the pointed end in the front.

She looked up and I waved before my view of her was blocked as more people filtered in, pulling carts with their stock. There was a lot of activity going on all over as everyone tried to ready their booth for the late afternoon kickoff of the show.

"We better get going on this," I said to Adele, grabbing one of the white bins of yarn. I pulled out an armload of yarns in shades of red. Adele was standing around crocheting.

"Excuse me, but there's been some kind of mistake," a woman said in a sharp tone. I looked up from my work and saw an attractive woman with short, wavy dark hair held back by an orange knitted headband. "This front spot is mine." Her hand was resting on a rack covered in a sheet. "At least this much of it is," she said, measuring off the first third of our booth.

"And the problems begin," I muttered as I walked closer to her. Adele came with me for backup as I assured the woman there was no mistake and that we were in the right spot.

The woman was not to be dissuaded. "I've been in the show since the first year, and I've always had this first spot." She looked at the structure Mr. Royal had built. "Maybe you can just push the whole thing down."

She introduced herself as Rain Bergere and waved a greeting to Thea Scott. "You can ask her. My booth has always been here." When I looked at Thea, she turned away and it was clear she didn't want to get involved. I tried to calm Rain down by complimenting her on her long, soft gray knitted vest and mentioning how everyone seemed to be wearing something they'd made but me. I heard Adele making harrumphing sounds in the background and guessed that she was probably jealous that I hadn't made a fuss over her sweater with all the flower embellishments.

"This is just a sample of the long vests I have available. If you like this . . ." Rain said, pulling back the sheet on the rack she'd brought in, exposing a whole row of garments on hangers.

"Wow," I said, moving the hangers as I admired the long vests like the one she was wearing. "I thought the vendors just sold supplies to make things," I said.

"I'm the only one who sells finished items. Now I really need to get my space ready." The woman seemed to be holding her ground, and I didn't want to be the heavy, but I was sure we were in the right place.

I saw an official-looking woman with a clipboard and called her over. I explained the confusion and she consulted her map of vendors.

She looked at Rain and shook her head. "Nope. This space isn't yours." She showed her the map on the clipboard and pointed to the correct location. Rain didn't seem happy, and I was relieved when she pushed her rack down the aisle and disappeared.

"Sure, this was supposed to be her booth," Adele said in a sarcastic tone. "More like she wished it was." Mr. Royal had smartly stayed out of the whole thing and hung the list of the bookstore benefits on one of the wood supports in the front.

"It doesn't matter. She's gone. We should set up the front table," I said, feeling a little scattered. Adele looked at her watch and her eyes flared with her usual drama.

"I have to go and meet my boyfriend, Eric." As if either Mr. Royal or I didn't know who Eric was. She dropped what she was doing and took off.

Our booth was designed so that there was plenty of space for customers to come inside and look around. But the table across the front was where all the important action was going to take place. The Hookers were going to offer free crochet lessons there, and it was also where the granny square pin making was going to take place. Adele had positioned her logo in the middle of the table and left her crochet stuff next to it. I was surprised she'd been so careless with her special hook. I considered moving it but decided to leave it be. I had made signs announcing the free crochet lessons and chance to make a granny square pin. I put them in with the supplies. I was just shoving the box with the hooks, crochet thread and beads under the table when I heard a thud.

When I straightened, K.D. and her assistant, Delvin, were staring at Adele's crossed hooks, which now seemed to be askew, as though someone had picked them up but then dropped them. K.D. turned to Delvin. "This won't do. What is wrong with these people?" She looked up at the banner and shook her head. "This all has to go." It was then that she noticed me. She repeated that the logo and banner had to go. "We attract the knitterati from around the world. We go for class, like our logo. This is a crass and cheesy imitation," she said, handling the two giant glittery gold-painted crochet hooks. It did something to the light control and they started to blink more quickly. The magazine mogul stared at it and shook her head with disgust. "This has no place here, no place at all."

I was put off by her high-handed manner and wondered if she had the right to dictate what we had in our booth. I was going to say something, but a dark-haired woman who looked like a younger version of K.D. joined them. From overhearing their conversation, I got that her name was Lacey and she was not only K.D.'s daughter but also handled the social media for the magazines and the show. There seemed to be some kind of disagreement over an announcement K.D. was going to make. I couldn't help but eavesdrop. They made an odd group. K.D. wore a designer black velour tracksuit. I don't know why they called them tracksuits. She certainly didn't look like she was going to take off on a sprint. Delvin had one of his oddly matched outfits and had traded the fedora for a newsboy cap. I guessed that was supposed to make the look more casual. Lacey had on jeans and a blazer.

"I'm not going to tell you what it is," K.D. said in a sharp tone. "I don't want it tweeted and put on Facebook before I've made it public."

"I don't know why you won't share it with me, at least," Delvin said.

K.D. seemed to have forgotten about Adele's logo for the moment—and me, for that matter. She seemed to be considering something and then shook her head like it was an internal answer. "I'm not telling anyone before I make it. I will just say that it is something that is going to change everything around here."

Neither Lacey nor Delvin seemed happy with what she said.

"Did I hear you say you were going to make an important announcement?" a woman asked, joining the small group. I recognized the Channel 3 reporter Kimberly Wang Diaz. She was holding a microphone with a "3" stuck to the top, and between the heavy makeup and sprayed stiff black hair, she seemed ready to film.

K.D. answered the question by avoiding it entirely. "Thank you for coming. Do you think you could get something for tonight's news? It would be nice if you could include the location and all the free parking."

"We've got it scheduled for the eleven o'clock," the newscaster said. "And then there will be a feature piece on Saturday, covering my award." The reporter attempted to appear self-effacing as she said how honored she was to be getting an award for excellence in reporting on the craft world.

It was hard to keep my eyes from swirling in my head. As I said, my late husband had worked in public relations, and I knew all about making up fake top ten lists to spotlight a client and giving reporters awards to be sure an event got coverage on the news.

K.D. was using her body to block our table as she pointed off in the distance and suggested the reporter set up there.

When Kimberly and her cameraman had moved on, K.D. stepped away and looked back at our table. "I'm glad she didn't see this." She glared at Adele's creation. "That monstrosity is not the image we want for the show. You'll take it away and remove that banner, right?" It was clearly not a suggestion but an order. "They better not be here when the show opens," she said in a warning tone. As if to punctuate it, Delvin gave me a decisive nod. I was relieved when they moved on.

Joshua Royal came up to the table when they'd left, and we both looked at the offending pieces. We discussed what to do and decided that it was better to keep the peace. He took down the banner and I removed the logo. We put both of them in a bin and shoved it under the table.

"Why don't you take a break," he said. "There's a coffee wagon set up in the back." He pointed off in the distance. The caffeine from my red eye at breakfast had worn off, and a fresh cup of coffee sounded good.

As I got ready to go through the maze of aisles to get to the back, I noticed a pair of open doorways near the administration table. Curious, I wandered into the first one. There were two long tables and two sets of dress forms, a few of which had been dressed in some yarn items.

CeeCee swept into the room, followed by a woman with a clipboard and a volunteer badge. As soon as the actress and fellow Hooker saw me, she smiled and reached out to hug me.

"Dear, it's good to see you're here," she said. "I'm not so

sure about judging the crochet competition." She pointed toward the left of the two setups, and it was clear that it was light on entries. "Adele wanted to bring something in, but K.D. nixed it. Said it wasn't right because she was one of the teachers."

We were interrupted as K.D. and a woman came into the display room. The woman looked familiar, although it took me a minute to place her. Then I saw the butterfly tattoo on her hand and realized she was the woman that K.D. had banished from her store for bringing in yarn she hadn't bought there. This time she was holding a soft pink jacket that looked like it was made out of mohair. We couldn't help but overhear.

"Julie, you can't enter that jacket again. You won an honorable mention with it last year," K.D. said. I felt for Julie as once again K.D. was embarrassing her. Though the woman spoke up.

"It only looks like the jacket I entered last year," she protested and held it out to show off the stitches. "The pattern is similar, but this time I did the bottom half in crochet."

K.D. seemed unmoved and then noticed CeeCee. "Maybe you can enter it in the crochet competition." I was glad that Adele wasn't there. The tone when K.D. said *crochet* would have set my coworker off. I had to admit that it got to me, too, particularly after the whole fuss at our booth. If it bothered CeeCee, she didn't let on, but then she was an actress who had Oscar buzz about her last performance.

K.D. was out the door back into the main room before CeeCee finished saying she'd accept the entry.

"Thank you," Julie said. "It really isn't the same jacket I entered last year. The color of that one was sunset pink and this one is rosy dawn."

"K.D. could use a class in dealing with people," I muttered when Julie had gone. CeeCee leaned in close.

"Putting on a show like this has to be a strain. And she is used to being the boss and ordering people around." CeeCee brought up some role she'd played as head of a department store empire and how the character went ballistic when the staff used the wrong kind of hangers. When I left, CeeCee was graciously accepting a traditional granny square afghan as an entry.

I peeked in the other room. A man looked up and asked if I was bringing in an item for the auctions. He gestured toward one table. "Those are all the silent auction items, and the other table has the real valuable stuff for the live auction."

"Sorry. I didn't realize there was an auction."

"The money all goes to a women and children's shelter. You can bid on the silent auction pieces until closing time on Saturday, and the live auction is at the banquet that night."

I thanked him and said I'd check back later when all the donations were there.

I started down the main aisle and saw that everything was still in setup mode. There was an open space at the back of the room. Some chairs had been scattered around rather randomly, and there was a snack bar and a coffee wagon. I was glad there wasn't a line and ordered my drink.

The smell of the red eye was perking me up as I turned to go back. For the first time I noted there were some booths on the ends of the aisles that faced the open area and was glad we weren't stuck back here. I recognized the rack of knitted pieces in one of the spots. Maybe Adele was right about Rain Bergere just pretending she was supposed to have part of our space. This was yarn show Siberia.

Mr. Royal was standing in the entrance to our booth when I returned. "I'm just about finished," he said, showing off his work. I knew he wanted to get back to the bookstore. With me and Adele both gone, Mrs. Shedd was going to need his help.

"You can go now, if you want," I said. "Adele should be back any minute." I glanced toward the entrance to see if she was on her way in. There was no Adele, but my mouth fell open when I saw who had walked in.

Mason Fields? Was I seeing things or was the solidly built man in the beautifully tailored gray suit really him? And if it was him, what was he doing here? I'd told him that I was tied up for the weekend with some yarn thing for the bookstore, but I hadn't given any details. Had he somehow tracked me down? When I saw the lock of dark hair that had fallen across his forehead, I knew for sure it was him. I always thought it made him appear hardworking and earnest. He said it was just what his hair did on its own.

It had been months since I'd seen him in person, even if we had been talking on the phone for the past couple of days. I was all set to catch his eye and then do one of those movie things, where you see each other and are drawn together like there is this giant magnet at work. In the movies it's often in slow motion, but in real life, I thought I'd just run into his arms. But then I saw that he wasn't alone. A tall, elegant-looking woman accompanied him.

I felt a pang of jealousy until I got a closer look and recognized her as Audrey Stewart. She'd been the "It" girl for a while and starred in a string of romantic comedies with titles like *Love, Really?*, *Sweet Home Iowa*, *Sleepy in Cincinnati* and *You've Got a Tweet*. Now that I thought about it, the only thing I'd heard about her lately was that she'd gotten into some kind of trouble. It was one of those really non-news items that got stuck in with real things like a typhoon hitting India. Now I was sorry I hadn't paid attention to the details since she was obviously the client Mason had referred to.

It was impossible to miss K.D.'s mane of silvery hair, and I saw her come to a stop next to Mason and Audrey. Delvin had rejoined her, but it seemed K.D.'s daughter had gone off to tweet or post on Facebook by herself.

All I could see was their body language. Mason got ready to speak to K.D. and appeared a combination of calm and friendly. But Audrey moved a little in front of him and said something first. Whatever the actress said, K.D. seemed to be annoyed and actually shook her finger at Audrey. Mason physically stepped between them and took over. Even at this distance, his effort to smooth things over was apparent. And just as apparent was that it wasn't working.

Thea Scott had come out into the aisle and was watching with me. "Any idea what's going on?" I asked, noticing that the Knit Style Yarn Studio manager appeared worried.

Thea muttered something to herself about K.D. being so hardheaded before she turned to me. "I'm surprised you didn't hear about it. Audrey Stewart is part of our celebrity circle who meet at the yarn store. And she shoplifted one of those sets of jeweled silver knitting needles you were admiring." Thea paused for a moment, shaking her head as she thought it over. "She claimed it was an accident. That she just happened to drop the satin roll of needles in her knitting bag and forgot to pay."

The three of them seemed to be at a standoff, and Thea let out a sigh. "I thought we should let her pay for them and forget about it, but K.D. sort of snapped. She took it way too personally and insisted we press charges against her. I'm guessing that Audrey and her lawyer are trying to change K.D.'s mind." As Thea said that, things seemed to get worse between the three across the room. Audrey appeared angry and actually stamped her foot. "I tried to talk K.D. out of it, but she absolutely wouldn't listen. Audrey's lawyer is wasting his time."

"I don't know about that," I said, feeling protective. "I know Mason Fields, and he is very persistent."

"What a mess," Thea said as Audrey stamped her foot again and Mason grabbed her hand and led her away. She seemed unhappy with him and pulled free. He glanced back for just a moment, and this time he saw me. His face broadened into a smile. He stopped, and I thought we were going to have that movie moment, but then he saw Audrey marching toward the door. He held his thumb and fore-finger to his ear, mimicking a phone call, and then pointed at me before rushing after his client.

"It was mission definitely not accomplished," Thea said before going back into her booth.

CHAPTER 6

"Pink, our booth has been vandalized," Adele said, arriving back just as I walked into the interior. She appeared horror stricken as she stared at the front table. "They've stolen our logo and taken our banner." Joshua Royal had his tools all packed up and left quickly. I'm sure he didn't want to be there when Adele heard what happened.

"Not exactly," I said, pulling out the box where I'd stowed the things before explaining why.

"No," Adele said in her most dramatic form as she grabbed the pair of crochet hooks and held them against herself in a protective manner. "That's just nonsense. We have every right to put what we want in our booth as long as it isn't offensive," my coworker said.

The problem was that K.D. found Adele's handiwork offensive. I was trying to find a way to explain it when we were interrupted. Rain, the woman who'd tried to claim we were in her space, had returned. She was holding a dress form wearing a white knitted jacket. A sign hung around its neck with her business name and a number on it.

"I wonder if I could leave this here. So people looking for my booth will know where I am." She said it in a polite way, but this was not the time to wave anything knitted in front of Adele or ask for any help.

"Have you seen the schedule?" Adele said to me. "It's one knit fashion show after another with a bunch of knit demos in between. There's brioche knitting and intarsia, whatever that is. Do we really need to help the enemy by having a dress form modeling a knitted jacket in front of our booth? We are the beacon of crochet in the knitted darkness." Before I could mention that what Adele had said didn't quite make sense, she'd plunked her crochet logo on the table, before pulling over a chair and rehanging the banner. "That's it. I'm going to go talk to K.D. Kirby and tell her these things are staying." Both Rain and I stepped back as Adele rushed out of the booth.

"You can leave the dress form," I said when Adele was gone. Not only was I not as nuts about knitters, I felt for Rain after I'd seen the location of her booth. Though after Rain left I did push it over to the side so it was at the very edge of our spot. Things had begun to quiet down as the vendors finished setting up. I did a little rearranging of our area. I made sure the supplies were ready for the granny square pin venture, along with a sign to put up when we were featuring the activity. I did take out the sign announcing free crochet lessons before I opened the tin of Bob's Oatmeal Power Squares and made sure the café menu was visible. I did a little rearranging of the yarn and the crochet tools, and then the booth was ready for the opening.

When I looked around, I noticed the aisle was empty. Apparently everyone else had finished setting up and left. I had lost all sense of time and was surprised to see that it was almost four. The kickoff of the show was at six thirty.

Although Adele and I along with the other Hookers were all sleeping at home, we'd gotten a mini suite to act as a place for us to take a break during the weekend and to keep some extra stock. Mr. Royal had taken care of checking us in and provided keys for Adele and me. It had already been arranged that the rest of the Hookers would meet up in the room and I'd hand out their badges. I left a note for Adele and went there to freshen up.

I walked through the lobby and took the elevator. The carpeted hallway was silent and empty as I looked at the room numbers. I expected an empty room and was surprised to find Adele already there redoing her makeup. I quickly discovered the operative word in the suite was *mini*. It was really one large room with a seating area in addition to a bed.

I was going to castigate her for not coming back to help, but she was all discombobulated.

I asked if she'd talked to K.D. and Adele gave me a funny look.

"Let's just say it's taken care of. The banner and the crossed hooks are staying. I'm even thinking we should add another banner that mentions the free crochet lessons and the granny square pin," Adele said, but she seemed somehow preoccupied.

"Is there something else?" I asked.

"It's Mother Humphries," she said. "She's staying in the

hotel for the whole weekend. I know she is going to be watching me. I know she wants to mess things up with me and Eric," Adele said. She seemed close to tears, and I was glad she didn't give the usual speech about how he was the yin for her yang—her soul mate.

Adele took off the crocheted sweater with all the flower embellishments and said she was going to wear it again on Saturday. She had brought something else for the show opening. She took out a long white vest that was embellished with hearts in different sizes and shades of red and pink, many of which had a lot of sparkle. Adele was crochet crazed, but she certainly made some stunning items, though I'm not sure I would have been comfortable wearing the vest. Something like that guaranteed you the spotlight—her favorite location.

The Hookers began arriving and it was hugs all around. Rhoda and Elise came together. Elise had a carrier on wheels with the crochet kits for the booth. She'd brought the one to make her vampire-style pieces and the ones she'd helped Sheila put together. This was the first time Sheila had assembled a kit to make a scarf in her trademark style of muted blues, greens and lavenders. Eduardo made quite an entrance. He'd done as we asked and dressed in the pirate outfit from his cover model days. The leather pants and billowing white shirt unbuttoned most of the way down along with his abundant black hair tied into a ponytail would definitely attract attention to our booth.

Dinah came in a few minutes later. I was so glad to see my best friend and wanted to tell her about seeing Mason, but there was too much confusion as I tried to straighten up my appearance and hand out the badges. Elise said she needed one for her husband. She was vague about what he was going to be doing, but she assured us his being in the booth was going to be a help.

"I hope he doesn't mind being Joshua Royal for the night," I said, handing over my boss's badge as a loan.

"I'm sure Logan won't mind," she said in her birdlike voice. None of us had seen much of her husband lately, so I was surprised that he was going to be hanging out at the yarn show.

"Where's Sheila?" Rhoda said in her matter-of-fact manner. She always got right to the point of things and wondered if our other Hooker was lost and having an attack of nerves somewhere in the hotel. Sheila had been handling her anxiety a lot better, but not finding her way could definitely set off an attack. I volunteered to go look for her.

The corridor of the hotel seemed quiet after the clatter of voices in the room. I was relieved to see Sheila coming down the hall. It wasn't her round face or chin-length dark brown hair that I recognized her by; it was her wrap. From a distance it reminded me of an Impressionist painting. When she saw me she picked up her pace.

"At last I found you," she said in a frantic tone. I assured her that Elise had brought her kits and pointed her toward the room. I was going to follow her when Delvin Whittingham came down the hallway behind her.

Apparently, the afternoon outfit had been his more casual attire and he'd changed into what I suppose he must have considered something more formal. The hint was the white dinner jacket, which was in direct contrast to the collarless knit shirt he wore underneath. I'd call it a T-shirt, but the fabric seemed too fancy for that lowly term. It was shiny black and seemed like an exotic blend of fibers. He'd changed his hat again to a white fedora with a black band and a rather large red feather stuck in it.

He picked up his pace when he saw me. "I'm glad I ran into you," he said. "I got a message that K.D. wants to speak with you about your coworker."

I saw him give me the once-over, and I'm pretty sure he didn't think much of my khaki pants, white shirt and black sweater, even if I'd been stylish enough to let the tails of the shirt hang below the sweater and had added a red cowl with a dash of sparkle.

"You mean Adele?" I asked, as if there could be any question who the Great One meant. What was it now? Maybe she wanted to cancel Adele's class or bar her from the show. I told him to lead the way.

He pointed toward the end of the hall and an alcove in front of a double door. "That's her suite. She has a before-show ritual of sipping a glass of champagne while she takes a bubble bath with her special blend of oils, but I'm sure she's done by now."

When we got to the door, he knocked and we waited, but nothing happened. He tried calling her on his cell phone, but it went right to voice mail.

"If she's still in the tub, she might not have heard either the phone or the knock," I said. "Maybe we should come back." I wasn't that happy about the summons and certainly didn't want to tick her off more by interrupting her ritual.

Delvin shook his head in response and said she'd been specific about wanting to talk before the show opened. His knock had been on the soft side, so I suggested I try. He had used his knuckles, but I gave the door a pound with the side of my fist. Both of us were surprised when the door slipped open a crack.

He pushed the door open wider and walked in with me

following. "Hello," he called out. "K.D., it's Delvin." There was just silence as an answer.

We'd walked into the living room of the suite. There was nothing mini about it. The floor-to-ceiling windows had a panoramic view over the eastern San Fernando Valley. It was just getting dark and the sky was a soft pastel lavender. The lights were just coming on in all the houses and buildings below. Off in the distance the Verdugo Hills and the San Gabriel Mountains looming behind them were a darker shade of the color of the sky.

The room was lit with recessed lighting and had a coffee table between two small couches. A bucket with a green champagne bottle sat on the coffee table next to some balls of yarn and other stuff. I wanted to step closer to have a better look, but Delvin pointed me toward the open door to the bedroom.

"Would you mind? In case she's undressed."

"K.D., it's Molly Pink from the bookstore," I said, taking a tentative step into the bedroom. The bed was made but strewn with clothes. I saw that the bathroom door was ajar. Delvin had come in behind me and glanced around the room. I heard him swallow as he touched my arm and urged me to check the bathroom.

It was too quiet, and I knew there had to be something seriously wrong. I took a deep breath and crossed the room to the open door. I didn't step in but rather leaned in tentatively. I was going to call out a greeting, but the room appeared empty.

I stepped in all the way to get a full view of the room. It was a luxury bathroom with an oversize tub in front of a window. At first all I saw was a mound of white bubbles and a champagne glass on the ledge. When I looked closer,

I saw that some of the light color was actually hair. K.D.'s iconic silvery hair. I started to rush in, but then I saw some water on the floor and the black cord that went from the tub to the wall socket.

"You better come in here," I said.

CHAPTER 7

MOMENTS AFTER DELVIN CALLED THE HOTEL OPERATOR, there was a flurry of activity as two hotel security men rushed in and pushed us back, letting a pair of paramedics pass by. I trailed behind them as they went through the suite to the bathroom. The action stopped when they reached the doorway and saw the black cord still plugged in.

"I think it's a hair dryer," I said, pointing out that it seemed the most likely appliance, since all hotels provided them. The group turned and glared at me.

"We can handle it from here," one of the security men said, taking my arm and leading me back to the living room. Delvin was standing in front of the window with his back to me. This had to be a terrible shock to him.

A man in a gray uniform came through, and when he met up with the others, I heard some conversation about making sure the wire was dead. A man in a suit with furrowed brows came in followed by a bunch of uniformed cops. The security man who'd grabbed me came into the room and conferred with the man in the suit, who I assumed was the hotel manager. A moment later all eyes turned to Delvin and me.

I started to say something but was shushed by the officer who had taken charge. He directed another officer to take charge of me. I saw he did the same with Delvin. The next thing I knew we were both being led out of the suite as yellow tape was strung across the double doors.

It was weird the stuff I noticed. I'd passed right through the small alcove on the way in without a thought, but now it occurred to me that this area set apart from the rest of the hall was a deliberate attempt to give the suite an entryway and make it seem more exclusive. There were a couple of chairs and a cabinet that seemed to be for decoration.

My cop took me into the main hall, and we stopped against the wall. Delvin's cop apparently thought the sitting area was for real and had him sit on one of the chairs. I watched, wondering if the chair would collapse when it was actually used. It only wobbled a little. It was hard to see Delvin's face in the shadow of his hat, but the color seemed to have drained from it. I imagined I probably looked about the same.

I knew the drill. They always wanted to keep witnesses separate until they got a statement from them.

I looked down the hall as my friends came out into the hallway. They were talking among themselves and went in the opposite direction without noticing what was going on at the end of the hall. Adele was leading the way, and I realized they were heading down to the marketplace for the opening of the show. The only one who hung back was Dinah. She looked up and down the hallway and then she saw me.

She began walking toward me, just as the uniform stepped in front of me, blocking my view. "I need to talk to my friend," I said, attempting to see around him and pointing toward Dinah.

"Not now," he said in a voice full of authority. "We need a statement from you first."

Dinah got close enough to see the yellow tape. Despite what the cop said, I waved at her and told her to go downstairs and that I'd be there soon. She reluctantly left after giving me a wave.

The hall got quiet again, and it began to sink in that no one had left the big suite. The paramedics hadn't rushed out, pushing K.D. on a gurney. For the first time, I began to think about K.D.'s condition. I asked my cop about her.

"I don't have that information," he said in a businesslike tone. I didn't know if he was telling the truth, but the more I thought about it, the less likely it seemed that K.D. was okay. There was another alternative for them not rushing her to the hospital. I didn't want to think about it.

My cop had a metal clipboard with some sheets attached and began to get my personal information. I was relieved that he didn't seem to recognize my name. Let's just say that it wasn't the first time I'd been questioned at a crime scene, nor the second time, either. I'd been taken to the police station a few times, as well, though never really arrested.

"Can I go now?" I said after giving all my information and the basics of what had happened. I explained my relationship to K.D., which was pretty slim, and how I'd happened to find her in the bathtub. The cop didn't seem to be in any hurry to let me go and called over a middle-aged cop who came out of the suite and seemed to be in charge.

"I really have to get downstairs. The yarn show is just

opening, and the place where I work has a booth there. It was very expensive, and I have to make sure it succeeds or my boss is going to be upset." I looked the middle-aged cop in the eye. "I'll be downstairs all evening, all day tomorrow and Saturday and Sunday. You can ask me anything you want anytime during that, but I really need to go."

I think Delvin was saying something similar to his cop. There was a bunch of discussing among the cops, and finally they let us both go.

By the time we got downstairs, it was completely dark outside. Floodlights lit up the grounds along the glass corridor that ran across the front of the event building. A crowd of mostly women was gathering near the doors, waiting for the opening of the show

I threaded through the crowd with Delvin. "K.D. would want the show to go on no matter what," he said solemnly as we reached the entrance to the marketplace. As soon as we got inside, we parted company, and I went to my booth.

"You're here," Dinah said, hugging me and sounding relieved. "I didn't know what to think when I saw you with the cops." I didn't see any point in telling the others. With the exception of Adele, they didn't know K.D., and why ruin the moment for them? I did pull Dinah aside.

"How awful," my friend said when I told her about finding K.D. in the tub and the black cord plugged into the wall. "What do you think happened?"

"I'm guessing there was a hair dryer on the other end of the cord, and I don't think it got in the tub by accident." I took a deep breath. "I think somebody threw it in there." Then Dinah asked the obvious question: Was K.D. dead?

"Nobody has confirmed it, but I have to believe that if

she'd survived, they would have rushed her off for emergency care," I said.

"What are you going to do?" she asked.

"There's nothing for me to do. I gave my statement to the cops." Dinah gave me a knowing look.

"You're not going to try to find out what happened?" Before I could answer, she spoke again. "You know I'm always available to be your Watson."

"For right now we'd better just concentrate on making our booth a success."

Sheila, Rhoda and Elise were in chairs behind the long table. Adele was just finishing adding a second banner that said "Free Crochet Lessons." Eduardo had found a bench and put it in front of the booth and was sitting on it with a supply of yarn and hooks.

"I hope you don't mind if I offer lessons here," he said, gesturing at the setup. "This should be fun."

I tried to pull myself together and pick up on the excitement of the show opening. I reminded them of the pin making enterprise and began taking out the supplies and putting them on the end of the table. I noticed that half of Bob's Oatmeal Power Squares were gone already.

"All the vendors wanted to try them," Sheila said.

Adele got down from hanging the banner and zeroed in on the dress form with the knitted vest. "Pink, I can't believe you let that woman leave it here. It threatens the whole crochet concept."

"Don't worry, it's going." I looked up to see the woman with the short hair and knitted headband picking up the dress form almost in front of me. Rhoda admired the jacket on the dress form and the long gray vest the woman was wearing and inquired about the patterns. I struggled to re-member her name.

"Sand doesn't sell yarn and patterns. She has the items already made up," I said.

The woman gave me an odd look. "My name is Rain," she said.

"I'm sorry," I said. "I knew it had something to do with water, and then for some reason I thought about the beach." In the background, Adele was muttering something about people with weird names.

Rain shrugged it off and said she had to get back to her spot. She did a double take as she passed a man approach-ing our booth.

"We're not open yet," Adele said as the man walked right in.

"Adele, don't you recognize Logan?" Elise said. I looked at the man again, and the only part of him that seemed fa-miliar was the hair. Logan had a funny hairline that always made him look like he was wearing a hat. As for the rest of him—I should have known. With Elise's obsession with the crocheting vampire it made perfect sense that she'd make her husband dress up as Anthony to hang out in the booth. Mr. Royal had left a prominent display of all the Anthony books. Luckily, he hadn't brought the cardboard cutout that we had in the store. Even though it was sup-posed to be the character in the books, the artist had based it on the movie version of Anthony, Hugh Jackman.

Logan was a shorter and a much less sexy Anthony than Hugh Jackman. Elise had covered his face in pale makeup and glitter. He was dressed all in black with a red handker-chief stuck in his jacket pocket. Would she really have made him wear fangs? He greeted me with a smile, and I saw that she had. So we had a cover model pirate and an overdone vampire in our booth. Was there any chance our booth wouldn't get attention?

I stepped out of the booth and checked out the far end of the huge ballroom. A stage had been set up with a walkway that led out into the open space. Delvin was adjusting a microphone and testing that it worked. A large board next to the stage had a schedule of the evening's events. After the opening ceremonies, there were to be several fashion shows and some knitting demos. Lacey Kirby came in and headed for the stage. I wondered if anyone had contacted her about her mother.

From a distance she had the same build and way of moving as K.D., but without the silvery white hair. Hers was a very dark red. She and Delvin conferred, and after a moment she seemed to slump, and he put his arm on her back in a supportive way. Then she straightened and left the stage.

I tried to follow her with my eye, but she got lost in the crowd of people flooding in through the open doors. I went back to our booth and got ready for the onslaught.

Above the din of conversation, I heard Delvin over the microphone. He welcomed everyone to the show and introduced himself, explaining that there'd been an accident and he was taking over temporarily for K.D. Kirby. The opening ceremonies were basically him talking about this being the tenth annual show. He told the attendees how lucky they were to have the opportunity to take some of the fabulous knitting classes that were being offered and to rub shoulders with so many of the knitterati from all over the country. He reminded the group of the auctions and the banquet.

I could hear Adele grumbling behind me about all the

knitting references, and when he announced the beginning of the first fashion show, she said she and her heart-covered vest should really be up there.

I ignored it all and focused my attention on our temporary store. Thanks to the location and the flashing lights on Adele's crochet logo and Eduardo and Logan, we instantly had a big crowd. Yarn and books started moving, the Hookers gave some lessons, and Dinah handled the granny square pin making.

"Where exactly is your yarn store?" a woman said as she approached me.

"We're actually a bookstore and more," I explained as I started to reel off that the "more" included a yarn department and we hosted crochet parties.

"Crochet parties, hmm," she said as she glanced at the front table and saw Adele's flashing logo. "But not knitting parties." She held up her flowered tote bag and showed off the yarn and knitting needles inside.

I gave her a crochet pitch, saying that was easier and faster than knitting and because you worked with one stitch at a time instead of a whole roll, there were lots of possibilities.

"Excuse me, Molly, when you have a minute I need to speak to you." The male voice startled me both because there were mostly women milling around and because I recognized it.

I handed the woman a book on crochet, taking an extra moment before turning to face the voice's owner. It had been months since Detective Barry Greenberg had walked out of my life. I had figured that I'd have to tell my tale to a detective after being the one to find K.D. I just hadn't expected it to be him. This was awkward with a capital A.

When I finally turned to face him, I felt a familiar rush. No matter our difficulties, there had always been an automatic reaction when I saw him. It was some kind of force that drew me to him in the first place. I wondered if he felt something similar. Not that I could tell by looking at him. He had his cop face on, and it made his handsome features seem stoic. Even his dark eyes didn't flare with a hint of emotion.

The last time I'd seen him was when he'd come by to tell me that he was stepping away, that I deserved more than he could give, that I ought to go with Mason.

Even with the cop face, his tiredness showed. There was a worn look around his eyes, and I wondered if he'd been up all night. But, I reminded myself it was none of my business anymore. He was dressed in his work uniform of a conservative suit, white shirt and striped tie.

"I suppose you're here about K.D. Kirby," I said, avoiding looking at his face. I didn't have a cop face to hide behind, and I didn't want him to see my reaction to his presence.

"We need to talk." He had the cop voice going, too. It was all business.

I felt a hint of guilt for not trying to do something to help K.D., but as soon as I saw the cord going into the water, I was afraid all I would do was electrocute myself.

Detective Heather came up behind him and leaned in close to say something to him. When she stepped back, she looked at me directly. "Molly. So you're involved in this case."

I should explain that I was the only one who called her Detective Heather. And it wasn't out loud, either. I only called her that in my head. To everyone else she was Detective

Gilmore. If there'd been a homicide detective Barbie, it would have resembled her. Heather wasn't all just good looks, either. She was smart and reputed to be a great shot at the gun range. She'd always had her eye on Barry, and now I guessed he was finally hers.

"So, you guys are partners now?" I said, trying to keep the snarky tone out of my voice.

Was it my imagination, or was there a little triumph in the way Heather nodded in answer before suggesting that maybe she should handle the interview with me and he could talk to Delvin Whittingham.

"I've got it covered," Barry said to her, and after a moment she walked away. He turned back to me. "Yes, we're partners, Molly." There was a slight lapse in his cop face. "At work only. I'm doing the single thing now. Just concentrating on work and dealing with a teenage son." He blew out his breath. "I don't seem to be very good at relationships."

His comment hung in the air for only a second before he became all business again.

"I understand you were the one to find K.D. Kirby." His cop face broke again. "You can't seem to stay out of trouble, can you?" he chided before resuming his professional demeanor. "How about you tell me what happened."

Before I could even begin to answer, we were jostled by shoppers coming into the booth. A woman touched my arm. "Could you tell me about the crochet parties you put on?"

Barry gave the woman an arresting stare and said she'd have to wait. When he flashed his badge at her, the woman's eyes widened and she began to back away, mumbling something about how she'd heard I was some kind of sleuth and she didn't want to interfere.

"Did you have to do that?" I said with a touch of annoyance. "She might have wanted to set up a party at the bookstore." I broke away and snagged the woman, pressing a card on her and urging her to call me.

"This isn't going to work," Barry said with a sigh. Not only were we being jostled, but the din of noise made it hard to hear. "I could take you down to the station for the interview."

"No way," I said, shaking my head vehemently for emphasis. Not only did I not want to be away from the booth for a long time, but I'd seen the rooms they used. They were claustrophobic with locked doors. "We have a hotel room for the weekend. We could go there," I offered.

"A quiet hotel room is just what we need," he said. I glanced up at him to see if there was some double meaning in his phrase, but he was all detective.

Dinah had been watching the whole thing while helping a woman start a granny square pin. She gave me a funny look when I said we were going up to the room, but she agreed to handle the sales in my absence.

The noise level dropped abruptly when we went out of the marketplace and into the windowed corridor. I suggested we talk there and pointed to a corner. The words were no sooner said than a woman stopped next to me, read my badge and asked for directions.

"Let's stick to the plan," he said, leading me toward the elevator. We rode up in silence, both of us looking at the floor.

I unlocked the door to the room and he followed me in. I stopped abruptly to feel for the light switch and he walked into me. There was an awkward moment as we made contact. He apologized profusely and stepped to the side.

The room had signs of a lot of people being there. There were coats strewn on the bed and a number of empty coffee cups. We took the two chairs in front of the window. This room didn't have the floor-to-ceiling ones that K.D.'s suite had, but there was still a view. The lights of the Valley twinkled below like jewels on velvet.

He had his notebook out. The cops were still old school, using paper and pen. He was keeping up his cop demeanor, but now that we were alone I was having a hard time playing the part of the impersonal witness. While it was true that I hadn't seen Barry for months, I had seen his son Jeffrey.

It was a complicated story—one of the dogs living at my house was supposedly theirs. Jeffrey came by once a week to deliver dog food and play fetch with Cosmo in my back-yard. He never spoke about his father and I didn't ask.

"Jeffrey seems to be doing well," I said, and Barry looked discombobulated.

"Molly, this is official business. Let's start at the beginning—what were you doing in Ms. Kirby's suite?"

I know I should have probably just answered his questions and gotten the interview over with, but I couldn't help myself. "The fact that you're questioning me means she's dead, doesn't it?" I said. I was pretty sure of the answer, but I wanted to hear it from him. He didn't respond. "And this isn't just a death investigation, is it? You suspect foul play. Was the thing in the tub with her a hair dryer?"

Barry sat straighter and put up his hand. "We're not doing this. You are not going to answer my question with a bunch of your questions." He was doing his best to sound like a tough cop, but he sounded more frustrated than angry. "I'm here to get information from you, not give it. I'm not even going to remind you that interfering in this case could get you arrested and charged. No more sharing of information." He leaned toward me. "Now just tell me what happened."

"At least tell me if she's dead?" I said. Barry groaned in frustration and finally nodded his head before I continued. "You know that Delvin Whittingham said she had an accident and he was taking over temporarily."

Barry tried to maintain his calm and spoke in a terse tone. "Maybe he did that as sort of a cat's on the roof thing. Then, when it comes out that Ms. Kirby is deceased, it won't be such a shock. Now if we could get to what you were doing in the victim's suite."

"I knew it. You called her 'the victim.' You do think it's foul play, though to be honest I can't imagine how a hair dryer in a bathtub could be an accident. It was a hair dryer, wasn't it?"

Barry closed his eyes for a second and blew out his breath. "Molly, please, just the facts."

"All right, but even without you confirming, I'm assuming it is foul play and a hair dryer was at the other end of the black cord I saw," I said finally. After that I went ahead and answered his question and told him that K.D. had said she wanted to talk to me and that Delvin had had me go in first. As I said it, it occurred to me that it could have just been a setup. I remembered reading something about that in *The Average Joe's Guide to Criminal Investigation*. It was a common ploy of killers to get someone to go with them and discover the body. If Barry wasn't going to share with me, I wasn't going to share with him, either. Though he'd probably already thought of it himself.

"You said she wanted to talk to you about something. What was it?" he said with a glint in his eye.

I had assumed that it had something to do with Adele's

giant flashing crochet hooks, but the truth was I didn't know for sure. Barry seemed vexed when I shrugged and said I didn't know.

"How well did you know her and what kind of person was she?"

I explained my dealings with her. "She wasn't a very pleasant person," I said. "You know, didn't play well with others."

Barry's antennae had gone up. "Anyone in particular? Maybe someone in your group?"

The truth was anyone who'd met K.D. seemed to have some kind of problem with her. I didn't feel like putting the spotlight on the Hookers—well, one Hooker in particular. The best way to get his focus off my people was to push him in another direction.

"There was a woman, Julie, whom K.D. outed about her yarn the other day. I saw her here, too. This time K.D. gave her a hard time about her entry into the competition. I don't know her last name, but she's pretty easy to spot. She has a butterfly tattoo on her left hand."

Barry's expression softened into a smile. "Do you want to translate. *Outed her yarn?*"

I explained the setup, that women hung around the store working on their projects, but only if they'd bought their yarn at the store. "The yarn is very pricey, and I heard this woman had some financial problems and was trying to be one of the group." As soon as Barry heard where the store was located and the kind of clientele they had, he got it.

"I suppose being embarrassed like that could be a motive. And you're saying the victim embarrassed her a second time?"

"Yes, K.D. claimed the woman was trying to enter the same piece in the competition again." I saw Barry's eyes do the slightest roll. "I know all this sounds petty, and it probably is, but it was very important to Julie."

"I've made note of it," Barry said.

As he was writing, something else occurred to me. "K.D. was going to make some kind of announcement," I said more to myself than to him. "Another reason to talk to Delvin." Even though I mumbled it, my ex made another groaning noise.

"Oh no. I know where you're going. Remember what I said before about interfering with a police investigation. Let the professionals handle it, Molly." He flipped his notebook shut. "That's it for now. If you can think of anything else." He started to offer me his card, then took it back. "You know the number."

We both stood up and walked to the door. He got there first and opened it. "So, you're with Mason, huh?" he said in a calculated, casual tone. I swallowed and nodded in response.

CHAPTER 8

"I UNDERSTAND YOU ARE THE ONE WHO FOUND the body." Kimberly Diaz Wang stuck her microphone in my face just as I got back to our booth. There was no avoiding the Channel 3 reporter since she basically blocked my way.

"No comment," I said, trying to get around her.

"What do you mean no comment? You're such a . . ." I cringed, afraid of what she might say next. This wasn't our first encounter when I'd been at a crime scene. "Crime scene groupie," she said, finishing her thought. It was useless to point out that it was an incorrect statement. *Groupie* implied someone who was a follower of something or someone. I certainly didn't want to show up at murder scenes; it just happened.

"How'd you know that K.D. is dead?" I said, glad that she'd lowered the microphone. Delvin had only said the magazine mogul had had an accident.

"I'm a reporter. I have a nose for the story behind the story. Do you think I just bought that line Delvin Whittingham dished out about her having an accident?" As she was talking she dropped her cell phone. She rushed to retrieve it, but I got it first. When I looked at the screen, there in black and white it said: "Knitting legend K.D. Kirby found dead #murder?"

"Your news source is a tweet?" I said incredulously.

"But look who sent it," she said. I read it over and saw the sender was KnitStyleMag, or Lacey Kirby.

Chalk up one for Kimberly. K.D.'s daughter was a credible source.

"What a lucky break for me. Here I was getting some sound bites about the opening of the yarn show for a story that I thought would be thrown in at the end of the broadcast. But with K.D.'s death and a question of murder, it ought to be flashed during the breaking news segment." The newscaster stopped for a moment. "I didn't mean that to be as cold as it sounded." She looked at me to see if her comment had gotten my approval. But before I could react, she started talking again. "I wonder if this is going to impact my award."

"You must have missed it, but Delvin assured everyone the show would go on as planned, which I'm sure includes your award." I tried very hard not to sound the least bit sarcastic.

"You really think so?" Kimberly said, dropping the reporter persona. "I sure hope so. I have a spot all picked out for the trophy." Her eyes started to move back and forth, and it was obvious she was thinking about something. "This is definitely going to impact the feature story I was doing. I'll have to rework what I have."

I made a move to get away from her, but she grabbed my arm. "C'mon, give me something. If you're the one who found her, you must have some inside dope, like how she died."

"No comment," I repeated. "Why don't you talk to the cops? I'm sure they'll tell you what happened."

Kimberly rolled her eyes. She knew what little information she'd get from the cops, if they even agreed to talk. "The facts aren't enough anymore. The public wants color, gore, grisly details and hopefully some kind of video." She looked at me hopefully. "Did you get something with your cell phone?"

I gave her a no on the video but finally relented on giving her a comment on one condition: She'd get our booth in the shot. She called her cameraman over and took out the microphone again. "I'm talking to Molly Pink, who discovered the victim. Tell us what you saw," Kimberly said, expectantly.

I positioned myself next to the long table across the front of the booth. There were some crochet lessons going on, and Adele's logo was blinking. Eduardo in his pirate garb was in plain view as was Logan's version of a vampire. I cleared my throat and began. "It's a sad day in the yarn world with the passing of K.D. Kirby. She was a knitting legend."

It wouldn't show on camera, but Kimberly made a face and muttered something about how she never would have made the deal if she knew that was all I was going to say. Then she gave herself a whispery pep talk, saying that she wasn't just a pretty face, she was a hard-hitting reporter.

But with nothing of substance from me, Kimberly had no choice but to read the tweet out loud for the camera. "I think it's pretty clear there was foul play if you consider this tweet that appears to have come from the victim's daughter. 'Knitting legend K.D. Kirby found dead hashtag murder?'" She turned back to me. "What do you have to say about her death being murder? Surely the police have talked to you."

I nodded as noncommittally as I could. "I'm sorry, I didn't hear you," she said, pushing the microphone closer.

"Yes, I did give a statement to the police about what I saw."

"And that was?" the reporter said.

"No comment," I repeated.

"Do you have any idea who did it?"

"I'm sure there is a whole list of suspects," I said, trying to back away.

"Since you've become known as the Miss Marple of Tarzana, I bet you're already on the case and talking to the suspects."

I did my best to appear shocked at her statement. The last thing I needed was for Detective Heather or Barry to hear something like that. Detective Heather would love the opportunity to arrest me for interfering with an investigation and, well, who knew how serious Barry was about his threats. He certainly had been tight-lipped about information.

Kimberly seemed disappointed when I said I was sure the cops had it under control. I tried to move aside to give a better view of our booth, complete with the sign, and even slipped in a little gesture pointing it out. "I'd love to help with a list of suspects, but I'm staying out of this one."

"So, then you do have a list of suspects?" Kimberly said.

She'd boxed me into a corner. "No comment," I said with a sigh. When she realized that was all she was going to get, she left and waved to her cameraman to follow her. Once they were gone I gave all my attention at the booth, realizing it looked like a windstorm had gone through.

"What happened? I was only gone for a little while," I said. The tin of Bob's goodies was empty, the granny square pin operation seemed to have shut down, but the table was littered with balls of yarn and scraps of crochet. Elise was putting out more of the vampire kits. Sheila was talking to someone and showing off the muted color wrap she was wearing. Eduardo was sitting close to an artsy-looking young woman, demonstrating Irish crochet made with yarn instead of thread. Rhoda was trying to demonstrate single crochet to a couple of women, but they were more interested in Logan. He'd struck a pose next to the Anthony books almost like he was the cardboard cutout we had in the bookstore. He held a hook in his hand with a trail of blood red crochet dangling off it. I noted that the supply of vampire books had gone way down. There were some bald spots in the yarn supply, and the number of hooks had also decreased.

Adele rushed inside and began rearranging things on the table as Dinah came to the front, holding the computer tablet we were using to check out customers. "We were really busy. So many people wanted to make the granny square pins, the line was blocking the aisle and I had to shut it down. And the free lessons . . ." Her eyes went skyward. "Everybody wanted them. The good part is they led to us selling a lot of yarn and hooks." Two women squeezed past us to get inside and headed to the display of crochet tools, and Dinah shot me a quick look. "So, tell me, how did it go with Barry?"

"It was a little weird," I said. "But he was all business and just wanted to find out what I saw and what kind of person K.D. was." I mentioned that he had asked if I was with Mason. "It was the only personal thing he said."

"And you said?" my friend asked.

"I didn't give him any details, but then there aren't any details to give yet. The only in-person contact Mason and I have had was seeing each other across the marketplace as he was trying to control his client. I wasn't about to tell Barry that. I just nodded as an answer and let it go at that."

I looked around all the activity in the booth again. "I think it was a wise move to pay the extra money for this location. And Eduardo in his leather pants out front helps."

"Don't forget Logan Belmont," Dinah said. "He might not have the appeal of Hugh Jackman, but the women are still going nuts for him."

"And we can't forget Adele's golden crochet hooks." I glanced toward the table and saw that the colored LED lights had started blinking faster. Adele was hovering over the table fumbling through all the yarn and generally disturbing the lesson that Rhoda was giving a twenty-something girl with an elaborately tattooed arm. I let my glance move over the group. "I don't see any point in mentioning that K.D. is dead since most of the group doesn't know her. But Adele is a different story," I said. "I better tell her before she hears it from somebody else."

I swooped in and slipped my arm through Adele's and pulled her away from the table. Rhoda looked up with a grateful nod.

"Pink, I can't find it," she said in a teary voice. "My hook, the one Dr. Wheel hand carved, is gone." She stopped what she was doing and looked me in the eye. "You know how much that means to me. It's irreplaceable and it's the only thing I have left of our moment."

Her drama was a little hard to take. Yes, the hook was handmade and one of a kind, but that moment she was talking about was probably on her side only. She'd been all over Dr. Wheel when he'd done a book signing at the bookstore, once she found out he had a passion for crochet.

"Maybe someone stole it. It was here this afternoon. It's my lucky charm. I need it to teach the class."

Dr. Wheel wasn't local, and I didn't even know if he'd be willing to give her a replacement so I didn't even bring it up but offered to check around the table. I cleared everybody away and pulled out all the boxes we were using for storage from below. Logan offered to climb under the table and run his hand over the floor.

We found nothing. Adele was so panicked I thought she might not be thinking clearly, and I tried to calm her by asking her where she'd seen it last.

"Pink, I'm sure it was here on the table this morning." Adele's voice cracked as she spoke.

She was close to having a complete meltdown, and I didn't know what I would have done if Mother Humphries hadn't come along. Instantly Adele reeled in the hysteria and greeted her.

"So, this is your booth," Leonora Humphries said, looking over the interior and then the front table. Her gaze stopped on the flashing crochet hooks, and then she looked around at us. "Whose idea was this?" Poor Adele wasn't sure if she should take credit for it or not.

I cut to the chase and asked the woman what she

thought of it. As soon as she said she thought it was definitely a good attention getter, Adele relaxed and told her she'd made it. Then to my great relief, Adele suggested they tour the marketplace together.

I realized I never got the chance to tell them about K.D.

CHAPTER 9

MORE YARN LOVERS SURGED INTO THE MARKETPLACE of the yarn show. Since ours was almost the first booth everyone saw as they came in, and we had something of a circus atmosphere with the flashing lights and men in sexy costumes, the crowd flowed directly to us. Adele had returned and was making the best of being without her special hook as she took over the crochet lessons. She made sure there were two people in addition to herself and Eduardo giving lessons at any one time. Dinah and I resumed the granny pin making, and the line grew so thick, I could barely see across to the Knit Style booth. When I did catch a glimpse, Thea Scott and her helpers had nowhere near the crowd we did.

"We need to make more kits for the pins," Dinah said. The small packets with lengths of thread and beads we'd made up were almost gone. I let her continue to oversee the operation, while I got out the box of supplies.

"Where are the scissors?" I asked, holding an orb of turquoise thread. Dinah looked up and then shrugged.

"Here, use this." She took something from around her neck and hung it around mine. The pendant hung low on the long cord. I was mystified until she showed me that the round metal piece had a cutting edge hidden in the design.

"This is fantastic." I pulled a length of thread and made a clean cut as I pulled it over the hidden blade.

I heard a voice over the loudspeaker saying there was an important announcement. Actually, the voice, which I was pretty sure was Delvin's, had to repeat that in increasingly louder tones a few times before the din died down. All the action in our booth came to an abrupt stop as everyone turned in the direction the sound was coming from.

I stepped out of our booth to the long walkway that went across the front of the room. I could just get a view of K.D.'s interestingly dressed assistant on the end of the catwalk. People had begun to gather around the stage, and I saw Kimberly Wang Diaz move in close with her cameraman. Apparently this crowd was more interested in yarn shopping than gazing at their cell phones, because it was immediately clear that they hadn't read the tweet about K.D.

"I am very sorry to have to announce the passing of our beloved K.D. Kirby," he said. There was an instant gasp through the crowd then a titter of conversations. Delvin started to speak again and everyone fell silent. "I know this is a shock to all of us, but I also know that the best way we can honor her memory is by making the Tenth Annual Southern California Knit Style Show the best ever."

"What happened?" someone from the crowd shouted out. "You said she had an accident."

"All that is immaterial. We should just focus on her legacy." He gestured around the marketplace. "I want to reassure you all that everything will go on as scheduled. As K.D.'s assistant, I was in the middle of all the planning." He glanced up nervously, as Lacey had joined him on the stage. It was a little eerie, because she looked so much like her mother with the same self-important walk that was all shoulders.

She stopped next to Delvin, and he put his hand over the microphone as they spoke. Lacey stepped up to the microphone and introduced herself. "I will be taking my mother's place with Delvin Whittingham's assistance. I know that is what my mother would want me to do."

Delvin wrangled the microphone back. "What a valiant offer at a time like this," he said. He put his arm around Lacey in a supportive manner. "But I can't let you do it in your fragile state. K.D. had it in writing that if something happened to her, I was to step into her place." Lacey looked like she wanted to say something, but he kept the microphone out of her reach. There was a surge of sympathetic comments and then a round of applause.

"You'd think she'd be a little more stunned," CeeCee said, coming up next to me. Since CeeCee's function seemed to be taking in the entries in the crochet competition and hanging around the administrative table, I hadn't spent much time with our celebrity Hooker.

"I'm so sorry," I said to her, thinking she had a relationship with the magazine mogul. CeeCee seemed surprised at my comment, and I explained I thought they were friends. It was CeeCee who'd gotten us involved with the show because of her relationship with K.D.

"I don't know that she had any *friends*," the actress said.

"Or that friendship meant much to her, even in her younger days. Rumor has it she stole her sorority sister's boyfriend and married him. Even then all she cared about was getting what she wanted all the time. It seems so odd for someone who was involved with yarn. As a rule we are such a friendly bunch." Delvin was continuing to speak, but the crowd's attention had dissolved into a bunch of smaller conversations. "And as for my relationship with her," CeeCee remarked, "K.D. couldn't see me for dust until I was in the Anthony movie. I think the whole reason she even added any crochet to the show was because she saw how successful the movie was and that it had inspired people to pick up the hook. You saw how she was in her yarn shop, trying to get me to join the celebrity circle who met there. It was nothing personal."

"Do you know anything about an announcement she was going to make?" I asked, and CeeCee shook her head.

"I heard that you were the one who found her," my fellow Hooker said. When I seemed surprised she knew, she mentioned Kimberly Wang Diaz trying to get a comment from her. It wasn't a surprise, really. There wasn't a better draw than getting a celebrity to talk on camera about a news event.

"How terrible for you, dear," CeeCee said, patting my hand when I'd repeated my story once again. "I'm sure you're right about it being murder. That was just the method the killer used in *Mad Day at Murray's*." CeeCee fluttered her eyes at the memory. "I played the victim. It was the beginning of my career, and I was just glad to get any screen time, even if most of it was me slumped against the tub." She let out a small chuckle. "In my case, the weapon was a toaster. It was so long ago, they didn't even have those handheld hair dryers."

CeeCee continued on for a few moments, reliving her role. She'd been fully clothed beneath the mound of bubbles, and apparently they'd had to do the scene a bunch of times and the floor had gotten quite slippery from the toaster being repeatedly thrown in the tub. I laughed at the image and said it sounded more like the setup for a slapstick comedy than a serious mystery.

"I wanted to take a look at the booth," CeeCee said when she'd finally finished her trip down memory lane. We walked back together, and the actress did a rendition of her musical-sounding laugh when she saw Adele's golden crochet hooks.

"K.D. must have had a fit about that."

"That's an understatement," I said. "She insisted we remove the hooks and that." I pointed at the banner.

"And yet they're still here," she said. Adele was deeply involved with showing a young woman how to hold her hook and had no idea we were talking about her.

"Adele put them back," I said, rolling my eyes. And in the back of my mind I thought of something. Hadn't Adele said she was going to talk to K.D. about the crochet additions?

CeeCee made a tour of the booth and did a double take when she saw Elise's husband dressed up like Anthony. "He's not exactly Hugh Jackman's double," she said to me with a smile. Not that it seemed to matter. As we stood there a dewy-eyed woman went up to him and asked him to do a little crochet for her.

I hadn't thought about that, but thankfully Elise had, and her husband pulled out a hook and the crochet strip he'd been holding before and began to do a row of treble crochet. The woman seemed almost weak-kneed as she watched him. There seemed to be some magic appeal to vampires, even an imitation one with funny hair that looked like a hat. The woman got all gushy when he handed her the little swatch. Logan seemed very comfortable with the whole scenario, and it made me wonder what went on at Elise's house.

"Things are a mess, dear," CeeCee said. "K.D. was supposed to be the judge of the knitting competition."

"That woman had her finger in every pot," I said, going over how she ran the magazines, had the yarn store, and made all the decisions about the yarn show. "Didn't she ever hear of delegating some responsibilities?"

"Delvin Whittingham is stepping in to do the judging, though Ruby Cline came by and volunteered." It was the first time CeeCee had met her, and she seemed quite taken with the yarn company owner. "I wish I could stay here. This looks like much more fun," CeeCee said before she reluctantly went back to the contest area, since contest entries were still being brought in.

By then, Delvin and Lacey had long finished their statement, and as promised, things went on as planned. There seemed to be a running commentary announcing knitting demos, door prizes and assorted other details.

Business continued to boom for us. I acted as the mainstay in the booth, and as the evening wore on I needed a break.

"How can I ever thank you?" I said to Dinah when she offered to take over.

"You've been here all day. I just came this evening. Besides, this is fun. Now go on and check out the place." Dinah gave me a friendly nudge toward the aisle.

Even though it was getting toward closing, there were still lots of people wandering through the temporary shops.

There was so much to look at. Not only were there all kinds of specialty yarns, there were spinning wheels and supplies, special designer patterns, beads and buttons, knitting needles in all different materials and wonderful accessories like shawl pins and fancy stitch holders. I was just looking and did a complete tour without stopping. I was glad to see that our booth definitely had the most action.

I walked through the last aisle to the front and was about to return to the Shedd & Royal super booth when I noticed a woman holding up a long white vest and realized I was next to the booth of the woman who had insisted we were in her space. I struggled trying to remember her name. I remembered that it reminded me of water. Right, it was Rain. Something seemed off, and then I realized she was in a new spot. I stepped into the small enclosure at the front of the aisle. Rain looked up immediately, ready to offer assistance.

"Molly, isn't it?" she said with a friendly smile. "Just to let you know, I give a discount to fellow vendors."

"Good to know," I said, glancing around her space, curious to see how it compared with the arrangement of ours. She had made the most of the small area. The four dress forms wearing knitted items were placed around the perimeter. The racks of finished items were in the front, and a table covered with a cloth that went to the ground had some wire shelves holding more of her stock at the back against the curtained divider.

I took a moment to look through what she had and quickly ascertained that there were only six different designs, but she had made them up in a variety of colors. I complimented her on how much she'd managed to get into her booth.

She thanked me and modeled the gray-toned jacket she was wearing, explaining that to save space she acted as one of the models. She kept glancing toward a woman who had taken a long white vest off of one of the dress forms and was holding it up against herself and suggested she was welcome to try it on, gesturing toward the full-length mirror toward the back of the space. Two other women were admiring an exquisite jacket in shades of reds, pinks and orange. It took me a moment to realize it was the same design as the one Rain was wearing. She modeled the style for the two women and invited them to try the one they were holding.

"It's a fine line between being helpful and too pushy," Rain said in a soft voice. She let out a sigh. "It's hard to keep going like it's business as usual. It's such a shock about K.D."

I remembered that Rain had mentioned being at all the shows from the very beginning. "You must have known her pretty well."

"We were what I'd call business friends. I'd helped her out when she first started the show and needed vendors. She appreciated my loyalty. That's why I knew there was some mistake when you were in my spot."

As Rain said that, I realized why I'd been surprised to see her booth in the front. When I'd seen her setup before, it had been in yarn show Siberia.

The women were all trying on the knitted pieces and taking turns in front of the full-length mirror.

"It looks like you worked it out. This spot is much better than the one in the back."

She kept her eyes on her customers while she talked to me. "Do you know what happened to K.D.? One minute Delvin was saying she'd had an accident and then he said she'd died. I haven't been able to talk to him to find anything out."

When I said I'd been the one to find her, Rain's eyes widened. "How terrible. What happened?"

"Did you know about her ritual of the bath and champagne?" I asked, and she nodded. "None of it is official, but it seems like someone threw a hair dryer in the tub while she was in it."

"But who would do that? K.D. did kind of rub a lot of people the wrong way, but kill her?" She put her hand to her forehead in dismay and rocked her head. "I was up there. I went to her suite to talk to her about the mix-up with my space." She seemed stricken as she explained that K.D. had said she would take care of it and then Rain had left.

"Do you know if anyone else went up there?" I asked.

"Probably K.D.'s daughter and Delvin. Maybe someone else, too. She said something about toasting a new beginning with someone. She kind of bent my ear about it. It was someone she'd gone to college with and then, because of something with a man, they hadn't spoken for years. Only recently had they mended fences. When I left, the waiter was at the door with the champagne."

I asked her how well she knew Delvin. She understood where I was going. "You think that he might have been the one?" She stopped to consider for a moment, but the woman with the long white vest made a move toward her. Rain dropped our conversation like a hot coal at the prospect of making a sale.

I left her to make her transaction and headed across the front walkway. I'd been gone long enough, anyway.

When I got back to the Shedd & Royal booth, things

had quieted down as closing time approached. And not a moment too soon for me. It had been quite a day.

Most of the Hookers had already left, and the booth seemed quiet without them. Adele was giving a last lesson to Thea Scott, who'd come over since it had gotten so quiet. My coworker seemed to have gotten over her lost hook, for the moment, anyway. Dinah sat back in a chair, looking exhausted. When I checked the small bin where we'd kept the packets to make the pins, it was empty.

"Nothing like something free to attract a crowd," Dinah said.

"There's no reason for you to stay," I said, taking off the pendant and handing it to her.

"Keep it," she said. "It's better than looking for scissors all the time." I thanked her and put it back around my neck. She took my suggestion and wearily went to the exit.

I got ready to close down the booth. Mr. Royal had devised a series of roll-down duck cloth curtains to cover the whole front of the booth when it was closed. It was more for look than security. As I got ready to let them down, Eric and his mother came by. They certainly made a strange pair. Eric seemed twice as tall as his diminutive mother, but both of them carried themselves with the same ramrod-straight posture.

"Cutchykins, after what happened, I wanted to be sure you were okay."

When Leonora Humphries heard the pet name her son had for Adele, her eyes went so far back in her head, I thought they were going to disappear.

Adele seemed stricken. "How did you know?"

Eric shrugged his big shoulders. "It's common knowledge now."

Adele put her hand on his shoulder. "You mean everybody is talking about it? It isn't what it seems. I'm upset about losing it, but not because he gave it to me."

Eric seemed perplexed. "I'm talking about K.D. Kirby's murder," he said. "What are you talking about?"

"Oh," Adele said a little too loudly. "She's dead?" She seemed totally surprised by the news.

"Didn't you hear Delvin's announcement?" I said. Adele shook her head.

"You said you lost something?" Eric sounded concerned. "Maybe I can help you find it."

Adele shook her head quickly. "It's nothing. He means nothing. Don't worry about it." I tried not to roll my eyes, realizing that Adele had been talking about her lost hook and its connection to Dr. Wheel. Only Adele would think everybody was talking about something that happened to her. She looked at her glittering logo and snapped the flashing lights off. It seemed like she let out a sigh of relief as she patted the oversize gold hooks. Her eyes grazed the rest of the front table, littered with balls of yarn and hooks left from the crochet lessons. She muttered something under her breath. It sounded like she said she had an idea. I shuddered to think what it might be.

"Now that you've seen she's fine, why don't we go," Eric's mother said. "I'm sure Adele wants to go home and rest up for tomorrow."

"No," she said forcefully. "I'm coming with you." She grabbed her things and rushed out of the booth to join them.

I finished closing up, letting down the coverings for the booth. The lights were already going off and a man in a gray uniform was waiting to lock the door when I left. It was easy spotting my car since the parking lot was almost completely empty. I gratefully headed for home.

When I opened my kitchen door, both dogs ran out. It was strange not to have to coax Blondie outside, but then they'd been left alone longer than usual. Cosmo had registered his discontent by knocking over the trash again, and this time spreading it around the floor. The cats walked in the kitchen with their tails held high and gave me a dirty look.

I checked their bowls and understood the unhappy faces. Other than a few stray pieces of dry cat food, their bowls were empty. I didn't have to be Sherlock Holmes to deduce what had happened. The footprints near the bowls were too big to belong to either cat. I'd left a chair too close to the shelves. Blondie would only have eaten the cat food if it was easily accessible, but Cosmo was a different story. I was sure it was the little black mutt who'd figured out how to jump on the chair and help himself. I refilled the bowls and moved the chair to the other side of the dining room.

I was back in the kitchen sweeping up the coffee grounds and food scraps that Cosmo had spread around when the phone rang.

"Don't you check your messages, Sunshine?" Mason said when I picked up. I took my BlackBerry out of my purse and checked it.

"I don't see any on my cell phone," I said. I scrolled around and random things began to open.

"That's it, I'm getting you a new one," he said. "I left a message on your house phone as well."

I explained I'd just gotten home and was too busy with the animals to check it yet. "It's about what happened, isn't it," I said, assuming he was calling about K.D.'s death.

"Did something happen?" He sounded concerned. "Are

you all right?" He offered assorted services in case I wasn't, including bringing over anything I needed or giving me a lift to the ER.

He was half teasing and I laughed, though I knew if I'd said yes to any of them, he would have come through. "I'm fine. Well, maybe a little tired. But it's K.D. Kirby who has the problem. She's dead." I started to explain who K.D. was, that she was the woman his client Audrey Stewart had the issue with. There was a moment of silence on his end. "She is your client, isn't she?"

"I'm not sure if I should confirm that," he said. "Attorney-client privilege and all."

I almost laughed. He'd managed to tell me Audrey was his client without actually saying it. Then he wanted details—when did it happen, how did it happen and most of all was it natural causes or murder.

"I think the word you're going for is *homicide*. Is *murder* even an official police word?" I said, and he chuckled. I told him what I knew and he listened without comment before abruptly changing the subject.

"I can't tell you how happy I am that you called me and that you're finally ready to start things between us. You really do bring the sunshine into my life. I know it's late and we said we'd wait until after this weekend, but I could come over," he offered.

"I know Audrey stole some knitting needles. I don't suppose you could tell me what you were doing there this afternoon."

"Allegedly stole," he corrected. "And you're right; I can't tell you what I was trying to accomplish. Do you know if the cops have any suspects?"

"I've lost my in; nobody would tell me anything." The

first part of my response must have gotten him to thinking, because he suddenly wanted to know if I'd seen Barry. He didn't sound happy when I said Barry had been the one to question me since I'd been the one to find K.D.

"I just bet he was happy to interrogate you."

"He was all business. It was as if we'd never been a couple. He didn't call me Babe once and he might have even referred to me as ma'am." Mason seemed to relax and started talking about seeing me in the afternoon.

"I'm sorry I couldn't stop and talk. At least now I know what you're going to be doing all weekend. I saw your booth and it's very impressive." The dogs had come to the back door and were scratching to get in and be fed. I let them in and tried to cradle the phone while I opened the dog food can, but it required two hands. I told Mason I had to go.

"Are you sure? Last chance. I could come over and give you a preview of my attention." Then he stopped himself. "Sorry if I'm being too persistent. After everything that's happened, I'm just afraid you're going to change your mind."

"No way, I have really thought this through. And you're the one I want to spend time with." I hesitated. "Starting on Sunday night."

CHAPTER 10

It seemed like I'd barely been asleep when the alarm went off and I opened my eyes. For a moment I lolled in bed and thought of sleeping a little longer, but then I remembered the show. I almost ran across the house and started in on animal chores. Water bowls needed to be changed, the cat box attended to and food for everyone. In the end, I barely had time for a cup of coffee and a container of instant oatmeal.

I stopped at the bookstore on the way. Mrs. Shedd gave me a dark look. "Molly, not another body. I thought for sure you could get through one weekend without ending up in the middle of a crime scene."

"How'd you know?" I asked.

"The eleven o'clock news. Kimberly Wang Diaz's story was the top one. Imagine my surprise when I looked up and saw her talking to you. You could see the Shedd & Royal booth in the background. Joshua outdid himself," she said, smiling with pride. "I wish you had just talked about our booth though instead of mentioning the dead woman."

I had forgotten all about the newscast and regretted missing it. I wanted to ask Mrs. Shedd for more details, but I thought it better to get off the subject of my relationship with dead bodies. I particularly didn't want to bring up that I'd been the one to find the victim. I changed the subject to how well the booth was doing. "That's why I'm here. We sold all the Anthony books Mr. Royal brought over. It helps that we had a real live Anthony in the booth." I mentioned that Elise's husband had dressed up as the character.

Mrs. Shedd shook her head and said something about it being a stretch, and I realized she'd seen the man with the hair that looked like a hat. "You'd be amazed what a little glitter makeup does."

Mrs. Shedd laughed at the image, and then we got a supply of all three of the books and a freestanding cardboard holder. She even helped me load it into the greenmobile. "I'm almost afraid to ask, but how is Adele doing?"

I knew Mrs. Shedd wasn't referring to her health, but rather the level of trouble Adele was generating. You might wonder why we all kept Adele around if she was so much trouble. Though none of us had actually talked about it, I think we were all on the same page. Adele was like that troublesome cousin, a bunch of bother, but family all the same. And she certainly kept things interesting. But I decided there was no reason to stir things up by mentioning the fuss Adele's logo had made and her drama over the lost hook, so I simply said Adele was doing fine.

"I'm surprised you don't have a list of suspects. Not that

I'm complaining. I'm glad you're focusing all your attention on running the booth instead of playing detective."

I started to react to the word *playing*. There was no playing involved, and I reminded her that I'd solved quite a few murders.

We'd gotten to the greenmobile and were loading things in the backseat and trunk. "But maybe this time you really should leave it to the professionals," my boss said.

The words echoed in my mind as I drove across the San Fernando Valley, avoiding the rush-hour clogged freeway by taking Burbank Boulevard. The view was enough to take your breath away as the wide roadway wound through the Sepulveda Dam area. The Los Angeles River looked like a real river here and not the concrete channel it was in so many other areas. A hawk coasted on the wind, circling over the wild open space. The air was cold and crystal clear, and the peaks of the San Gabriel Mountains were so sharp, it was almost like they'd been outlined in black ink. Who killed K.D. really wasn't my business, and then there was the issue of Barry's threats. Not that I really believed he'd arrest me, or at least I didn't think so. And yet it had happened almost under my nose. The killer was probably someone I'd seen, maybe even someone I knew. How could I ignore that?

The Buena Vista parking lot wasn't as quiet as I'd expected, considering that the show didn't open for another hour. A group of cars were parked close together, and the women were standing around drinking coffee. Some of them had brought baked goods that were being passed among the group. My first thought was it looked like a tailgate party for yarn fans.

As I passed by them I saw there was a lot of admiring of

each other's handiwork and I heard snippets of conversation. Some of it was about yarn they'd bought or classes they were taking that day, but the biggest topic of conversation was last night's news and the murder at the yarn show. What was that saying about publicity? Bad publicity was still publicity. Of course, the facts had gotten wildly distorted. I heard one woman say that K.D. had died in the midst of the marketplace and another say K.D. had been modeling a sweater when she'd keeled over and that it was probably some fast-acting poison. I almost wanted to stop and correct them, but I forced myself to keep going with my bin on wheels to the event center. As I prepared to go in, a deliveryman came out pushing an empty dolly. He let the door slip but then caught and held it when he saw me.

Inside, the people running the registration booth were just arriving and went behind their temporary stand near the entrance. Several easels were being set up with large placards presenting the day's schedule of classes. I scanned it quickly and noted that most of them had to do with knitting. The few crochet offerings were taught by people I'd never heard of. Another placard had the day's schedule of knitting demonstrations, fashion shows of knitted designs and special events at some of the booths. I noticed there was no mention of our free lessons or pin making.

I started to get annoyed at how crochet was being ignored. I didn't understand why K.D. had included it in the show and then excluded it from all the demonstrations and events.

"Oh no, I'm turning into Adele," I said under my breath as I went inside the exhibit hall.

The first thing I noticed was that a large floral wreath had been placed just inside next to the administration table. A picture of K.D. was beside it with the words: "A Knitting Legend Gone Too Soon."

I went directly to the Shedd & Royal booth and began rolling up the coverings on the front. I wheeled the books inside, and it only took a few minutes to set up the free-standing holder. Now that I was viewing the booth with less tired eyes, I saw that we'd sold so much yarn that the extra Mr. Royal had left up in the mini suite wouldn't fill all the empty spots. I certainly didn't want to miss out on sales because we didn't have stock. What to do?

I had a good view of the other vendors as they filtered in, drinking their morning coffee. Paxton Cline came in looking like he wasn't sure he wanted to be there. But then I'd felt from the start he was working in the family business because he had to, not because there was yarn in his blood.

Perhaps he could offer a solution to my problem. He was pulling back the coverings from the Cline Yarn International booth as I approached him. He looked up and, when he saw it was me, appeared stricken. "I didn't do it," he said as I got closer.

It was so funny that someone with such an unusual name was so bland and ordinary looking. He had medium brown close-cut hair and a soft, roundish face, which would probably become more defined when he got out of his twenties. I didn't get what he was talking about at first, but he continued on. "If you're coming to question me about K.D. Kirby's death, I have an alibi. My grandmother made me stay in the booth the whole time so she could wander around."

"I don't know what you're talking about," I said.

"I saw the interview on the eleven o'clock news. I know all about your detective work."

I told him I'd missed the broadcast. He took out his smartphone and with a few swipes of the screen had brought up the Channel 3 site and found the story. He went right to the part where Kimberly read the tweet out loud and mentioned that it seemed like her death was murder. The picture went directly to me after that. It was weird to see my name in tiny letters scrawled across the screen.

"I look horrible," I said, focusing in on myself more than what the newscaster was saying. I'd never realized how bad I looked from the right side. My hair was askew and my complexion was as pale as a ghost. "It doesn't even look like I was wearing any makeup," I muttered. I only tuned in to the report at the end when Kimberly said the part about me being the Miss Marple of Tarzana. "Could you play that again?" I said and he obliged. When I listened to it carefully, I realized it had been edited. They had cut out my statement about a loss to the yarn world and left in the part where I said something about a list of suspects. It really made it sound like I was on the case.

"Paxton, I'm not investigating K.D.'s death, and even if I was, you wouldn't be on my list of suspects." Maybe I had wrongly suspected him in the past, but that was over and done with. He looked instantly relieved. "I'm here about yarn. We're doing so well, I need more stock and now." I figured that Paxton kind of owed me. He'd been mostly a gofer until I said I wanted him to be the contact for the bookstore's yarn department and he'd been elevated to sales.

We walked into their booth and he looked over their stock. "I'm sure it wouldn't matter to Gran if I sold you some of our yarn. The end result is the same whether your shop or ours sells it." Then he had a change of heart. "Maybe I better not. There's something weird going on. The very fact we have this booth is strange. We only sell wholesale to yarn stores. I asked Gran about it and she refused to say anything."

He finally offered to call in a rush order and pick it up when he took a lunch break.

I asked him if his grandmother knew K.D., and his face fell. "Please don't investigate her. She wouldn't take it well. She'd probably sue you for character assassination or something."

He looked at me for some kind of acknowledgment, but before I could say a word, he went off talking like a runaway train.

"Okay, Cline Yarn International bought ads in the knitting magazines. And the *Knit Style* magazine sometimes used our yarn in the patterns they featured. They bought yarn from us for their store. It doesn't mean anything that Gran always made a face when she mentioned K.D. Kirby's name."

Poor Paxton realized what he'd just said pointed out how his grandmother and K.D. were at odds. "Forget I said that."

"Don't worry, I'm not investigating anything," I said, putting my hands up in capitulation. "I only came here to ask you about buying some yarn for our booth."

Adele was just coming in when I went back to our booth. She was wearing a sample of the stash buster wrap her upcoming class was based on. It had a variety of colors and textures of yarn, but at a distance it was the reds that stuck out. She wore it over a navy blue pencil skirt that brought out the bright colors of the wrap. She'd brought another sample and laid it on the front table with a pitch about the class.

She noticed me staring.

"I'm trying to show off what students can learn to crochet in my class," she said as she bustled inside. I expected some kind of fuss about the hook, but she said nothing. I decided it was best not to bring it up. She rushed off a moment later and said she had to take care of something.

I didn't expect the Hookers until later and was glad when Rhoda came in. She set down her stuff and took up a position to give crochet lessons. Adele was back by the time the doors opened and people began to come into the marketplace. Delvin took the microphone and welcomed everyone to Friday morning. I tuned out what he said after that, figuring it was all just stuff about knitting.

The morning crowd was lighter than the night before, but all of them stopped at our booth. Several people commented on seeing me on the news and asked for details about K.D., although it seemed like what they were really interested in was my reaction to coming across a dead person. Other people asked me if it was true I was some kind of amateur sleuth.

"She is," a woman with brown curly hair said. "She's like our own Nancy Drew."

There was a lot of interest in the crochet parties and the fact that the bookstore had a yarn department where people could hang out. Adele modeled her wrap and tried to get sign-ups for her class. She seemed a little frantic, and it occurred to me the class might still be a bit low on numbers.

"We've got to get enough people to sign up," Adele said finally, and I realized I was right about her concern. "With all these knitters, we can't have a crochet class canceled. The embarrassment of it all," she wailed. I was pretty sure she was most concerned about Eric's mother finding out.

"It's not until tomorrow, so there's lots of time for people to sign up," I said. Adele seemed slightly calmed by my words. The crowd grew steadily, and then there was a lull as the morning classes started on the upper floor. When I looked around, Rhoda had disappeared. I took the opportunity to straighten things up while the booth was relatively quiet.

Across the way, I watched as Thea Scott and her helper did the same. I think everyone who'd come to the marketplace had stopped over there, too. It was, after all, K.D.'s yarn studio booth. I imagined it was a combination of people wanting to pay their respects and a certain level of curiosity.

I was surprised to see Audrey Stewart march into the booth and stop next to Thea Scott. I checked to see if Mason was behind the alleged shoplifting actress, but she was alone. I was curious what was going on and moved to the bench outside our booth to get a better chance at overhearing. The actress had a pixieish look with her short chopped haircut and slender build, but she seemed all business.

Delvin joined them, and then K.D.'s daughter Lacey came into the booth as well. Now I was really curious about what was going on.

Audrey first gave her condolences to all of them on the passing of K.D., and I wondered if *passing* was the right term when someone was murdered. Wasn't that more like being pushed? Then the actress got down to the real reason she was there.

"I'm sure at a time like this, the last thing any of you want to be dealing with is the whole fuss about the silver knitting needles. I got the impression that it was K.D. who was so insistent about pressing charges, anyway. I think I've come up with a good solution." She made sure she had their attention.

"It doesn't matter how I got the needles, even though it was really a mistake. Why not turn this into something positive?" Her audience nodded at the idea. "So, here it is. I've donated the silver needles to the auction. With all the attention they've gotten, they will probably go for more than the selling price, and all that money goes to charity. At the same time, I will pay the store for the needles. And as a little something extra, I'll hang around for the weekend. We all know how celebrities attract attention. I can do autographs, take pictures with people, even help them with their knitting." She paused for it all to sink in. "Then at the end of the weekend, the slate is clean."

The store manager stepped forward. "You're right that at a time like this the silver needles hardly seem important. Why not keep it simple and you just pay the store for the needles." Thea Scott looked to Delvin and Lacey for agreement.

"It's too late for that," Audrey interrupted. "I already donated them to the auction." She pushed a check toward the manager saying it was for the needles.

Delvin turned to Audrey. "I think that is a great idea." He glanced at all of them. "Since I'm in charge now, I'm giving her the okay." In case they'd forgotten, he brought up that there was something in writing that if K.D. was incapacitated, he was to step in. Lacey argued that it was only meant to be temporary.

Delvin disagreed. "Your mother probably didn't tell you, but I know she wanted to step back from the business. Once everything is settled, I expect to be permanently in charge. I'm sure that was what the announcement K.D. was making was all about, and I'm sure she left it in writing with her attorneys." He looked very self-satisfied. "I've been covering for her for years. All the pieces supposedly written by her were done by me. I supervised the photo shoots. She was the face of the business, but I did all the work."

Lacey jumped in. "Delvin, if my mother was going to turn anything over to anybody, it would be to me."

The trendily dressed man appeared shocked. "You must be kidding. You have no interest in yarn. You don't even like to wear sweaters. I have been your mother's right-hand person for years. I know the ins and outs of everything. All you know is how to post tweets and manage a Facebook page."

Lacey gave him a haughty stare. "I have a degree in business. I don't need to know about yarn to run things." She turned to Audrey. "I think your suggestion about the needles is an excellent solution." Lacey took out her phone and began to compose a tweet. "I'm going to let everybody know about your donation to the auction. It will generate a lot of attention. There's nothing like a story to go with a donation to make it seem more valuable."

But something in Audrey's proposal didn't seem right to me. After watching how Mason had accompanied her the day before and spoke for her to K.D., I couldn't believe he would tell Audrey to come make this deal herself. Unless he didn't know what she was doing. I felt a little like a tattletale, but I called his office anyway.

"Miss me, huh?" he teased when he came on the line.

"Well, yeah," I said, meaning it. Seeing him just for the few minutes at a distance had made me long for more time with him. But this wasn't the time to get all gooey and romantic. I told him about his client, and I could hear his breathing change and could tell he wasn't happy.

"I just hate it when my clients think they can handle

something themselves and end up making a mess that I have to clean up. Sorry I can't say anything specific. But there's nothing wrong with you talking."

"She sort of admitted to taking the needles," I said, and I heard him groan. "But she seems to have come up with a plan they're all happy with in exchange for dropping the charges against her."

I described the plan to Mason, and he made more upset noises when he heard that the people who agreed to Audrey's plan probably didn't have the authority to drop the charges against her. "And she's going to be there all weekend?" he said.

"That was her offer."

"It looks like I'll be seeing a lot of you this weekend, Sunshine, from across a crowded room."

CHAPTER 11

AROUND MIDDAY, THE CROWD SWELLED AS THE classes finished and the newly inspired students went looking to buy more yarn. As if any crocheter or knitter ever needed a reason to add to their yarn stash. Most of the people coming into the marketplace made a stop at the wreath and picture of K.D. The usual reaction was a concerned head shake and a worried look around. Once Kimberly Wang Diaz had mentioned murder on the newscast, it changed everything. The questions on everyone's mind were probably something like, who did it and were they still there? I suppose there might have been a third one—would the killer strike again?

Thanks to our primo position, the Shedd & Royal booth was their first stop after that. And thanks to Mr. Royal's great design, everyone wanted to wander inside the booth. I snapped some photos with my BlackBerry and sent them to

Mrs. Shedd. I knew she was worried about the cost versus profit for our presence at the yarn show, and I wanted to reassure her we were getting lots of customers.

At first, I'd just given out cards to anyone interested in the crochet parties, but then I'd set out a sheet where people could leave their information and I'd contact them. We were already on the third page.

Adele had wandered off, mumbling that she had to take care of something. I was certainly glad when Rhoda reappeared and took over the crochet lessons. With her New York accent and slight bite to her voice, people were a little hesitant at first, but her no-nonsense manner turned out to work very well for teaching. The best part—there was no lecture about the wonders of crochet that Adele always gave out with her lessons. Elise arrived without her husband but with a fresh batch of her vampire kits. She joined Rhoda to help with the lessons, but her first priority was moving the kits.

Since Dinah wasn't there, I'd shut down the granny square pin making. I was left to help people with yarn, tools and books and doing the cashiering. It didn't take a whole lot of thought to handle it, and my mind started mulling over who could have killed K.D. Kirby. Apparently lots of people. Even Rain had mentioned how the knitting mogul rubbed a lot of people the wrong way. Including Audrey Stewart, I thought with a start. Her pixie-ish appearance could be deceiving. I viewed her as a headstrong actress who thought she could handle things better than her lawyer, who was an expert at fixing messy situations. But now the timing of her appearance struck me. Of course . . .

My train of thought was interrupted by something coming over the loudspeaker. I'd gotten used to the constant flow of announcements and descriptions of knitted items in the numerous fashion shows, so I'd mostly tuned it out, but this time something cut into my attention. Or someone.

There were no customers at the moment, so I ventured out of the booth and walked to where I could see the catwalk. Adele was standing in front of Delvin, holding a large turquoise plastic crochet hook that I recognized as a size Q. She grabbed a strand of thick yarn that I saw was coming from the bag on her shoulder. She held it up over her head and made a slip knot. She gave a nod and music began— something that sounded like an Irish jig. And then Adele began to rock back and forth to the music as she made a short foundation row of chain stitches. Thanks to the big hook and thick yarn, it was easy to see what she was doing. She joined the row of chain stitches and formed a circle. I was pretty sure I knew what was coming next. She turned single, double and triple crochet stitches into the petals of a flower and then they exploded into crazy shapes that had no name. The music quickened and Adele with it.

"What's that?" a woman next to me asked her companion. "It looks like fun."

I butted right in and answered her question. "It's free-form crochet. Sometimes called scrumbling." I didn't mention that the addition of the music was all Adele's idea. More people joined them, and I heard the women repeating what I'd said Adele was doing. I saw several women heading to our booth and rushed back to help them. There seemed to suddenly be a lot of interest in the big-size hooks.

"Hey, Sunshine." I looked up just as Mason stopped by the edge of the front table. "Thanks for calling me," he said, going past the crochet lessons in progress and coming into the booth. The women left with their crochet supplies, and there was a lull in customers. Mason took the opportunity to put his arms around me. The familiar scent of his subtle cologne filled my senses, and despite where I was, I settled into his embrace and hugged him back. Very simply he felt like home. It was our first physical contact in months, and neither one of us wanted to let go.

But we both had things to attend to and reluctantly separated as I heard someone clearing their throat rather loudly. It was the kind of throat clearing someone did when they wanted to be noticed. Both Mason and I looked up at the same time. Rhoda and Elise glanced up from their lessons, too. Barry Greenberg was standing in the aisle, shifting his weight, seeming impatient.

"What's he doing here?" Mason said in an unhappy tone. It probably wouldn't have mattered if I'd reminded Mason that not only had Barry walked out of my life, but he'd actually encouraged me to go with Mason. Even if they hadn't been vying for my attention, the fact that Barry was a homicide detective and Mason was a lawyer made them natural adversaries. Me being in the mix just stirred the pot a little more.

I was going to answer, but Barry spoke before I could. "I'm investigating a homicide. And I'd like to speak to Molly. It's official business." Mason looked to me, and I reminded him that I'd found K.D. and that Barry had already questioned me once.

"Do you want me to stay as your lawyer?" Mason asked. I was sure the best chance for peace was for him to leave. I assured him that I wasn't a suspect. "I'm one of the few people who doesn't have a motive. I had no problem with K.D."

Mason reluctantly left, but not without saying that he'd

try to stop back later. I followed him outside the booth and stopped next to Barry.

"What's he doing here?" Barry asked. He was trying to sound like it was just an informational question, but he couldn't quite hide the edge in his voice. I mentioned one of his clients was at the yarn show. Barry knew the kinds of clients Mason had and also that if Mason was there, the client must be in some kind of trouble. He asked for details. I had no attorney-client situation to keep me from talking, but I didn't want to get in the middle, either, so I only gave her name.

We were still standing in the aisle. Barry was staring at the administration table, and I followed his gaze. Mason had just caught up with Audrey Stewart. He hugged her in greeting and then put his arm around her shoulder and led her to the back wall.

Barry smiled. "And you're not jealous?" I shook my head, and he stopped to think for a moment. "Right, I did hear something about Audrey Stewart. There was a fuss about some knitting needles she shoplifted. Mason's clients certainly know how to make a mess out of anything." He turned to me. "Are you sure it doesn't bother you that he has to spend all kinds of hours with women like her? All that hugging doesn't look that professional to me."

"I gather you're here for a reason," I said, ignoring his comment. Barry had said it was official business, and I was more comfortable dealing with details of a murder than comments on my personal life.

"Right," Barry said. He pointed to a quiet corner in the back of the booth and suggested we go there. "I have something to show you," he said. He waited while I cleared a spot on a display table before laying the file down and opening it.

He extracted a photograph and set it down on the closed file. "I wondered if you recognized this."

I did my best to appear neutral, but I certainly did recognize the subject of the photo. The wooden hook was thick around the bottom and was clearly handmade—and—the hook Adele had been frantically looking for.

"Where was it taken?" I asked. Barry let down his cop face and smiled while shaking his head. "Some things don't change. You can't answer my question with a question. Molly, this is serious business. I'm investigating a homicide. Now, just tell me anything you know about this hook, like who it belongs to."

I took a moment to consider what to say. The fact that he was asking about the hook meant it was somehow connected with K.D.'s death. Adele had been angry with K.D. and said she was going to talk to her, and throwing a hair dryer in a bathtub probably was the kind of thing Adele would do if she was going to kill somebody. But I still wasn't going to hand her over to Barry.

"It's obviously a rather large crochet hook," I said. "It looks like it's made out of wood."

Barry groaned and was all serious cop now. "That's not what I meant and you know it. I know you know who it belongs to. I could arrest you and take you down to the station."

"For what?" I said.

He narrowed his dark eyes. "For not talking, ah, withholding evidence. Something like that."

I rolled my eyes. "You'd really do that, all that time and paperwork? And you know that charge would never stick."

"What's going on?" he said. "You used to tell me stuff."

"And you used to tell me stuff," I said. "You clammed

up first." I reminded him that I'd asked him unanswered questions when we'd spoken before.

He seemed totally frustrated, and I thought he was going to drop it. Elise left to take a break as Adele came barreling back in the booth, exuberant from her performance. She even had a following of people.

"Pink, I'm so glad it occurred to me to talk to Delvin. It was so much easier dealing with him. He completely got why they should include crochet demos. Not like some people." I tried to be like Barry and do the cop face thing, but I don't think I succeeded. It might have been the little gasp that escaped my lips despite my best effort to keep it in. Or it might have been the way I rushed to block Adele's view of the photo and tried to move her away. One look at the picture and she'd be sure to shriek something about it being her hook. Barry was a master at reading people's reactions, and there was a triumphant glint to his eyes. I knew he was up to something. I wanted to warn Adele, but that was too much of a giveaway.

"Adele, could you hand me a copy of the first Anthony book?" he said. I yelled, "Don't!" but she just looked at me like I was nuts and picked up a copy out of the freestanding case.

"How about I get a picture of you holding the book," Barry said. Adele was clueless there was anything up and naturally just liked the attention. She even posed. When he was done she brought the book over and started to hand it to him, but he started fidgeting with something and asked her to leave it on the table. Without a second thought, she set it down and picked up one of the large hooks we had for sale and went back to show it to her group of followers.

"Ring me up," he said to me, handing over his credit

card. There was nothing I could do but take his card and run it through the thing on the computer tablet. Adele had gone back to showing off the freeform crochet piece to her followers.

"Do you want a bag?" I said after he signed the screen with his finger.

He was all cocky smiles now. "Just give me the bag and I'll do it myself." I handed over one of the paper bags with "Shedd & Royal" on the front and could do nothing but watch helplessly as he took his pen and pushed the book into the bag without touching it.

"Did I forget to mention that we found the hook in the victim's room and it was covered with fingerprints?" He looked at his package. "And now we have something to try to match them with and even a photo to show whose prints they are."

Poor Adele had no idea that she'd just contributed to cooking her own goose.

I waited until he was completely clear of the booth and Adele's crew had moved on before I went over to her. "What's up, Pink?" she said, looking at me with a wary eye.

"I need to know. Did you go up to K.D.'s room and talk to her?" Adele seemed surprised by the question.

"I was going to, but then I decided why bother, I'd just put the blinking logo back out and rehang the banner. If she came back to the booth and fussed, then I'd talk to her." Adele stopped and suddenly seemed suspicious. "Why are you asking?"

"So, you're saying that you didn't take your special hook and yarn and go up to her room?"

"No way." Adele put her hand on her hip, and then I watched as a cloud went through her mind and her expression dampened. "What are you saying—that the hook I've been looking all over for was in K.D.'s room?"

I didn't say a word, but my expression must have told it all, because Adele kept on going. "It couldn't have been there. It must have been an imposter hook. I wasn't anywhere near her room. How do you know the hook was in K.D.'s room?" Then the pieces began to fit together. She glanced toward the aisle and her eyes moved back and forth as she thought. "The cops have it, don't they? And now they have my fingerprints, too." She suddenly looked totally dejected.

We were interrupted by the arrival of Paxton pulling a cart with several big plastic bins on top. He wheeled it right to the back of the booth and had me sign for the order of yarn. "Please don't mention this to my grandmother. I can't see why she would mind, but she's been so jumpy, I don't want to take a chance on upsetting her."

When Paxton left, Adele came up to me. "Pink, you have to do something. I can't be accused of anything. That would be the final straw with Mother Humphries. I know I've teased you about doing the detective thing, but you've got to find out who really killed K.D."

CHAPTER 12

"THERE YOU ARE," DINAH SAID, CATCHING UP TO me as I threaded through people in the aisle between a booth featuring gorgeous handspun yarn studded with sparkle and one that had a display of little shopping bags with kits of organic cotton to make small items like washcloths.

"You made it," I said. The agreement had been that she would come after her day's class and help out with the booth. I was thrilled to see her, not only for the help she offered, but also for her understanding ear. I held up my coffee cup. "I just got this, but if you want we can go back and pick up a drink for you." She shook her head and we continued up the aisle together.

When we got to the front of the aisle, we walked to the area near the stage and catwalk. For the moment it was quiet, and it seemed like a good place to talk away from the

others. From there we had a good view of the administration table. Audrey Stewart was leaning over, talking to a
little girl who had some knitting in her hands. The girl's
mother was capturing the moment of her daughter talking
to the actress on her cell phone camera. Mason was propped
against the wall. CeeCee was watching from the end of the
table and appeared annoyed.

"So fill me in on what I missed," my friend said. I brought
her up to speed on the shoplifting actress's arrival and
attempt to get herself off the hook, along with my reporting
it to Mason. "We just had a moment together and Barry
showed up."

"Barry and Mason both here," she said with a laugh. "It
sounds like a handful."

"But I haven't gotten to the important part," I said. And
then I brought up Adele and how Barry had set her up.

"She must be hysterical," Dinah said.

"You would think so. But it's Adele we're talking about.
She dropped it in my lap and told me to find out who killed
K.D. Then she went on like it was problem solved." Just
then Delvin stepped up to the microphone.

"And now we're having an audience participation fashion
show. I know it is a tradition to wear something you've
made. This is your chance to show it. Do we have any vol-
unteers?" The words were no sooner out of his mouth than
a line of women and two men formed near the staircase that
led up to the stage.

I nudged Dinah and pointed. "See what I mean." Adele
was the fourth person in line and was adjusting her stash
buster shawl as she moved up. Delvin had repositioned
himself and his microphone near the short staircase. He
questioned the first person in the line and then turned to

the crowd. "First we have Becky from Chatsworth wearing a knitted mohair blend scarf." He gave a few more details about the design used as Becky made her way down the catwalk. I was sure Becky wasn't really a model, but it was amazing how quickly she picked up the swirling and holding out the scarf to show off the intricate stitches.

"That's the woman who thought we were in her space," I said as the second model stopped next to Delvin.

"I'm not sure if this is really fair," he said with a wink in his voice. "Rain is one of our vendors, and she's modeling one of the pieces she has for sale." He described the luxurious gray shawl as she walked the length of the narrow walkway. "Rain wanted me to be sure to mention that this was only the sample and that it comes in other colors."

"Maybe we should go up there," I said. I looked down at the multicolored cowl I'd added to my outfit. Dinah had on a long skinny scarf crocheted in pale yellow cotton. We traded glances and both shook our heads. "And maybe not."

We hung around the spot until Adele had her turn. "See what I mean," I said. "She doesn't seem worried at all that the cops have her hook and her fingerprints."

Dinah nodded in agreement. "If it was me, the last thing I'd be worrying about was showing off my crochet." We both rolled our eyes.

It took her quite a while to tell Delvin about her wrap, and he seemed a little uncertain as he began his patter. "And now we have Adele who belongs to the Tarzana Hookers." He paused long enough for the titter of laughter to subside. "I'm sure you all realize that is hooker as in one who crochets. She's modeling her own crochet design of a stash buster wrap. Adele wanted me to mention that this is the first year that we've included crochet in the show, and she is teaching a class in how to make her stash buster wrap to-morrow afternoon."

Adele was at the end of the catwalk now and turning and showing off the wrap. She undid the pin that held it closed and lifted it up to show off all the different yarns.

I noticed that Leonora Humphries was in the front and Adele was playing up to her. The problem was, Adele should have been heading back down the catwalk by now. Delvin cleared his throat into the microphone several times, no doubt trying to give her the message. But typical Adele didn't notice. Finally, she held up a crochet hook and started circling her hand in a triumphant gesture. I think she was trying to say that crocheters rule.

Delvin got tired of waiting for her to return and simply announced the next model.

When Dinah and I headed to the booth, Adele was still hanging on to the spotlight. As we walked, I went over the strikes against Adele. "As far as Barry is concerned, that hook places Adele at the murder scene." I looked at Dinah. "And she told me she was going to talk to K.D. and work things out about the logo and banner. But now she's insist-ing she didn't go up to K.D.'s suite."

"Do you believe her?" my friend asked.

"I think so. But it's hard to tell. She could think denying she went up there is the best policy. Not that I think Adele killed K.D. She's crazy for crochet, but even she has limits about how far she would go to promote the craft." I glanced back toward the fashion show. "Still, it is so odd how she seems to have dismissed being a murder suspect."

"Maybe not," Dinah said. "I think it makes perfect sense in Adele's world. She has so much confidence in your de-tective powers that she isn't worried anymore."

In a strange way, what Dinah said made sense. "I just wish I felt as confident as she does."

"We need a plan," my friend said.

"For starters, how about we play our Sherlock Holmes game," I said. Dinah had helped me in previous investigations, and one of the things we did was try to look at things the way the fictitious detective did. "Maybe if we put our heads together we can deduce something that will get her off the hook." The words were barely out of my mouth when I realized the double meaning.

Dinah laughed. "Get Adele off the hook? Never."

Something going on behind Dinah caught my eye. "It looks like Mason is back on duty." She turned and we watched together as Mason and Audrey stood near the administration table with Kimberly Wang Diaz. The reporter was holding her microphone, and her cameraman was close by. Audrey held up some knitting. From here, all I could see was something pink hanging off her long needle. Mason seemed to be intently listening to what she was saying.

The group began to move, talking as they went. I nudged Dinah and we caught up with them as they stopped in the doorway of the room that held the auction items.

Audrey seemed very animated as she talked. Mason's expression was unreadable. I suppose it was a lawyer version of a cop face. Then his face lit up and he tried to step in.

The newscaster held out the microphone toward Audrey Stewart, and Mason looked frustrated as his client continued to talk. Audrey had delicate features, which gave her a waif look and seemed to inspire people to want to take care of her. Even the newscaster seemed sympathetic as Audrey told her tale.

"My attorney doesn't want me to talk until everything is

settled, but I think it is important for me to explain how I've turned a bad situation into a positive one. How I got the needles isn't the issue. I feel bad about all the problems it's caused, and now with K.D. Kirby's death, I wanted to do something to help." The group started to move into the room, and Dinah and I followed along. They stopped in front of the long table at the back. The snowy white table-cloth made a nice background to the perfectly displayed auction items. Audrey gestured toward the prime spot.

"I've not only paid for the needles but donated them to the auction. All the money raised by the auction is going to charity. It's my way of trying to make things right."

There seemed to be a tear in Audrey's eye as she spoke, and she had just the right emotional tone. I heard an "aw" sound go through the crowd that was following her along with us. I stepped a little closer to get a view of the in-famous needles. The satin roll had been opened, and the recessed lighting in the ceiling reflected off the silver nee-dles and caught the sparkle in the diamonds on the end. Audrey was saying that she hoped that now that the nee-dles had a story they would bring in even more for the charity than the store value.

"She's playing them like a violin," CeeCee said. I saw that our celebrity Hooker had joined us. She was shaking her head as Audrey continued on, saying that she was going to be at the show all weekend. CeeCee seemed even more unhappy when the younger actress said she'd be helping with the auction and the fashion show at the banquet and would even assist attendees with their knitting problems.

"When K.D. approached me about being a judge, she said I was going to be the celebrity guest," CeeCee said. "I'm supposed to help with the auction and the fashion show at the banquet. After that story of hers, do you think anyone is going to pay attention to me even if I do have Oscar buzz about my performance in the Anthony movie?"

Then CeeCee admitted the whole reason she'd agreed to do everything at the show was for the publicity. "The Oscar nominations come out next week. You see how Kimberly Wang Diaz is hanging out here. It was a chance to get my face out there at a crucial time when people are voting."

I'd never seen CeeCee seem so upset. She was clearly dressed for her close-up. She'd kept the simple hairstyle she'd worn for years, which gave the impression that she hadn't really changed, though the perfect shade of golden brown was the artistic creation of her hairdresser. Her makeup was flawless, and her classic slacks and jacket had just the right look of authority to set her apart from the crowd. I could see her point. Audrey had definitely made herself the center of attention.

"You know that K.D. wanted to press charges against Audrey about the needles," CeeCee continued. "No matter what Audrey says, they had her on the surveillance camera putting the needles in her bag and then walking out of the yarn shop a few minutes later. K.D. thought it was as if Audrey figured she could get away with anything because she was a celebrity, and K.D. was going to show her that she couldn't."

CeeCee put her head down. "I'm sorry, dears. I must sound so petty. But I've waited a whole career for this chance at an Oscar nomination. And then to see my spotlight stolen."

Dinah and I both put an arm around CeeCee and told her we understood.

Mason was sticking close to Audrey, monitoring what

she said. Still, he looked over at me and our eyes met. His softened, and there was a trace of smile all meant for me. CeeCee saw it.

"I saw the detective here before and now Mason," she said, shaking her head. "You lead a complicated life."

We didn't get to play our Sherlock Holmes game. When we got back to the booth, there was a crowd gathered around the front table as Adele, fresh from her fashion show appearance, was helping several people make the granny square pins. I saw that "Anthony" was back and Eduardo had just arrived. This time he was dressed in the cowboy outfit from his cover model days. He'd worn the works—jeans with a silver belt buckle, blue denim shirt, boots and a Stetson. And all I could say was the man knew how to wear the outfit.

Dinah was supposed to be the one handling the granny square lessons but left it to Adele, and Dinah and I took over handling sales from Elise. She was glad to be able to put all her energy into moving her vampire kits. Having her husband dressed up as the crocheting vampire certainly helped.

"I'm glad we kept it simple," I said as a few people stood around the end of the front table and began to make the little squares. The original plan had called for them to be dipped in fabric stiffener at the end and a pin back glued on. But to keep it moving, we'd cut out the stiffener and the pin back and simply given each person a small safety pin to attach their newly made granny square to a shirt or scarf. I looked at the pile of packets of pin supplies I'd made earlier and was surprised they were almost gone.

Adele was using the opportunity to give people a close-up on the wrap she'd modeled in the fashion show.

"And to think this is all made with scrap yarn." She looked over the group huddled around the table. "And we all have lots of bits and pieces of yarn, don't we?" There was a ripple of agreement. "There are still some spaces in my class for tomorrow."

Adele stopped paying attention to the group around her and zeroed in on Leonora Humphries as she approached the table. It was obvious by the way the older woman was trying to see over the crowd that she was curious what was going on. "Mother Humphries, why don't you make one of the pins," Adele said, motioning her to join the group.

One of Adele's problems was she didn't pick up on cues from people very well and apparently didn't notice how the woman she wanted to be her mother-in-law stiffened at the name Adele called her. Could you blame her? Mother Humphries? And then it got worse.

Adele attempted to speak to the crowd, but she seemed focused on Leonora. "There might be a rumor floating around that a very precious hook of mine disappeared and then showed up in K.D. Kirby's room." In case there was any doubt about who K.D. was, Adele pointed to the wreath at the front of the large room and explained that she'd been killed just before the show opened. "I want to make it clear that I had nothing to do with her death and either the hook is an imposter or someone is trying to frame me."

Leonora Humphries fluttered her eyes in dismay and walked away.

Rhoda Klein came back into the booth late in the afternoon. She had a guilty look as she took a seat at the teaching table and slid her tote bag under it. Sheila joined us a short time later. She spread some of the kits she'd made in front of her spot, and I noticed she was wearing a mohair shawl in the Impressionist shades of blues.

I watched as people complimented her on her shawl and she directed them to the kits. Working in the lifestyle store Luxe had definitely helped her confidence, though I did still catch her taking out a hook and some yarn and soothing her nerves with a few minutes of crocheting.

As things were winding down, Dinah and I did another coffee run and toured the large room. It took all my will-power not to buy some of the handspun yarn with the sparkle. For once the catwalk and stage were empty. Delvin had finally closed up shop for the night and left the micro-phone. When we passed the administration table, K.D.'s daughter Lacey was sitting there sending out a last tweet. The rest of the table was empty. We went into the room with contest entries. Delvin was looking them over.

"I'd forgotten that K.D. was supposed to judge the knit-ting competition."

"You're doing this, too?" I said. Delvin stopped what he was doing and let out a tired breath. Up close his outfit seemed even more like a costume. He had all the layers of shirts and a vest with a bunch of chains hanging out of his pocket. He'd stuck with the white fedora with the black band and red feather.

"You should only know," he said, rolling his eyes. "I sup-pose I can say it now." He leaned closer as if to be sharing a confidence. "I have been more than K.D.'s assistant for years. Her name might have been listed as editor and pub-lisher, but I did most of the actual work. I think she was finally going to give me my due." He dropped his voice even lower. "And I think somebody didn't want her to do it, if you know what I mean. It seems coincidental that right after she says she's going to make a big announcement, something happens to her." He adjusted the sleeve of a pink sweater. "I just hope she left something in writing. Everything is on hold until the end of the show. Then the lawyers will straighten everything out."

"I suppose you told that to the cops," I said. Delvin made a face.

"Several times, to several different cops," the man said.

"They probably wanted to know if K.D. had any enemies." I let it hang in the air and then he took the bait.

"I didn't call them enemies. I just said that K.D. had standards and not everybody agreed with how she did things."

"You mean like embarrassing a customer because she wasn't using yarn from the store," I said and pointed toward Julie's entry in the crochet contest.

"I believe that when Julie brought in that cheap yarn, she no longer fit the description of a customer, at least in K.D.'s eyes," he said.

"What about Audrey Stewart?"

Delvin shrugged. "What about her?" He looked over another entry, a wine-colored shawl that was thick and scratchy looking. The distasteful shake of his head made it clear that piece didn't have a chance. "Do you mean the stolen needles? Yes, *stolen* needles. I'm not going to say alleged stolen needles no matter what that attorney of hers keeps saying. K.D. wanted her to see jail time. Personally, I thought K.D. was being a little extreme. All along, Thea Scott had been saying that as manager of the store, it should be her call, and she was in favor of letting Audrey pay for the needles and then let the whole issue die. I'm sure that's what will happen now."

"Was the bubble bath and champagne ritual of K.D.'s

common knowledge?" I asked. By now Delvin's patience seemed to be wearing thin. It had just seemed like we were sharing gossip at first, but now he appeared a little wary.

"Don't tell me you're one of those amateur sleuths who thinks they're smarter than the cops," he said.

"Me?" I said with my best absurd laugh. "Of course not."

CHAPTER 13

"THERE WERE SO MANY MORE QUESTIONS I WOULD have liked to ask Delvin," I said as we walked into Dinah's house carrying bags of food from the local Italian restaurant. The family-run neighborhood eatery had been about to close when we got there, and we had to get the food to go.

"There's always tomorrow." She set the containers down on the coffee table in front of her chartreuse sofa and went to get some plates. "And finally time to play our Sherlock Holmes game."

Dinah's house was within walking distance of the bookstore. It was nicely sized for one person with occasional guests like her ex's kids. Yes, her ex's kids. They had been there for the holidays. Her jerk of an ex wasn't with the kids' mother anymore and had gone off with his new girlfriend. The fraternal twins' mother had a new boyfriend who thought the kids were in the way. The situation for those kids would have been a mess if it hadn't been for Dinah. It showed what kind of a heart Dinah had. She loved those kids despite who their parents were, and the fact that the only way they were related to her was that they were Dinah's kids' half siblings.

Dinah pushed over the toy chest left from their visit. "I have to put all this stuff away," she said a little wistfully. "It was such fun having Ashley-Angela and E. Conner here."

Dinah's own kids were grown, and both had moved to the East Coast and were busy with their careers. Neither had produced any grandchildren yet.

Dinah brought back plates and silverware, and we both helped ourselves to the food. I didn't know about her, but I was starving. I vaguely remembered eating something before I left that morning, but the rest of the day had been fueled solely with coffee. We started off with Caesar salad with their homemade dressing and moved on to mounds of ravioli in pink sauce. We practically inhaled the garlic bread. And then her phone rang. My friend was now in a committed relationship with Commander Blaine, and they usually spent Friday evenings together putting on a fun program at the local senior center. He was calling to give her a report and see how her day went.

While she was talking I almost jumped at the sound coming from my purse. I'd actually heard my cell phone ring for once and started diving through my purse trying to get hold of it before it stopped. Anyone who knew me never depended on reaching me by cell phone.

I tried not to take it personally, but my smartphone just didn't work well for me. The ringer would mysteriously change to silent. Or if someone left a voice mail, my Black-

Berry rarely let me know, which meant I'd hear reminder messages for dental appointments weeks or maybe even months after the fact.

"Hello," Mason said in a surprised voice. "Is that actually you, Sunshine?" I could hear the laugh in his voice and, even without seeing him, bet his lips were curved in a grin.

I assured him it was really me and not my voice mail, and he said he'd tried my house and gotten no answer. "It seemed like a shot in the dark, but I'm glad I tried your cell."

"Are you still shadowing Audrey, trying to keep her out of trouble?"

"No," he said. I expected him to elaborate, but one word turned out to be his whole answer. He changed the subject back to me and asked where I was.

"Dinah and I just crashed at her house with some food from the Italian place. Then we're going to play Sherlock Holmes. The cops seem to have focused on Adele," I said. I was careful to say cops instead of mentioning Barry's name. I'd seen the look on Mason's face when Barry had shown up at the booth. No reason to start a problem.

"I'm assuming you two don't agree with them," Mason said. "From what I heard a hair dryer was thrown into K.D. Kirby's bubble bath. It sounds like it took minimal planning. It could have even been a spur-of-the-moment decision. Something done in the heat of anger. I suppose they have some evidence that points at Adele." Was it my imagination or did he put a weird emphasis on the word *they*? I guess he didn't want to bring up Barry's name, either. There was silence on the phone, and for a moment I thought we'd been disconnected.

"I just wanted to make sure you haven't changed your

mind about us," he said. There was no laughter or teasing in his voice now. It was a legitimate question, because I had sort of done it in the past. I rushed to assure him that we were still one hundred percent a go.

"When you hugged me, it felt like home," I said.

"Good," he said, adding a *whew* at the end. He was back to his fun self. "I hope that is a home full of excitement and passion, not a couple of rocking chairs on the front porch sort of home."

"I'm with your first description of home," I said with a laugh.

"Glad to hear it," he said. "And don't worry about Adele."

"I can't help it. They have real evidence against her. And more than once she's told me that I'm her best friend."

Mason laughed. "She has a weird way of showing it."

"Adele is just Adele. We're trying to come up with possible suspects, which is no problem. It turns out a lot of people had problems with K.D. Kirby, including your own Audrey Stewart."

There was dead silence on the phone. This time I didn't think we'd been disconnected, because I heard Mason take a breath before he spoke. "I wish you hadn't said that."

"Why?" I asked, mystified.

"I was going to suggest we get together tonight. Even for just a few minutes. But Sunshine, you know about attorney-client privilege. I can't say anything about her. And now I can't possibly spend any time alone with you. At least until they arrest somebody, hopefully not Adele."

"I don't understand," I said.

"I have great self-control; the best example is how long I've hung around waiting for you to make a decision. But even with my best of intentions, if we were together and you started to ask me stuff, which I'm pretty sure you being you, you would, I'm afraid I'd melt."

"What if I promised not to say anything?" I protested.

Mason chuckled. "I know you, Sunshine. You're determined to help Adele. You wouldn't be able to help yourself."

"Maybe you're right," I said. "Though the idea of a midnight rendezvous sounds romantic and exciting."

"I've got to hang up now, before I weaken. We don't want me to get disbarred," he said. He added a hasty "Love you" before he clicked off.

I sat back on the couch and looked at the phone, thinking about Mason and sorry that I wasn't going to see him. Dinah had taken her phone into the other room. When she rejoined me, she noticed there was something wrong. "Wow," she said when I explained about the obstacle with Mason. "All the more reason we hurry up and figure something out and get this case closed."

She went into the kitchen and came back carrying a cup of chai tea for each of us. "I think we've both had enough coffee for one day," she said as she set them on the coffee table before taking her seat again.

"We didn't get to play the Sherlock Holmes game before, but we can do it now. So, let's start deducing." Dinah was always up to helping me investigate. She found it interesting and exciting, particularly when we had to sneak around.

I recognized the eager look as she sat forward on the couch. "The obvious place to start is with K.D. It's not hard to deduce that she wasn't very popular. I barely knew her and I didn't like her. She was high-handed when it came to knitting over crochet, she didn't care about anybody's feelings, and I think her power had gone to her head."

"Are you sure you didn't kill her?" Dinah said with a grin. She waited until I'd acknowledged her comment with a hopeless rock of my head before she continued. "Since you get along with most people, she must have been really bad and collected a lot of enemies."

"I'm sure Sherlock Holmes would deduce there is something strange about K.D. adding crochet to the show," I said. "It seems very halfhearted if you consider the facts. None of the fashion shows or demos had crochet. She was really over the top in her reaction to Adele's logo. And why would she react so strongly about a banner saying our booth was pro crochet?"

"Maybe she really is one of those people who talk about crochet as the C word," Dinah offered. We knew there were lots of knitters who had contempt for crocheters, though neither of us had figured out why. And there were yarn stores that barely seemed to want crocheters' business, which really made no sense because crochet used more yarn than knitting.

"It's almost as if someone made her add crochet to the show and she did it begrudgingly." I thought about it for a minute. "But is that a reason someone would kill her?"

"If it was, it would have to be some crazy crocheter who got in an argument with her. . . ." Dinah's voice trailed off as we both knew who fit that description.

In an effort to change the subject I brought up something that was jiggling around in my mind. "I wonder what Sherlock Holmes would deduce about Mason. Maybe that Audrey Stewart is guilty and Mason knows it or at least thinks it." I answered my own question and my shoulders sagged. "I never thought his work would be a problem."

"Why don't we look for other suspects. People we don't have any emotional thing going on with."

"Good idea," I said, brightening. "Chances are it wasn't Adele or Audrey Stewart. Why not start with Delvin Whittingham. He's the one who knew K.D. always took a bubble bath and had a glass of champagne before the show, which means he of all people would have known exactly where to find her. And getting me to go with him to her room could have just been a ploy to have somebody else find her body."

"What about motive?" Dinah asked.

"I've heard him say several times that K.D. was making a big announcement. He was talking like it was something that was going to benefit him but that other people might not be happy about it. He implied they might be unhappy enough to try to keep her from making the announcement. What if he was really talking about himself? Maybe the announcement was really something that was going to hurt him and he kept her from making it."

I thought about it for a moment. "About Adele's hook being found in K.D.'s suite. What if somebody figured out how to commit the perfect crime but wanted the cops to pin it on somebody else?"

"Why?" Dinah asked.

"Maybe they wanted the case closed. And maybe they had it in for the person they pinned it on."

Dinah's eyes went skyward. "I know a lot of people find Adele annoying, but . . ."

"What if they wanted to really make sure their son

broke up with her?" We both said, "Mother Humphries," at the same time, and then I said, "But why would she want to kill K.D.?"

"It does sound like an extreme way to mess things up between Eric and Adele," Dinah said. "What about considering the kind of person K.D. was?"

"It's pretty easy to deduce from her behavior that she was someone who had rules and standards and she didn't bend." I brought up how she'd confronted Julie twice basically for breaking the rules that K.D. had made and described the encounters in the yarn store and at the show when Julie had tried to enter the knitting competition. "But K.D. was willing to rectify a mistake. When Rain talked to her about the mix-up with her booth, K.D. got Rain moved out of the horrible spot at the back of the room. Then there's the case of Audrey Stewart. The fact that K.D. wanted to press charges instead of just letting the actress pay for the silver needles seems vindictive."

"It seems pretty obvious what Delvin Whittingham could have gained by killing K.D., but what would Julie have gotten out of it?" Dinah said.

I thought it over a moment. "Maybe K.D. humiliated her one time too many when she wouldn't accept her entry in the knitting competition and it pushed Julie over the edge." I didn't really want to talk about Audrey, but I had to face facts. "And it's pretty clear what Audrey Stewart thinks she's going to gain by K.D.'s demise. I'm not sure who ultimately has the power to make the decision about pressing charges, but the manager of the yarn store, ah, I mean studio, seemed anxious to let the actress pay for the needles and let the whole thing go." I thought over the scene I'd witnessed. "It was a little strange. Thea Scott seemed almost upset that Audrey had donated the needles to the auction rather than just return them to the store."

All the deducing on top of the long day had left me with a headache, and we decided to call it a night. Dinah wouldn't even let me help clean up before I headed for home.

CHAPTER 14

BY NOW THE STREETS OF TARZANA WERE QUIET and I didn't pass another car as I took the back roads to my place. I did a start when I saw that the outside lights were on as I pulled into the long driveway that led to my carport and garage. Of course, I'd realized how long I'd be gone and remembered I'd asked my son Samuel to stop by and look after the animals. He must have left the lights on for me.

No upturned garbage can this time. Or if there had been, Samuel must have cleaned it up. The kitchen was as clean as I'd left it. I almost wished my son had made a little mess while he was there. I laughed at myself, thinking about how long I'd wished for this on-my-ownness and now I didn't like it at all. But I reminded myself I had Mason, or I would have once K.D.'s murder was settled.

After Dinah's cozy house, my place seemed enormous with the vaulted ceilings and large rooms. My footsteps echoed on the wood floor as I crossed the living room. I was keyed up from the day and not ready to sleep yet.

I settled onto one of the leather couches in the living room to consider my options. I thought about a nice scented bath but quickly let it go when a vision of K.D. in her bath floated through my mind. For a second I could almost smell the cloying fragrance I'd encountered.

What else was there? Crocheting? To be honest, after the day I'd had, I really didn't want to do anything with yarn. I thought of watching a movie, but the decision of what I was going to do was pretty much made for me when the animals, glad for company, gathered around me, locking me in place. Holstein climbed onto the back of the couch and came up behind me, putting his paws on my shoulders, kneading them. He rested his head on top of mine and began to purr loudly. Who said cats weren't affectionate? Cat Woman jumped up and settled next to my leg. Cosmo wasn't about to be left out, and the small black mutt took up a position on the other side and draped himself over my thigh. The only one who didn't join us was Blondie. I heard her claws on the floor as she headed out of the room. Even after years of living with me, the terrier mix hadn't lost her aloofness. I knew she was heading for her chair in the bedroom.

I hoped the cuddling of the pets would be calming, but I started thinking about Adele. Really I started worrying about Adele. Her hook had been found at the murder scene. Now they had her fingerprints, which might match those on the hook. She hadn't done herself any favors when she made a disparaging remark about K.D. in front of Barry. Though he hadn't come out and said it, I was sure Adele was Barry's prime suspect. It didn't matter that he knew her. Actually, it was almost worse. It wasn't that much of a stretch to imagine Adele being enraged at K.D. about the stupid crochet logo and doing something on impulse, like waiting until K.D. was in the tub and then throwing the hair dryer in. But Barry hadn't come back and arrested her. And then a troubling thought surfaced—she hadn't been arrested yet.

I knew how the cops operated. They liked to take people in when there was the least resistance and when they had the advantage. I knew they favored doing it late at night, like right around now.

As Holstein purred louder and started to massage my neck with his paws, I pictured Barry and the SWAT team. They were all wearing bulletproof vests that said LAPD in big letters and were gathered outside Adele's condo door. They had their weapons drawn as one of them pounded on the door and yelled out, "LAPD, open up." They were ready to break through the door if she didn't follow their command.

I imagined Adele inside dressed in one of those filmy cream-colored peignoir sets out of an old movie from the 1940s. But knowing Adele she would have embellished the nightwear and sewn on some giant doilies done in an eye-searing fluorescent pink.

My mental picture fast-forwarded to the crew of cops escorting Adele to jail. My last image was of her in the peignoir, sitting in a cell with a couple of angry DUIs whom she was trying to teach how to crochet using their fingers. Outside the cell Mother Humphries had an I-told-you-so look on her face and Eric waved a sad farewell at Adele.

I shook my head to get rid of the image. Maybe my imagination had taken it over the top, but the idea of the cops being at Adele's door was all too real a possibility. I couldn't let that happen.

Barry's homicide detective crazy hours had been a problem when we were together, but now they were a benefit. It didn't matter that it was almost midnight; he was used to getting calls at all hours. Holstein's massaging turned into grabbing with a hint of claw as I tried to stand up to get the house phone. I reached for my cell phone instead.

"Greenberg," he said in his cop voice.

"It's me, Molly," I said, not assuming he'd recognize my voice. "I need to talk to you about Adele." I wanted to ask him where he was or more specifically if he was outside my coworker's door, but instead I just apologized for calling so late.

"No problem about the hour," he said in an even tone. "Actually, I'm not far from your place. Do you want to talk in person?"

I hadn't thought about that, but it seemed like a good idea. I'd have a better chance of pleading her case if we were face-to-face. I invited him over.

A few minutes later there was a soft knock at the front door. It was so strange to have all the familiarity between us gone. He'd always come through the yard to the kitchen door and called me by an affectionate nickname. I suppose I should have been glad that he said, "Hello, Molly," when I opened the door instead of calling me Mrs. Pink.

Barry had obviously accepted the situation as strictly professional. No more was he trying to win me over by being anyone other than who he was. The overhead light on the porch made the shadows on his face even deeper, only enhancing how tired he looked. The dark gray suit, white shirt and striped tie gave it away that he was still working.

I saw the black Crown Victoria parked at the curb, which confirmed it.

"Do you want to talk here?" he said, not making a move to come inside.

"Why don't you come in," I said, stepping back to clear the way.

"Good," he said, accepting my offer and letting down his professional demeanor for a moment. "It's cold out there." He shut the door behind him and we stopped in the entrance hall.

He waited to make a move until I invited him into the living room. It seemed inhospitable not to offer him something.

"I was going to have some tea. Would you like to join me?"

"That sounds good," he said. He was standing in the living room, glancing around. I caught a glimpse of his eyes, and they had definitely softened. Was he thinking about all the cups of tea we'd shared and memories connected to my place?

My house held a lot of memories for both of us. I watched his gaze move in the direction of my crochet room, which I'd converted into a bedroom for him when he'd been recuperating from being shot. I stopped looking at him as he turned toward the other side of the house and my bedroom. I didn't want to conjure up any memories connected with that room and started to walk toward the kitchen.

"Something is different," he said, and I turned back.

"Samuel moved out," I said and continued on my way. As I took out a teapot and some loose-leaf Darjeeling, I began to wonder if I'd made a mistake agreeing to us talking here. It was more uncomfortable than I thought it would be. It wasn't that we'd broken up in a fit of anger. It had really come down to wanting different things. For him, first and foremost was his job, or as he said, his calling. Not only did he love it, but he felt like it was his duty to find justice for the dead. The erratic hours, the knowledge that something else would always come first didn't work for me. Even though he was the one who made the decision to walk out of my life, I ultimately agreed with that choice.

When I came back with a tray, he'd settled on the couch. Cosmo remembered Barry and was lying across Barry's lap. I doubt that the black mutt realized he was supposed to actually belong to Barry. I was curious how Barry would react to the dog's demand for attention. He didn't exactly rub his tummy and go into baby talk, but he stroked the dog affectionately, though his attention seemed elsewhere and he appeared to be examining everything in the room.

I poured the fragrant tea into two mugs and pointed to a plate of cookies. I knew it wasn't a social call, but the tea seemed a little bleak without something to go with it. The way he took a handful of the sugar cookies, I was sure he'd missed dinner. It was really hard for me not to offer to scramble some eggs for him, but this wasn't that kind of visit.

"So," he said, after eating the cookies and taking a sip of the steaming tea, "you said you wanted to talk to me about Adele."

"You didn't just arrest her, did you?" I blurted out. I told him about my image, well, most of it. I didn't mention the peignoir set or crocheting in the cell. I also didn't mention Mother Humphries and Eric standing outside it.

Barry broke his cover and laughed. "Arresting Adele would hardly take a SWAT team in the middle of the night."

"But you haven't arrested her, right?" I said.

"No," he said, going back into cop mode.

I launched into my pitch, saying that I was sure that Adele hadn't done it and it would ruin everything if they arrested her now. I needed her to help me run the booth and she had a whole slew of people signed up for her crochet class. Maybe I fibbed a bit on that one; the sign-ups were still pretty light. I ended by telling him about Mother Humphries, although I referred to her by her real name. "She's just here for the weekend. If she sees Adele getting arrested, can you imagine what she'll say to her son about his girlfriend? It'll be over between them. And he's the yin for her yang, her soul mate."

"I thought Adele was a thorn in your side and now you're standing up for her?"

"Well, I guess I am. She thinks we're French toast sisters," I muttered, and he gave me a strange look. "She says I'm her best friend." He still seemed a little incredulous. "You should be looking for other suspects. There certainly are enough of them."

Barry let me finish and then leveled his gaze at me. "As I've told you before, killers don't always look like killers. Nice people can do bad things in a moment of anger." He paused and let his breath out. "Thea Scott, the woman running the booth across from yours, told us about the victim insisting you take down Adele's crochet banner and some kind of blinking crochet hooks. She also told us that she'd overheard Adele say that she wasn't going to let Ms. Kirby dictate what was in your booth and that she was going to talk to her and tell her the crochet things were staying."

"Oh," I said, with a worried groan in my voice.

"Ms. Scott also told us that K.D. Kirby would never

have let the crochet banner stay or the hooks with the blinking lights, no matter what Adele said to her. I'm sorry, Molly, but the timing of it all puts Adele with the victim around the time of death." He took out his notebook. "I talked to the room service employee who brought up the bottle of champagne. K.D. Kirby was alive to sign for it, so she was killed between that time and when you and Mr. Whittingham found her."

"Maybe she was up there before the champagne came. Did you ask him if he saw a big hook on the table?"

"No, but I doubt he would have been that observant."

"There are lots of other people who didn't like K.D. Kirby. Any of them could have gone up there and tossed the hair dryer in the tub."

Barry sat a little straighter and had his notebook open and his pen poised. "And they are?"

I hesitated and his eyes narrowed. "You have to tell me. Remember I mentioned that charge of withholding evidence?"

"Is that a real charge or did you just make that up?"

"Real, of course," Barry said and then waited for me to proceed.

I mentioned that I'd heard that K.D. was supposed to be making a very big announcement that evening. "Delvin seems to think it had to do with him being promoted and that K.D. was going to lighten her load. What if that isn't what she was going to announce at all and he found out and killed her before she could say anything? I heard him say there was something in writing that if she was incapacitated, he was to take over. Dead is the supreme way to be incapacitated."

"I need more evidence than that, especially when I have a crochet hook loaded with fingerprints that puts Adele at the crime scene."

My offer of other suspects wasn't working, so I tried my last card. "How about this? Could you promise not to arrest Adele until the weekend is over and the show closes? I would let you know if I heard her talking about buying a ticket to Brazil or anything." The last comment was supposed to lighten the moment.

"Are you asking because you need Adele working in your booth, or are you trying to buy some time so you can investigate more?"

I almost laughed. Did he think I was going to tell him the truth with his constant hints that I could get arrested for interfering? I insisted it was all about the booth and Eric's mother. Since both Barry and Eric were cops, I thought he'd understand. "Put yourself in Eric's shoes. Having your mother see your girlfriend taken off in handcuffs is pretty hard to smooth over."

Barry's mouth was in a straight line, but his eyes were almost rolling. "I never met your mother," I said, defending myself. "And even if I was in handcuffs a few times, I was never really arrested. This is different. The charge would be some kind of homicide. And you aren't as straight an arrow as Eric is."

"Fine, I won't arrest Adele until Monday."

"Then you really are going to arrest her?" I said incredulously.

"Part of the deal is you can't tell her anything," he said, ignoring my question. He set the mug down on the tray and peeled Cosmo off his lap. "Sorry, buddy," he said, giving the dog an affectionate pat before he turned to me. "Thanks for the tea."

We both stood, he from the couch and me from a chair, and I picked up the tray prepared to walk him to the door and then take it in the kitchen. When we got to the door, he showed me the balled-up napkins in his hand.

"I'll just throw this away." He went ahead to the kitchen, and I came in after with the tray. He was doing the same thing he'd done before in the living room. He seemed to be examining the counters, the table, the whole room.

"Okay, what are you looking for?" I said finally.

He seemed a little disconcerted at being caught. "I don't see any evidence of Mason being here." He shrugged and gestured toward the hall tree that just had one umbrella and my rain jacket. "I kept a jacket hanging there. And I left a lot of tools here." He pointed to the handle of the closet door in the hall. "One of my flannel shirts was always hanging there." He turned back to the kitchen and I busied myself with putting the things away. Even though we'd always drunk our tea plain, I put out milk and sugar just in case. I put the sugar bowl back and then opened the refrigerator to put the milk away. I didn't realize Barry was watching from over my shoulder until he spoke. "It looks like you've got a lot of dinners for one," he said.

I shut the refrigerator quickly, though of course it was too late; he'd seen the stack of single-portion dinners I'd made up for myself and stored in containers. "We could be spending lots of time at his place," I said defensively. Barry shook his head.

"No way. You'd never abandon your pets." Then he went silent and just let it all hang in the air.

I wasn't going to say anything, but the dead air and his staring finally got to me. "Mason and I are still at the beginning. We haven't quite worked things out, yet."

All he said in answer was, "Okay." And then he left.

Barry would have been very unhappy if he realized that

something he'd said had given me an idea how to get Adele off the hook. There was that double meaning again; well, almost a double meaning. I was trying to get them off her hook. All I had to do was prove that it was there when K.D. was still alive and their evidence would be irrelevant.

My intention was to deal with it first thing on Saturday morning when I got to the show.

CHAPTER 15

SATURDAY WAS THE MAIN DAY OF THE YARN SHOW. It was the day that got the biggest crowd, had the most popular classes (surprisingly, Adele hadn't figured that out yet) and ended with a banquet where, among other things, Kimberly Wang Diaz would get her award.

The other days had been long, but this was going to be a marathon. The banquet said black tie optional. I was definitely going for the optional, but there was no way my work clothes would look right. There was a time lapse between when the vendor floor closed and the banquet began, but I'd decided to bring my things with me and change in the mini suite. Actually, I was afraid if I went home and sat down for a few minutes, I'd never get up and leave.

I made a stop at the bookstore on my way in and picked up another load of Bob's goodies. We'd decided to give away one of his chocolate walnut shortbread cookie fingers with each purchase. When I arrived at the hotel I gathered everything up and headed inside. It was amazing how much I'd brought along for the change of clothes. My dress was in a garment bag, and I'd put the shoes and fresh underwear, makeup and accessories into a small duffel bag. First stop was the room, where I stowed my stuff and checked the extra stock we'd left there. I picked up the last of the pin-making supplies before I rushed downstairs to the event center, trying to get a little investigating in before the show opened for the day.

All my rushing came to a dead stop when I saw a small crowd of people gathered in the corridor near the entrance to the marketplace. When I looked closer, I saw there was a uniform standing in front of the doorway blocking the entrance. I glanced through the gathered group, saw Thea Scott and caught up with her.

"What's going on?" I asked.

She pointed to a cluster of people at the front of the waiting crowd. "It has something to do with them." I was surprised she didn't have more details, but then with K.D.'s death and all I supposed the yarn studio manager was too worn out to be curious.

Personally, I still wanted to know what was going on. I made my way to the front of the gathered group to see what I could find out.

Several uniforms were hanging around, and another one was talking to a man I recognized as the hotel manager. Next to him a man in a waiter's uniform with his hand on a metal cart kept looking off to the side like he wanted to make a hasty exit. I got close enough to eavesdrop.

The uniform had a metal clipboard and clicked his pen. "How about you tell me what happened again for the report."

The manager turned to the waiter and nudged him. "You tell him. You're the one who called 911."

The waiter appeared unhappy as the officer asked him for his name and then the details. "I was wheeling in some urns of coffee. . . ."

"It's an extra gesture the hotel does for the vendors," the manager said, butting in. "We know that Saturday is their big day, and we offer them courtesy coffee and donut holes." The manager stopped at that, and when the waiter didn't go back to his story right away, the manager nudged him to continue.

"I should have figured something was wrong when the doors were unlocked," the waiter said, gesturing in the direction of the entrance to the marketplace. "But it happens sometimes. I made the delivery and I was on my way out when I saw one of the inside doors was open. I knew it was supposed to be locked, so I went in to check. Somebody was standing over one of the tables. I said something like 'Nobody is supposed to be in here.' Next thing I know the person ran past me. I knew right away they were up to no good, so I called you." He nodded toward the cop. "All I saw was a sweatshirt jacket with the hood pulled up." I had the feeling the waiter added that last part to make it clear he couldn't identify the person.

The cop nodded. "Was anything missing?"

"I don't think so," the manager said, stepping in again. He turned to the waiter. "Standard procedure is you contact me before you call the police."

"When the person ran out, they dropped these." The waiter held up the satin roll.

"It doesn't look like anything else was taken," the manager added quickly.

The cop seemed to lose interest then. "I'm marking it down as attempted burglary. And you have no idea who the person was? Woman, man, someone you've seen around here?"

The waiter shook his head on all counts and repeated his story about the figure in the sweatshirt jacket. Delvin pushed through the small crowd. He was carrying a garment bag and pulling a bin on wheels. He made an odd contrast to the conservatively dressed manager in his layers of T-shirt, dress shirt and vest, topped with a blazer. The style now was so silly and called for a skimpy jacket, and he looked like he was wearing something he'd bought in the kids' department. He was wearing a gray hat this time, and the brim seemed a little bigger than the others, but as always he wore it at a jaunty angle. I honestly wondered if I'd recognize him if he ever went hatless.

"What's going on?" he demanded. The cop said something about a call about a break-in and then wanted to know who Delvin was.

"I'm in charge of this show." He made a lot of grunting sounds of displeasure, acting very much the person in charge. "First there's a murder and now a break-in. Not very good security." The manager apologized profusely, though I couldn't see how anybody could blame him for K.D.'s death unless providing his guests with hair dryers counted as a crime. He apologized some more and said that the main door to the marketplace had been opened earlier for a delivery to the snack bar at the back and must have been left open. He insisted his people had nothing to do with the lock on the door to the room with the auction items.

A maintenance man in a gray uniform tapped the manager on the shoulder, and they conferred for a moment. The manager seemed to shush him and went back to speaking to the group.

"Nothing was really taken. It's probably just some kind of misunderstanding. But I'll give you someone in security to stand outside the door to the room with the auction items just in case." While gesturing with his hand, the manager dropped the satin roll and it came undone. The cop leaned down to pick it up and saw what was inside.

"Knitting needles?" the uniform said. "I'm writing a report because you think somebody was trying to take those? My grandmother has tons of them and nobody ever bothers with them."

Delvin's eyes flared as he took the roll of needles and pulled one out. "Your grandmother's are probably made out of aluminum. These are sterling silver. And I doubt that your grandmother's have diamond accents." Delvin lowered the top so the light caught in the embedded stone and twinkled.

The uniform seemed at an impasse. "There's no sign of forced entry, nothing missing, and therefore nothing to report." He waved to his fellow officers and said they were done. They might have nothing to report, but I was convinced somebody had tried to steal the needles. It made sense to think it was someone connected to the show, because they would appreciate the value of the needles, and what's more, they might be in the crowd around me.

I surveyed the people just as the cop stepped away from the entrance and people began to go into the marketplace. I caught sight of Ruby Cline and her grandson Paxton before it got too hard to make out individuals.

I heard a rumble as the waiter quickly pushed the metal cart down the corridor. The manager and Delvin parted company and, thanks to his gray hat, I was able to follow the show head as he pushed through the group going into the vendor area. The uniforms were headed to the door when I heard Mason's voice.

"Sunshine, what are the cops doing here?" Mason said, stopping next to me. He put his arms around me in a welcoming hug and wrapped me against his solid build. He was dressed a little more casually in slacks, a collarless shirt and a sports jacket. He was taller than me, but not so much that he towered over me.

"What are you doing here?" I said.

"You don't sound happy to see me," he said in a teasing voice.

"I'm sorry, that didn't come out right. I'm just surprised to see you." I tried to smooth over my abruptness by snuggling against him.

"That's more like it," he said with a smile in his voice. "As to why I'm here, it's the same reason I was here yesterday." I'd let go of him by then and we'd moved apart. When I saw the grin on his face, I got it. It was his way of saying without saying that he was there to keep an eye on Audrey Stewart.

I realized that he had a lot more connection to the almost burglary than the rest of the crowd.

"I know you can't say anything," I said in a low voice, "but it seems to be okay if I talk." He leaned closer to hear and his arm touched mine. "Somebody tried to steal your client's donation to the auction. The knitting needles she shoplifted."

"Allegedly shoplifted," Mason said and then he let out a sigh. I was surprised he'd said anything after what he'd said the night before, but he explained that was common knowledge now and acknowledging it wasn't divulging a confidence. I saw him scanning the flow of people going into the marketplace. Just then Delvin came out of the doors, and a moment later, Audrey Stewart followed. The graceful actress tried to catch up with him.

Mason's smile faded. "I hate to hug and run," he said, giving me a last squeeze before he took off in pursuit of his client.

I watched him catch up with her and snag her before she had a chance to talk to Delvin. I admired her outfit. She'd gone casual, but on her the plain black slacks and loose white shirt with a silky-looking triangle shawl draped across one shoulder had an elegance I could never manage. I looked down at what I was wearing and shook my head. This was the big day of the show, so I'd done my best to dress things up. The nicest thing you could say about my look was that it was classic. The black slacks had never been in or would be out of style. I'd worn a turtleneck because the place was drafty and chilly. After seeing that everyone at the show was wearing one of their best creations, I found a shawl I considered my best achievement. Adele had coached me on it, and it showed her touch. It was made of small black granny squares. Adele's plan had been to sew a rosy pink crocheted flower on each square, but I'd gone a little more subtle and just added a few random ones.

Mason steered Audrey back into the marketplace. I wanted to get in there, too, and check on our booth. When I got inside, I did a double take as I saw a woman standing by the stage. Was I seeing a ghost? Then the fact that this woman's hair was blond, not white, registered, and I realized it was Lacey, K.D.'s daughter, and overnight she'd changed her hair color. She was talking to Delvin. Although I couldn't hear them, their body language said they were having some kind of disagreement. Delvin made some broad gestures, and it seemed he was trying to show her he was in charge, but she made a face and her eyes went skyward.

He'd laid the garment bag on a chair and went to open the bin he'd brought in. Lacey pulled out her smartphone and began typing away. He lifted out the Lucite box with the company logo of the crossed gold needles, climbed up on the stage and set it on the podium. Obviously, he hadn't trusted the hotel's security, which under the circumstances sounded like a good idea.

Paxton Cline waved at me from the Cline Yarn International booth on the other side of the entrance. Ruby Cline, his grandmother, was bustling around the interior, and I saw her put out a sign that said "Show Specials" next to a display of yarn.

I was in a hurry to check the Shedd & Royal mini shop. I lifted back the tarps we had covered it with and looked inside. I felt a sense of relief when everything appeared as I'd left it. The "Crochet Spoken Here" banner was still hanging, and the velvet pedestal with the big gold crossed crochet hooks was still intact. Only the blinking colored lights were turned off.

Seeing them reminded me of Adele and my plan to do some investigating before the show opened.

"Everything okay with your stuff?" Thea Scott had come across from her booth and stopped next to me. She must have seen me checking things over. I nodded and let out a sigh of relief.

"I was pretty sure it would be, but after what happened,

who knows." I glanced over at her booth. It seemed ready for business and she assured me everything was fine. She pulled her filmy, toast-colored mohair shawl around her shoulders and tied the ends together.

"I'd really like to know what happened, though I suppose we'll never know. The cops dropped it and the manager isn't going to tell anything he knows. Any ideas?"

"Someone could have tried to take the knitting needles because of their value. They're worth $3,500. Or maybe the person wanted them but couldn't afford to bid on them." Thea looked toward the administration table. "But if you want to know what I think—" The store manager held up her hand to shield that she was pointing at Audrey, who was leaning against the long table holding some pink knitting in her hand. Mason was standing a discreet distance away.

"Why would she steal them? She's already paid for them," I said, watching the actress and Mason do something.

"She might think that getting rid of the evidence would make sure the charges got dropped. I think she'd do anything to keep out of jail. Anything," Thea said. "In case there are any second thoughts about pressing charges." Thea explained the charges couldn't be officially dropped until the lawyers for K.D.'s estate determined who was in control.

I brought up that I'd heard K.D. was supposed to be making some big announcement at the show. Thea wanted to know who I'd heard it from. "I worked for the woman, managed her yarn shop and she didn't say anything to me about any sort of announcement. Well, things are going to change for sure now. I wonder how it's going to affect me."

She glanced toward the administration table again as

someone came up to Audrey and showed off something they'd knitted. "That's sure a joke," Thea said.

"What do you mean?"

Thea looked at me and rolled her eyes. "She's putting on this act like she's some kind of hotshot knitter." Thea laughed. "As if any of the regulars who come to the studio are. It's the in thing now for celebs and the Beverly Hills and Westside crowd. You should see the money they spend on yarn. And those needle sets."

"What did they make with all that fancy stuff?" I was just curious now.

Thea laughed. "It's more like what they claimed they'd made. The arrangement was that if they bought the yarn from us, they could be part of the regular group that met at the store and we'd help them with their projects. It was more like we made them for them. We had to keep them working on simple things like scarves and fingerless gloves to keep our sanity. Then K.D. had this idea they should make scarves for a homeless shelter, and they all picked out ridiculous, impractical yarns."

I was surprised at how hostile she sounded toward the customers. "The truth is," Thea continued, "the yarn that Julie slipped in would have been much more practical. That stuff lasts like iron."

I told Thea I'd seen the same woman have a problem with K.D. again right before she was murdered.

CHAPTER 16

"AM I GLAD TO SEE YOU," I SAID AS DINAH JOINED me in the booth and gave me a hello hug. As soon as I'd gotten back inside, I'd started making some more packets of thread and beads for the granny square pins with the supplies I'd picked up. "And thank you for this," I said, holding out the pendant that had hidden edges for cutting the thread.

She put down her things and started to help me. When I offered to share the pendant, she showed me she had one of her own. The doors were set to open soon and I wanted to get everything ready to go. "I don't know what I would do without you. It's my job to be here, but it's from the goodness of your heart that you are. And the help with the pins is the cherry on the sundae."

"Are you kidding, spending time with all these yarn people, surrounded by yarn and with my Hooker friends?

You couldn't keep me away," Dinah said. She finished several packets and dropped them in a plastic container.

"I don't know what happened to Adele. I thought she'd be here by now," I said. "Where is she?"

"You don't think she got arrested?" Dinah said. "It sounds like she is the main suspect."

"It's funny you should mention that," I said. "I made a deal with Barry about just that." Dinah's eyes widened as I continued. "He promised not to arrest her until the show is over."

"When exactly did you make that deal and what did you have to do to get it?"

"It's not what you're thinking," I said, rolling my eyes. "You don't really think I'd offer myself as some kind of bribe."

Dinah pretended to think about it for a moment and then laughed and shook her head. "Of course not." She wanted to know all the details.

I explained that I'd asked him over and basically pleaded with him to wait. "No matter what Barry says, I think he has his doubts, anyway. C'mon, it's Adele we're talking about."

"Right, right," Dinah said quickly. "So what happened when he left?" I knew she meant how did we say good-bye. She knew about all the ups and downs of our relationship and how he had taken himself out of the picture.

"Nothing. Not even a handshake or pat on the shoulder. He was strictly homicide detective Barry following up on a lead."

"Whatever you say," Dinah said.

"It's over. It really is this time. I only contacted him because of Adele." I hoped it didn't sound like I was protesting too much. But it really was over between us, and we both had moved on. I was glad that Dinah let it go, and we went back to talking about Adele and what Barry had that pointed toward her guilt.

"He said our booth neighbor had overheard Adele fussing about K.D. and saying that she was going to talk to her and straighten things out about the banner and the crochet logo. Adele is insisting she didn't really go to K.D.'s room, but that hook got there somehow." Dinah began to set out the hooks and needles that we let the people making pins use.

"Do you think Adele might be lying about going up to the suite?" Dinah said.

"I suppose she could be. Maybe the whole thing about not knowing where her hook was is just a charade. She could think that denying she was even in the room is the best policy. You never know what Adele will do. In any case, I figured out that if I could establish that the hook was there when K.D. was still alive, it would make the evidence irrelevant."

"Didn't you say K.D. drank champagne and took a bubble bath? I wonder if the champagne was waiting for her or if room service delivered it."

"You are such a good Watson," I said to my friend, giving her an impromptu thank-you hug. "It was delivered." I remembered the conversation I'd had with Rain. "The woman who thought we were in her spot told me she saw the waiter arrive with the champagne when she was leaving K.D.'s room." I thought back to what Barry had said. "And Barry talked to the waiter and K.D. signed for the bottle, so she was definitely alive then. I wonder if he'd remember seeing a hook on the table?" I shook my head in answer to my own question. "Probably not. But that woman, Rain, was in the room. She works with yarn and I bet she would have noticed the hook."

I looked out at the aisle and saw that the few people going by were wearing badges, which meant they were vendors. "I was hoping to do a little investigating this morning, and they haven't opened the doors yet. I'm going to go talk to Rain." I paused and looked at my friend. "That is if you don't mind keeping an eye on things here?"

Dinah laughed. "You're talking to a community college instructor who is used to being in front of a class of immature freshmen. Watching an empty booth is a snap. Go on." She waved her hands at me, urging me to go.

I remembered the new location of Rain's booth. When I approached it, I saw that she'd made some adjustments to it. The space was more defined with curtained panels on the side and a white picket fence along the front. She appeared to have just arrived. I was still working on my story as I got closer. Maybe the cops could be direct with their questions, but I'd found that didn't work for me. Whenever I'd tried, I'd gotten weird looks and questions about why I was asking. I needed to blend my questions into some kind of conversation.

Rain looked up and greeted me with a friendly hello. I glanced over the racks of knitted items. There seemed to be less than when I'd been there before. "It looks like you're doing well."

"Not bad," she said. She began straightening the pieces she had piled on some wire shelves on a table at the back of the small area. To break the ice I began to ask her about how she decided what items to bring.

"After all the years, I've got it down." She showed me that she had shawls folded and stacked on the shelves. A sample done in gray yarn was draped around a half torso in the middle of the table. She explained she had refined it down to bringing just six designs, a short vest, a long vest, a short jacket, a long jacket that was more like a coat, a poncho and a shawl. As she talked she took a short gray vest and put it on the first dress form, then a long blue vest on the next one. A long coat went on the dress form on the side. She shook a wrinkle out of the poncho before she put it on the dress form in the middle. "And I'll wear this," she said, picking up a gray jacket off the end of the rack. "I keep rotating the samples between the displays and me," she said with a smile.

She took off her own blue jacket and stowed it along with her purse behind the curtain hanging off the back table before putting on the knitted garment and then doing a model swirl to show it off. As she did one of the buttons fell to the ground. I rushed to pick it up and handed it to her.

"That's why I have samples. Let them get the wear and tear," she said. She took out a tote bag and searched through it until she found a needle and some thin yarn. She had the button sewn back on in no time. All this was very informative, but I needed to direct the conversation to what I wanted to find out.

And worse, when she finished with the button, it was clear she expected me to leave.

"Did you want something?" she asked finally when I didn't move on.

"My friend and I were here before, and she admired a shawl and her birthday is coming up." Dinah would be pleased. She was acting like my Watson and she wasn't even there. Dinah had liked something in the booth, but in all honesty I didn't even remember what it was. And her birthday was coming up. It was sort of true. August could be considered coming up, coming way up since it was only January. Sensing a possible sale, Rain was very solicitous and asked if there was a particular color I wanted.

I glanced at the sample quickly. "She liked that one."

"The gray pieces are all samples, but I think I might have brought one shawl in a shade close to that color," Rain said. She went through the pile and then, acting like I'd just won the lottery, pulled out a lighter gray shawl. She went into asking for the order mode, and I stalled by asking about the yarn.

"I use only the best quality. It's a bit of investment, but that's why I get a good price." I stalled more by asking about the time involved in making them and how she managed to make them so uniform.

"Experience," she said. An edge was starting to appear in her answers. She kept looking toward the doors, which would open any minute. She very subtly held it out toward me and then reminded me that there was only one of them and Saturday was the biggest day.

Segueing into the hook wasn't easy, and since I was running out of time I had to wing it. I pointed toward the fringe on the end of the shawls.

"Have you ever thought about adding a crochet edging instead?" I didn't wait for an answer. "You could use one of the bigger crochet hooks that are popular." I looked at her directly. "If you don't know how to crochet, I'm sure Adele would be glad to show you."

"You mean the woman who didn't want to let me leave the dress form?" When I nodded, Rain shook her head. "I don't think that would work, but thanks for the offer."

She held the shawl out again. "Shall I wrap it up for you?"

She had me in a corner. "Silly me," I said, looking down

and pretending to be surprised that I didn't have my purse. She offered to hold it until I came back, reminding me that there wasn't another.

"What about the sample?" I said.

"I don't usually sell them," she said. "But if you wait until the end of the show I could give it to you for a discount." I was just trying to get out of there without buying anything, but she thought I was negotiating.

I was definitely running out of time to talk to her. It was now or never. I had a plan that might work.

"It's amazing how everybody is just going on about their business around here," I said, trying to sound annoyed. Rain was still holding out the shawl, and I finally said I wanted to make sure my friend would be happy with it. I noticed she cooled quickly after I said that.

"You knew K.D. pretty well, didn't you?" I said, trying to keep my voice calm, like I didn't know that she was trying to get me to leave. "Don't you think that putting a wreath in the front of the vendor area is a pretty lame tribute?"

Rain put away the shawl. "K.D. and I had a professional relationship. I hadn't really thought about the wreath, but now that you mention it, it does seem a little lame."

"Didn't you say you went up to her suite?"

"Well, yeah, I knew there had been a mix-up with my booth, and I thought the best way to straighten it out was to go talk to her."

"So then you were actually in the suite," I said. Rain nodded and glanced toward the double doors that were still closed, but even here we could hear the din of the crowd waiting to get in.

"You probably heard that I'm the one who found her. I

did my best to look around at things. You know, so when the cops talked to me, I could tell them about anything I saw."

"That sounds like a good idea," Rain said in a dismissive tone. "They're about to open the doors. I'm sure you want to get back to your booth."

She was definitely showing me the door this time, but I'd come so far and I didn't want to have to start from scratch with her again. Just a few more minutes and I'd ask her about the hook so naturally she wouldn't even notice.

I did the politician thing and merely ignored her comment and continued on. "You know, personally, I was kind of surprised. All that talk K.D. did about knitting like it was the only yarn craft that mattered and then to see that thing on the coffee table in the living room of the suite." I looked at her. "You must have seen it."

Rain seemed puzzled. "Must have seen what?"

"What was on the coffee table when you were there?" I said.

"I don't know. There was some stuff. Some copies of the magazine, I think."

I didn't want to ask her directly about the hook. I was hoping she would volunteer the information, but she was not cooperating and I had no choice but to be direct. "You must have seen the crochet hook. It was big and made out of wood."

"Crochet hook? K.D. Kirby with a big crochet hook? I certainly didn't see one." Rain laughed at the absurdity of it.

I didn't have to worry about trying to hide my disappointment at her answer. She was instantly distracted as the doors opened and the crowd surged in. I don't think she even noticed when I left.

I'd barely taken a few steps when I heard Delvin on the microphone announcing the beginning of the day's programs.

Rain's booth was on the front end of the last aisle, and the open area with the stage and catwalk was just beyond. I stopped to watch. Delvin had walked to the end of the catwalk and had a handheld microphone. I suppose a headset version would have interfered with his hat. A smattering of people had gathered around the end of the long, narrow walkway. He directed his comments at them as he reeled off the morning's schedule and listed the knitting classes that still had room for last-minute sign-ups.

"And in case you're new to the show, we've added crochet classes this year. I know you've all heard of our celebrity crocheter CeeCee Collins." She joined him then, and he put his arm around her as though she were some kind of treasure. I was sure that CeeCee was glad that instead of talking about how long her career had been and calling her a veteran actor, which was another way of saying old, he went right to her current work. "Not only is she the host of the reality show *Making Amends*, but she costarred in *Caught by a Kiss*, the first in the Anthony the Vampire movies. Incidentally, Anthony is a crocheter. Fingers crossed that when the Oscar nominations come out later in the month, CeeCee's name will be on the list." He looked over the crowd with a bright expression. "She is the leader of a local group, the Tarzana Hookers." He paused to let the usual response of laughter over the name go through the crowd. "The group focuses on making items to give away, either to charity sales to raise money or directly to those who benefit." There was no loud whoop when he said that CeeCee was the head of our group, so I was sure Adele was still AWOL. No way would she have let that pass without some kind of noise.

Before he turned the microphone over to CeeCee, he

added that not only was she the judge of the crochet design competition but she had generously offered to step in and give a class on crochet pieces for charity. CeeCee did a little bow of her head and let out a dusting of her musical-sounding laugh as she accepted the microphone. "Delvin, you're making me blush with all those kind words."

CeeCee was playing the part of the modest actor, but I knew she was loving every complimentary word he had said about her. Her little talk was very nice and, I knew, heartfelt. She was an excellent actress, but when it came to crocheting items to help others, all the emotion was real. She went on to describe the impromptu class she had decided to teach, and I saw several women racing each other to the administration table to get the last few spots.

I had to hand it to CeeCee. She had figured out how to get the spotlight away from Audrey and back on her. Best of all, it was through positive action.

I watched Delvin as he took back the microphone. He seemed so at home in front of the crowd. It was hard to imagine how he was handling K.D.'s death and the added responsibilities so well. Either he was a really good actor, or he had shoved any grieving over his boss to the back of his mind. Of course, there was another possibility: Maybe he wasn't that upset at her demise.

There was no time to think about it at the moment. I needed to get to the booth. Dinah was there all alone. Just as I turned to go, I saw a maintenance man pushing a cart through the crowd toward the back of the large room. He was the same man I'd seen whispering to the hotel manager after the whole almost burglary attempt. At the time I had the definite feeling that the manager wanted to just close the door on the whole incident, and I was betting the hefty man in the dark gray uniform had said something to him that would have stirred things up.

Dinah would be okay for a few minutes more, I thought, as I began to trail behind him. I would just wait until he stopped and then see what information I could get out of him. He was good at threading through the throng of people in the aisle. I didn't have his talent, and my progress seemed to be constantly thwarted by the meandering gait of the thick crowd.

The maintenance man had gotten quite a lead, and I rushed through the people, trying to catch up. He seemed to be headed to a pair of doors at the back of the room. I was blocked by a knot of women who'd stopped to show each other the handspun yarn they'd just bought. By the time I pushed my way around them, he'd almost reached the back wall. A space opened up and I rushed to catch up, following him through a doorway.

He stopped the cart abruptly and I bumped into him. "Excuse me, I need to talk to you," I said, hoping I'd think of something to say after that. He turned with a surprised look.

"You can't be in here. They sent you from corporate, didn't they? I told them it was all a mistake," he said nervously.

I was afraid he was going to move on, but he stayed glued to the spot. "I know I should have checked it, and from now on I will." I saw his dark eyes widen with worry.

I was pretty sure the mistake he was talking about had to do with whatever he had told the manager about earlier, and I wanted to know what it was. But the only way to find out was to act like I knew what he'd done.

"I'm sure we can work something out, if you tell me the

whole story," I said, wishing I had CeeCee's acting ability. I had no idea how someone from corporate would act, so I did my best to be authoritative, which meant standing as tall as I could and lowering the timbre of my voice. I think it worked, because he began to remind me that he'd worked there a long time and one mistake didn't seem so bad after all that time.

"I have to know all the details," I said. I had lowered the tone of my voice so much, I almost sounded like Darth Vader.

He began to stumble over his words, telling me that during the setup, he'd forgotten to check that the wall panels that had been used to divide off the space for the auction item room were locked in place. And what was worse, he'd seen someone slide the end panel away from the wall and then do something to the door. "I figured it didn't matter, but now with the burglary . . ." His voice trailed off.

I had reached an impasse. I wanted to know who the person was who'd been messing with the temporary wall, but it didn't exactly fit in with the scenario I'd created. And then . . . genius struck. "You know, Michael," I said, reading his name off his shirt in my creepy deep voice. "I'd like to help you. But I need you to help me help you. If I could just talk to the person. We could make this all go away." I was getting a little caught up in the part I was playing and wished I had something to write on. I saw that he was holding a package of paper towels and grabbed one. I took a pen out of my pocket and held it poised. "Just give me a name."

"I can't," he said as his expression crumbled. "I don't know who it was. It was just some lady with a yarn thing wrapped around her shoulders."

That's a big help, I thought. He'd just described most of

the women wandering around the yarn show. I'd have to try a different angle

"Do you have any idea how the door to the marketplace got unlocked?" I asked. Now he looked anguished.

"That wasn't really a mistake. I unlocked it for the snack bar delivery guy." He dropped his voice after that and mumbled something about how he meant to check it after the guy left. "This isn't a very good place to talk. You really shouldn't even be in here," he said.

My total focus had been on talking to him, and I'd just assumed we were in some back room. For the first time I took in the tile floor, then the row of sinks and finally the row of urinals. Oops.

"Molly!" a deep voice said. I tried to slink back and hopefully disappear, but Barry grabbed my arm. "Do you want to explain what you're doing in the men's room?" He gave a sympathetic nod to the maintenance man and escorted me out.

"I can't talk now," I said, pulling free. "I've got to get back to my booth." I hoped that whatever had made him go into the men's room would make him go back, but he followed behind me and then finally got in front of me and blocked my path.

"You're investigating, aren't you?" he said. His voice didn't have a touch of playful to it. He was all serious. "We had a deal. I agreed to wait until Monday to arrest Adele, and you weren't going to investigate."

"I never said that," I argued.

"I thought it was an understanding."

"More like a misunderstanding," I said with a smile, hoping he'd lighten up. Instead he blew out his breath and looked like his blood pressure had just gone up.

"Why aren't you worried that I'm going to arrest you? I could, you know. Suspicious activity in the men's room." He blew out his breath again, and when I looked up at him, I saw just a hint of a smile in his eyes. "My job is so dull without your interference." He seemed to be weighing what to do. In the end, he steered me to a quiet corner in the large space, not far from the scene of the crime. "The least you can do is tell me what you found out."

CHAPTER 17

"THE WORST IS, I HAD NOTHING TO SHARE," I TOLD Dinah. "Or should I say, nothing to share that he wanted. As soon as Barry heard that the employee had to do with the burglary that wasn't, he wasn't interested."

"Barry might not be interested, but I'd like to know," she said.

Rather than tell her what the maintenance man had told me, I told her my scenario of what had gone down. "I think someone at the show had a plan to take the knitting needles. She slipped in the room where the auction items were. Maybe she would have taken them then if the maintenance man hadn't seen her. But I definitely think she did something to the lock, like put a piece of tape across it so it wouldn't engage. She probably saw the opportunity to slip in when the door to the marketplace was unlocked for the deliveryman." I stopped while an interesting thought surfaced. "One thing we know for sure: It wasn't Audrey Stewart."

"What makes you so sure?" Dinah asked.

"She might not have been in a movie for a couple of years, but I'm sure the maintenance man would have recognized her. All he said was that it was a woman with some knitted thing around her shoulders."

"Good thinking," Dinah said. "I'm sure you're right." I went back to talking about Barry. "I was actually relieved when he mentioned our supposed deal," I said. "With Adele not showing up, I was getting worried. Now I can just be annoyed."

"I bet Barry's job is pretty dull without you popping up." Dinah adjusted the end of her long red scarf. Her short hair was gelled to spiky attention and she was bubbling with energy as usual.

"He said something to that effect, but then he threatened to arrest me again."

"Yeah, and I bet he'd take the long, long route to the police station just so he could spend time with you," my friend joked. "Where exactly did you say Barry ran into you?"

I made a face and told her. She burst out laughing. "I told you his life was dull without you." She reminded me that I'd originally left to see if I could find out about Adele's hook in K.D.'s suite.

It didn't register what she was talking about at first. The whole Barry encounter had thrown me off. "Of course, you mean the trip to Rain's booth. No luck. She didn't see the hook in the suite, but I did see a gray shawl you would love." My mind drifted back to Barry. "It's a good thing he's here." I noticed Dinah's puzzled expression and realized I'd jumped from talking about a shawl to talking about Barry with no explanation. I apologized, then explained why it was a good thing Barry was at the show. "It means he's still investigating and maybe he's not so sure Adele is the culprit."

"Or he's looking for a way to see you," my friend offered.

"The thought had crossed my mind, but other than an almost smile that only registered in his eyes, he'd totally kept up the cop facade. I think it's just about the case."

Dinah had taken good care of the booth in my absence and rung up a few early sales. She had put off starting our offer of making a granny square pin until I returned and she had some backup. Elise arrived without her husband but said he'd be there in the afternoon and for the banquet. She didn't mention if he'd be wearing the vampire outfit to the dinner. Rhoda followed her.

"I'm just checking in to let you know I'm here," she said. Everything about Rhoda was no-nonsense, including her loose-fitting black pants and long powder blue top. Even her brown hair was cut into a neat style that just required combing. She set down her cloth tote on one of the chairs. It started to lean as if it was going to fall, and Elise made a grab for it. I was surprised when Rhoda swooped in first, not only snatching the bag, but holding it against herself as if it contained something precious and secret. I wasn't the only one who noticed what she'd done, and Elise gave her a funny look.

"What's going on? You're acting like you have the crown jewels in there." Elise leaned toward Rhoda and reached out to pull the end of the tote free so she could see what was in there, but Rhoda actually turned her whole body so Elise couldn't reach the bag.

Rhoda pretended to laugh at the crown jewels comment and said it was something she had for the class she was taking. "Another one? I didn't realize there were that many crochet workshops," I said, surprised, mentioning she'd taken one the previous day.

"There are people here who've come from out of town and some of them are taking more classes than me." I hadn't expected her to get so defensive. She pointed out a couple of women going by and said they'd come from Chula Vista. Since most of the people were local, I'd forgotten that some of the people actually traveled to the show and stayed in the hotel.

"I'm sorry. Go on to your class. What did you say you were taking?" I asked as an afterthought. Rhoda didn't seem to have heard me and just said something about being back later to help, and then she was gone.

Dinah had smartly not started the free pin making yet, but now that she had backup, she put out the sign. There was an immediate rush of people. Elise volunteered to teach the first group. I don't think either Dinah or I had realized how popular the pin making would be when we were planning what supplies to bring. When I saw the crowd and then eyeballed the packets we had left, I got worried.

Delvin was back at the microphone announcing the beginning of the morning classes. "We have a demo going on at the administration table," he said. "Audrey Stewart is showing off how to make a skinny scarf." On the chance that people didn't remember who Audrey was, he went through her credits, including the whole list of romantic comedies, conveniently omitting that the most recent of which was three years ago. Without explaining why, he also mentioned her donation of the sterling silver with diamond accent knitting needles in the auction. He ended by saying she would be glad to give out autographs or pose for pictures. I had a feeling this was because of CeeCee's offer to teach a class and all the attention Delvin had given her earlier.

I stepped away from our booth to get a view of the administration table. Score one for Audrey. Kimberly Wang Diaz and her cameraman were hovering around the young actress, who was showing off her knitting skills for the camera. Dinah had followed me, and I nudged my friend. "Even I can knit that well."

Nobody in the group talked about it, but I had learned how to knit, just basic casting on and off and the knit stitch, so I could make swatches for the bookstore yarn department. That was all Audrey was doing, but due to her celebrity status, she was getting oohs and aahs from the crowd that had gathered behind the news crew. Mason was standing next to her. I stepped even closer to hear what was going on. Mason looked my way, and I felt my heart do a little flutter. It was something about how our eyes met. Now that I'd made the decision about changing my life and having him in it, I couldn't wait for it to start. He did just the smallest roll of his eyes and his lips curved into a crooked grin for a moment, then he was back to business fielding the questions that Kimberly Wang Diaz threw at Audrey. It was the stupidest interview, with Audrey insisting that she was beginning a new chapter in her life and that between the whole experience from the misunderstanding about the knitting needles and now K.D.'s death, she'd realized she wanted to make scarves for the less fortunate. She was even considering starting her own charity.

I watched for a moment longer. "Audrey may be off the hook for trying to steal the needles that she donated, but she could certainly be a suspect in K.D.'s murder," I said to

Dinah. "The way Mason is sticking by her side means he thinks so, too. Thea Scott said she thought Audrey would do *anything* to stay out of jail."

"Watson sees your point," Dinah said. "I wonder if Audrey has an alibi."

I glanced back at our booth and saw that it was abuzz with activity. "We better take care of our own business," I said, leading Dinah back to the booth. Several people were inside looking through our yarn, and the line waiting to make the pins was more than Elise could handle.

And the people in line were getting fussy. I heard an argument break out between two women over who was there first.

Without saying a word, Dinah stepped in and directed the first five people in line to step to the end of the table. She handed out packets of the thread and beads and had them each grab a hook and a needle. In no time they'd strung the beads on the thin yarn and begun making the small granny square.

Adele was still a no-show. Just when I was about to give up on her, I heard her voice. Adele tended to be on the loud side, and even with the din, her voice carried over the top. A moment later she was standing at the entrance of the booth. She was flanked by Eric-her-boyfriend. Of course, his name was really just Eric, but she'd referred to him so many times as "Eric-my-boyfriend" that now the whole title stuck in my head. I was glad he wasn't in uniform. Eric was very tall, over six feet, and with his super-straight posture, the cop uniform would have been too much. He was a motor officer, which meant he got to wear black boots, ride on a motorcycle and give tickets. Or be a first responder, as Adele kept pointing out.

His mother, Leonora, was on the other side of Adele and carried herself the same way her son did. She was a little too perfect for my taste—the way she never ate sugar and had five grapes for dessert. What real person does that? Anyone would have had trouble winning the woman over, but Adele had the extra burden of being Adele. And that didn't even take into account that Leonora Humphries was a knitter.

Adele wore a long blue denim skirt that was embellished with large white doilies made out of thin crochet thread and another version of her stash buster wrap. No fascinator or big hat this time, just a simple black beanie with a pink flower on the side.

I heard just a bit of their conversation. Adele seemed to be telling Mrs. Humphries to come to her crochet class. I couldn't believe that Adele was so self-absorbed that she still didn't see the look on Eric's mother's face every time Adele called her Mother Humphries. Adele broke free of them and rushed up to me. "Pink, I'm sorry I'm late. Eric took us out to breakfast." She stopped talking and cocked her head, trying to hear what Delvin was saying this time.

"That's my cue," she said. She told Eric and his mother to wait while she got something. I was stunned. Here I was so worried about Adele being arrested in the dead of night, and she seemed to have forgotten the whole thing.

She dashed back in the booth, and I expected some hysterics now that Eric and his mother were out of earshot, but all she wanted was a rather large cloth bag. I couldn't resist. "Adele, what about the hook?"

She didn't get what I was talking about and said she had hooks in the bag and then she stopped. "Oh, you mean THE HOOK. No problem. I already emailed Dr. Wheel." Adele put on her drama face and said she couldn't take a chance talking to him on the phone in case he tried to convince her to come see him.

"He's sending me another hook." She sounded as if the main issue was that she didn't have her hook, not that it had been found at a murder scene.

I decided it was probably better not to enlighten her and let her know that Barry had decided that she was K.D.'s killer and was practically warming up a cell for her. She was already off the subject of the hook anyway.

"You should thank me," she said with a little proud jiggle of her head. "If it wasn't for me talking to Delvin, there wouldn't be any crochet demos." She tilted her head as if to hear better as Delvin announced that a demonstration of Tunisian crochet was about to begin near the stage. "That's me." Then she was gone. Adele was definitely a force of nature.

I would have liked to watch her demonstration, but there was too much going on in our booth. The number of pin makers had increased, and they were so enthralled with it, they wanted to buy supplies to make more of them. I'd brought in some orbs of the crochet thread in a number of colors and some beads, but I hadn't expected such a turnout.

"More bad planning," I said to Dinah. "We could run out of everything—the packets, the extra supplies, the whole thing—by lunchtime."

"Can you call Mr. Royal and have him bring over some supplies from the bookstore?" Dinah asked, and I shook my head.

"I took everything we had," I said. Dinah had a whole slew of pin makers working. I looked around, hoping an answer would drop in my lap, and for once it did.

"Hey," Paxton Cline said in greeting. He was carrying

drinks in a cardboard carrier from the snack bar as he passed our booth.

"Wait," I commanded, stepping out into the aisle. It might have been a little loud and a little frantic. He froze and I grabbed his arm, pulling him close. "I need more supplies." I was trying to be calm about it, but I think it came across like I was a junkie who needed a fix.

"Yeah, sure. I'll bring over an order form. You can fill it out and I'll get you what you need on Monday."

"It's not for the store. I need thread and beads. And I need them now."

He shook his head. "There's nobody there to fill the order today. When I went there yesterday, I just picked up the order." I saw him looking in the direction of his grandmother. "I'm not so sure she'd let me leave, anyway."

"When I said I would only deal with you, your grandmother took you off gofer duty and made you a salesman," I said. I didn't say it, but I implied he might owe me some extra consideration.

He looked at the drinks he was carrying, and his face clouded over. "You're right. I'm a sales representative. I don't do drinks." He paused and then added, "Except for this time."

I watched as he stood up straight and suddenly grew an inch or two. Nodding to himself, he said, "I'll just tell her I am taking care of one of our customers. A good sales representative takes care of their customers, right?" I nodded in agreement. "I'll just go up to the warehouse and grab some thread myself." His voice sounded a little shaky on the last part.

"Why don't I go with you?" I said. It wasn't that I exactly lacked confidence in his ability to find what we needed, but I thought it would be better if I were there.

Paxton appeared uncertain. "I'm not sure Gran would like it."

"And I'm sure she wouldn't like it if you brought the wrong kind of thread for a customer."

"You're right." His eyes grew troubled. "Gran's got a memory like an elephant. If she found out I'd made a mistake I'd never hear the end of it." He still seemed a little uncertain.

"Maybe the best option is not to even tell her," I suggested.

"Right, that's a good idea," he said, brightening. I quickly added that I wanted to bring Dinah along since she was the one running the pin making and would know best about the thread we needed. "Since Gran isn't going to know, I guess it's okay."

We agreed on a time and I let him go to deliver the drinks.

With that settled, I couldn't resist. I had to see Adele in action.

I stepped to the end of the aisle where I could keep an eye on the booth and see all the way to the stage and catwalk at the end of the room. Eric and his mother were in the small crowd that had gathered as Delvin introduced Adele. First she did a few minutes on crochet in general, saying it was the best yarn craft, et cetera. Then she explained that Tunisian crochet was done on a long hook, and unlike regular crochet, where you worked one stitch at a time, in Tunisian crochet you worked a whole row of stitches. Then she reminded the audience of her class that afternoon, saying she heard there was just one spot open. That was Adele the salesperson. She surveyed the crowd and smiled when she saw several people rush over to the administration table, presumably to sign up.

I hadn't realized how big a bag she'd picked up from the booth until now. "I'll need two chairs," she said to Delvin. I don't think he liked being treated like a stagehand, but he obliged. She plunked the huge bag on one and sat on the other. What had she brought? I was almost afraid to watch. A moment later she extracted a very big Tunisian crochet hook. It must have been an inch in diameter and a foot long. The yarn she took out was as thick as a sausage, and the roll of it was an armload. "I decided to go big so you could all see what I was doing," Adele said.

I don't know if it was the ridiculously large size of the tools or curiosity about Tunisian crochet, but she'd gotten everyone's attention. They must have been as fascinated as I was to see what she was going to do.

I had to hand it to Adele. She'd figured out a way to win the audience over. At least most of them. I could only see Eric and his mother from the back, but her body language was a giveaway. She looked like she had one foot out the door.

I waited until Adele finished her act and came back to the booth, then I announced I was leaving. You'd think I was abandoning her on a chunk of ice floating in the Arctic. She looked panicked and seemed to have suddenly remembered that she was a suspect in K.D.'s death.

"Nobody is going to bother you," I said, leaving out why I was so sure. Adele became even more upset when I said Dinah was coming with me. We were out of supplies, so there couldn't be any pin making anyway, and since it sounded like we were going to have to find what we needed ourselves, I wanted Dinah's help.

Luckily, as we left, Adele forgot her panic and stepped into the role of proprietor. I heard her ordering Elise around, and Sheila had just shown up.

Dinah and I passed the Cline Yarn International booth. Paxton was helping a customer, and I gestured that we'd be waiting by the door. I couldn't help but notice that Ruby Cline was off in a corner of their oversize space talking to a man in a suit. I really wished I could hear the conversation. I nudged Dinah. "He's either a cop or a lawyer."

Dinah looked closer. "I'm voting for a lawyer. The suit looks a little pricey for a cop."

Paxton caught up with us, and I asked him about his grandmother's company. He glanced back at their booth and shrugged. "She kept me out of it. I think maybe he's some guy she met online. You know, at one of those dating sites. I heard her talking on the phone about some boyfriend." He rolled his eyes, and Dinah and I both tried to get a better look at him.

"So she likes younger men," Dinah said. "Though I'd be careful if I were her. Maybe get a background check," Dinah said to Paxton. I figured the chance of his passing the advice on to his grandmother was about zero.

We'd decided to go before lunchtime while the classes were still in session and the crowd in the vendor area was lighter. I don't know what Paxton actually told his grandmother, but he seemed kind of nervous. He said he'd drive and took the van with "Cline Yarn International, Inc." on the side.

The business was located in a business park in Chatsworth, and since it was Saturday, the whole area was deserted. He pulled right in front of the single-story, plain-looking white building. It was dead inside, and the extreme quiet seemed a little eerie. We walked into a reception area, and I did a double take, thinking there were people lurking in the shadows.

"They're just mannequins," I said with a nervous laugh when I looked a little closer and noted their eyes didn't move. Paxton explained they were all wearing samples of things made out of Cline Yarn. Then he added it had been his idea. The wall had an artful display of framed items. Paxton was hurrying us along, but I looked at them long enough to see that they were ads for Cline Yarn from magazines. He shepherded us behind the reception counter and back into the warehouse. He flipped on the lights, and it was like we'd just found ourselves in yarn heaven. Everywhere I looked there were wire bins of yarn in glorious colors.

Paxton looked around as if he had no idea where to start. "We don't usually carry beads, but I think Gran got some samples the other day." He turned to the left and opened a door to an office. We waited for him to turn on the lights and then followed him inside. The office had the look of someone who really worked in it rather than had it just for show. The white desk and computer were the only things without color in the room. Wire bins of yarn were scattered about the room. Swatches were stuck to a corkboard on the wall. I noticed a basket with some balls of yarn and the beginnings of something pale yellow with the knitting needles stuck into the yarn. Some large pots of plants got their light from a tall window that looked out on a patch of grass next to the parking lot. Paxton took a small box off the table in the corner and showed us the contents. They were small pearls, and I said they would do fine.

"They're just some samples we got. We're not going to

carry them, and Gran told me to get rid of them, so you can just have them, no charge. I'll go look for the thread," he said, trying to give the image of being in charge. We offered to help, but he said we better stay there. Something about insurance rules dictating who could be in the ware-house.

When he left, Dinah started ogling all the yarn. I took a closer look at the desk and noticed a stack of old photo-graphs on it. Nosy should be my middle name, because I started looking through them. The black-and-white prints seemed fine, but the color ones had faded and turned odd shades. I was going to comment on what a relic film and prints had become, but one of the pictures caught my eye.

The picture featured a group of women as if they were in a club or organization. As I examined the faces, I stopped on one with a start. It was clear by the clothes and hair-styles that the photo had been taken decades ago. How could Lacey Kirby possibly be in it? I looked again and this time imagined the dark hair white and a face with a little more character, and I realized it was a young K.D. I exam-ined it more closely and saw they were gathered on the lawn of a big house that had some Greek letters on the front. Of course, a sorority. I was beginning to wonder why Ruby Cline would have a picture of K.D. Kirby as a young woman when I noticed the woman on the end. I was going to ask Dinah what she thought, but Paxton came in and saw the figure on the end I was pointing at.

"That's Gran," Paxton said, looking over my shoulder. He seemed puzzled that I was looking at the pictures, and I said something about being fascinated with photography. I used it as an excuse to look through the rest of the pile before it could register that I was snooping. I stopped on another photo from about the same time, but of a man and a young Ruby. The way the man had both of his arms wrapped around Ruby made it clear that he was her boyfriend. With Paxton hanging over me, I moved even faster through the rest of the pictures. I couldn't help myself from stopping on one of the prints. Even though there was no white dress or veil, I could tell it was a wedding shot. Maybe it was their expressions, and maybe it was the little bouquet of carnations the woman held as they stood in front of the Van Nuys courthouse. They looked young and starry-eyed, and I got the feeling they'd eloped.

"I don't know why Gran keeps that picture. She gets mad every time she looks at it even though it was a long time ago. I told you she has a memory like an elephant. We better get going," Paxton said, reaching to take the photos from me. I took a last close look at the wedding shot. The bride was K.D. and the groom was the man from the picture of Ruby and her apparent boyfriend. A thought stirred in my mind. Hadn't CeeCee said something about a rumor that K.D. had stolen one of her sorority sisters' boyfriends and married him? Paxton suddenly snatched the handful of photos and put them back.

"I shouldn't have left you in here," he said with a nervous edge to his voice. "We have to go." Dinah insisted on inspecting the contents of the bin he'd brought in. Paxton was clearly impatient and flipped the lid off to give her only a quick glimpse before he dropped the box of beads in with the different colored orbs of crochet thread. She asked about other colors. "This is the only thread we have. Do you want it or not?" Dinah nodded, and he herded us out of there and quickly snapped off the lights and shut the door.

Dinah and I traded glances as we got back into the van.

Something was definitely up with Paxton. The whole reason we'd come along was to make sure what they had would do for the pins and pick the colors. It had to be the photos.

"Your grandmother and K.D. were friends." I said it as somewhere between a statement and a question. Paxton responded by putting the van in gear and stepping on the gas so hard, both Dinah and I had to hold on to our seats.

Paxton kept the speed up as he turned out onto Plummer Street and headed east. I could just see the side of his face, but he appeared uncomfortable. When we stopped at a red light, he turned to me. "I know you're into that amateur detective thing, but don't start reading anything into anything."

"So then you know that your grandmother knew K.D.," I said and he winced.

"If I tell you everything I know will you promise not to bother Gran?"

"It's not me you should be worried about. Do the cops know your grandmother and K.D. go way back and, it's just a guess, but it looks like K.D. ended up with your grandmother's boyfriend?"

"Okay, I knew Gran knew K.D. I don't know why, but they seemed to have been talking to each other a lot lately. But Gran had nothing to do with her death," he said. "I'm sure of that."

I wasn't sure if he had some kind of real proof or it was just him commenting on her character. "Do you know where your grandmother was Thursday afternoon when everything quieted down?"

"I know what you're asking me," he said, taking a corner a little too fast.

Dinah suggested he pull over and let her drive. He was reluctant but did as she suggested. Though when they went to change seats, I thought he was going to take off, but he finally climbed into the jump seat in the back.

He put his head down when I turned around in my seat to face him. "Why don't you just tell me what you know," I said, borrowing one of Barry's interrogation lines.

Paxton blew out his breath and took a couple of deep ones before he finally answered.

"I'm not supposed to know, but she went up to K.D.'s suite."

CHAPTER 18

"ARE YOU GOING TO TALK TO RUBY CLINE?" DINAH asked. As soon as we'd gotten back to the event center, Paxton had rushed on ahead of us and was already back in their booth helping a customer by the time Dinah and I were passing it. I came to a full stop and glanced into the Cline Yarn International booth.

"I'd really like to ask her some questions," I said. A look of panic came over Paxton's bland face as he saw us standing there. His eyes darted toward his grandmother, who was talking to a customer and oblivious to his concern. Paxton waved his hand in the universal gesture that meant go away, and the rapid way he did it meant he wanted us to do it quickly.

"But I think Paxton would tackle me if I tried to speak to his grandmother. Besides, we need to tend to our own business right now anyway," I said. We were carrying bags of the crochet thread and beads Paxton had given us and continued on to our own booth. Even with the pin making sign down, there were several women lounging around the front asking Adele about making them. "It's about time," Adele said, looking up at us with relief. "I did what I could, but everybody wants to make those pins." There was a line before we even put the sign back up.

"I'm not making packets anymore. We'll just cut the thread as we go," I said, taking off a length of rosy pink crochet thread and rolling it around my fingers. As soon as I pulled it across the hidden cutting edge of the pendant, I handed the coil of thread to one of the women. Dinah doled out some tiny pearls. I was glad when Adele picked up the orbs of thread and said she would help. I let Dinah and her handle the enterprise.

For a moment I watched the passing crowd. This definitely seemed to be the prime time for the show. I could barely see the Knit Style yarn booth across the way. There was a break in the crowd, and I saw Lacey Kirby walking slowly with her head down. Her eyes were locked on the screen of her smartphone, and she was busy tapping away. No doubt a tweet about the show.

It occurred to me that she would probably know something about her mother's relationship with Ruby Cline. I called out her name and she looked up. I had never been officially introduced to her, so I began with that and then offered my sympathies about her mother. I could tell she had already dealt with a lot of condolence offerings because she seemed to have an automatic response.

"Thank you very much for your concern. My mother was quite a woman." Lacey started to move on, but I put my hand on her arm to stop her. It would have seemed a little

odd if I went right into asking about the relationship between Ruby Cline and her mother, so I asked something
Adele would have appreciated.

"I'm just curious," I began. "Your mother added crochet
to the show, but it still seemed like she was trying to ignore
it. Do you have any idea why?"

The question caught Lacey off guard. It wasn't something she could give an automatic answer to. She shrugged
and seemed mystified. "I have no idea. But then she did a
lot of things I didn't understand." It seemed like she was
looking in the direction of the stage and catwalk where
Delvin was droning on.

"Do you have any family to help you during this difficult time?" I asked. She shook her head.

"I'm an only child. The closest thing I have to anyone
helping me deal with this is Mother's lawyers, and they're
sorting through everything."

I asked about her father and she made a face. "Some
people aren't meant to be wives or mothers. K.D. was one of
them. My father was her second husband. I think the marriage lasted six months. I never had much of a relationship
with him and I certainly won't now. He died a couple of
years ago."

I was trying to look interested, but not too interested. So,
her father wasn't Ruby Cline's ex-boyfriend. I casually asked
about K.D.'s first husband. "That marriage lasted a couple of
years. I think my mother was angry and hurt that he left her
for someone else. But she once said that maybe it was pay-
back because he had left someone else for my mother."

It was hard for Lacey to keep her gaze off her smartphone, and she snuck a look and made a tsk-tsk sound before tapping something in. "My mother was so stuck in her

ways. I tried to tell her she should have digital versions of the magazines, but she said that wasn't going to happen under her watch."

I took a chance and brought up Ruby Cline, asking Lacey if she knew whether her mother was acquainted with the woman. Lacey gave me an odd look. "Go figure. They were college buddies but then didn't speak for years, until recently." In the background Delvin was giving some spiel, and Lacey looked angry.

"He doesn't get it. Maybe he was supposed to step in if my mother got sick or worse. But it's only temporary. When everything gets sorted out, I'm sure my mother's wishes were for me to take over. I don't know how to knit or crochet, but I went to business school and I know how to be a boss."

I didn't know quite how to respond, so I just nodded and said I was sure everything would work itself out. Lacey's smartphone began to make noise, and she muttered something about having to tweet that Audrey Stewart was a yarn goddess. She started typing the message as she nodded a farewell and went across the aisle to the Knit Style booth without looking up once.

A group finished making their granny square pins and wanted to buy supplies so they could make more of them at home, and I was suddenly busy ringing up sales. As fast as the women had left the table, new people had taken their place.

I had been tuning out Delvin's endless narration, but then he said something that caught my attention.

"We've got a special treat for you," he began. "You might not recognize his name, but I know you will all recognize his face, and maybe his chest. Eduardo Linnares is not only a former cover model and commercial spokesperson but he is also an expert in something called Irish crochet. It's all lace to me," Delvin said with an intonation that indicated it was supposed to be a joke.

A titter went through the crowd. Rhoda had just come into the booth, and she agreed to watch over things for a few minutes. I had to see this. Eduardo had been in the booth on Thursday evening and was to return this afternoon. I hadn't realized he was doing a demo, too.

Adele appeared out of the crowd and stood next to me. "Pink, I told you I'd take care of things. This Delvin guy is so much easier to work with."

Just then Eduardo made his way up to the stage and down the catwalk, which put him in the center of the growing crowd. No pirate or cowboy outfit today. He was in firefighter attire down to the boots. The outer coat was open as was the denim work shirt to midway down his chest. The firefighter helmet threw a shadow on his strong jaw and model good looks.

There was something about watching his big hands take out a tiny steel hook and some fine white crochet thread and then begin making a delicate flower motif that still struck me as amazing. What the crowd didn't know was that Eduardo was so much more than a pretty face. His Irish grandmother, having no granddaughters to teach, had taught him how to do the lacy patterns of Irish crochet. He'd been a member of our group for a long time and took part in all our activities and fiascoes.

I heard Adele making grumbly noises next to me. "How come he has a much bigger crowd than I did when I did my demo?"

"Do you really not get why?" I said, turning to her to see if she was serious. She was.

Eduardo stopped his crocheting and brought out some finished samples of Irish crochet. An appreciative aah went through the crowd when he held up what he called a wedding shawl made up of the standard motifs of flowers and leaves joined together by chains made of stitches almost too tiny to make out. Eduardo had a sense of humor and made some jokes about his outfit.

Actually, he could have said anything and they would have listened with rapt attention. The best part is that he did a pitch for our booth and said he'd be offering free crochet lessons.

Delvin stopped next to us. He surveyed the crowd around us and their reaction to Eduardo. I guess he was used to being the rooster around so many hens, and I could see he was jealous of the attention Eduardo was getting.

"Maybe I should try one of those Stetsons like he wore yesterday," he said half to himself. The audience didn't want Eduardo to leave, and women kept asking questions and suggesting he crochet more. Finally, when he stepped down, they crowded around him, wanting pictures with him.

Delvin had started to pout, and I realized this was my chance to talk to him about K.D. and Ruby. Since he acted like he was practically K.D.'s right arm, he probably knew something.

It was always hard to know how to start. Since I was not a real detective, I had no cred to just start asking questions. I had discovered that acting like a busybody worked pretty well. As soon as I brought up K.D., Delvin got very defensive. "I told the cops everything I knew. But I don't think they were satisfied. They kept asking me the same stuff over and over."

I pulled him over to the edge of the room where it was

quieter. Before I could bring up Ruby, he began with his details of what happened. He stopped for a moment and cocked his head. "I know you have an in with that Detective Greenberg. I'm going to tell you exactly what happened so you can tell him again in case he can't read his notes."

I started to object, but Delvin didn't buy it. "I saw him talking to you. I know that look he was giving you." I decided it was useless to argue about it and like before with Dinah it would sound like I was protesting, too. And even more, I wanted to hear what Delvin had to say.

"It was crazy all day," he began. "But then it is always that way before the start of the show. Glitches and problems. I told K.D. to let me handle it, but she was insistent on being in the middle of things, even more than usual. You probably saw the problem she had with a woman who comes into the shop, Julie. No matter how she tried to change that jacket, it's just like the one she entered last year. Except, of course, for the crochet on it. I was surprised she even showed up after the way K.D. outed her at the studio.

"And there was that whole problem about Rain and her booth. She's a regular at the show. I thought that K.D. was going to be a hardhead about it, but she reached me on my cell and told me to work out a better location for her."

He moved on to the confrontation between Audrey Stewart and K.D. "Well, it was more between her attorney, who seems to be another friend of yours," he said with a little too much emphasis on the word *friend*. "I don't know why K.D. was so adamant on pressing charges against her, particularly when these days, actresses like Audrey are ending up in real jails." He shuddered at the thought.

I didn't say it, but I was pretty sure that was the point. K.D. had wanted to see Audrey behind bars. "Not that she consulted me on any of it. You'd think as her right-hand person she'd include me. But no. There was something going on. People looking through the books and asking a lot of questions. I tried to find out what was happening, but she said I was imagining things." He seemed at the end of his spiel, and I took the opportunity to ask about Ruby. "Of course they knew each other. She has a yarn business and we have knitting magazines and a major yarn studio." But when I asked if it was personal, he shrugged it off, saying he didn't think so. He noticed that Eduardo had finally broken free of the crowd, and Delvin went to reclaim his microphone.

Eduardo went by and a whole crowd trailed behind him. Adele and I took a shortcut and got to the booth first. As he stepped behind the table with Rhoda for the free crochet lessons, we were inundated with business. The pin people got relegated to the end of the table, though they seemed more interested in watching what was going on with the crocheting firefighter.

I watched Adele watch how much attention Eduardo was generating. There was a little gleam in her eye as she moved in on his territory. She had slipped on the wrap that was the project in her upcoming class and was basically hanging all over Eduardo, pretending her curled hand was a hose and she was dousing a fire as she kept announcing that her class would be starting soon and she thought she might be able to sneak in a few more people.

When that didn't have much effect, she crouched next to him as he gave an up-close demo of the Irish crochet. Adele was so busy cuddling up to Eduardo, she'd stopped paying attention to the crowd in front. Until there was a loud throat clearing. "I wonder if Eric knows what kind of a hussy you are," Leonora Humphries said in a loud voice.

Adele bolted upright, knocking Eduardo's helmet off and exposing his glossy black hair and ponytail. "Mother Humphries, this isn't what it looks like," Adele said. "Whatever Eduardo and I had together was in the past." She said it in a dramatic tone like it was coming out of one of the romance novels Eduardo had been the cover model of. Anything between them was strictly in Adele's imagination. Eduardo, ever the nice guy, tried to play along by saying there'd always be a place in his heart for her.

"I stopped by here to see if I need anything to bring to your class," Leonora Humphries said, trying to compose herself as she glanced over the supply of yarn and tools.

"You're taking my class?" Adele said, and then she turned to the rest of the people and said in a loud voice, "You must have gotten the last spot." When no one rushed up to beg to get into the class, Adele turned back to the woman she hoped would someday be her mother-in-law.

"I brought some odds and ends of yarn and rather large knitting needles," the older woman said. Adele's eyes bugged out.

"Needles. It's a crochet class. You need a hook. No, don't worry, I'll bring you one of mine."

"Oh," Leonora said, sounding genuinely confused. "It would be nice if I could use that handmade one you have."

It was at that moment that Adele remembered how much trouble she was in. "I have lots of hooks you can use. There's no reason to dwell on that one." Adele pulled out a bamboo hook and handed it to the woman. "Here, this is a nice one." Then she grabbed her large bag and suggested they walk to the class together.

I hadn't told Adele, but I was worried about the class being empty, so I'd signed up for it. I didn't want her to have an empty class or just one student like Leonora. Dinah was ready for a break on pin detail and took over sales. Rhoda said her husband was coming by in a while and she was going to show him around, but in the meantime she could stay. Sheila said she'd be glad to help Dinah out. Eduardo was too busy with his crochet groupies to notice that I was gone.

The classrooms were all on the second floor. They all had names that came from local communities. Each had a placard out front with the name and details of the up-coming class. Adele's was being held in the Studio City room. As I went inside, I realized the classrooms had been shaped by dividing a larger space. Move all the folding walls and there was a large ballroom. It amazed me how temporary it all was. The room had been set up with four tables with four chairs at each of them. A long table was in the front for Adele.

Leonora chose the first seat at the first table. I hung back and was relieved to see more women than I'd expected come in and take their seats. I heard several people remark that before this show with our booth and the demonstra-tions, they'd only thought of crochet as being picot stitches for edging. I felt a sense of pride. We actually were getting the yarn world to notice us.

The class wasn't full, but there were enough people not to be an embarrassment. Adele began by modeling the wrap and then talking a few minutes about why crocheting it was so much better than knitting it. "You could never knit this horizontally," she said. "All those stitches would never fit on knitting needles—even the circular ones." A murmur of acknowledgment rippled through the group. Even Leonora Humphries nodded in appreciation. The first thing Adele had them do was to lay out the yarn they'd brought and decide the order they wanted to add it to the wrap. Adele made her way through the group, suggesting different orderings of their yarn and, in one case, telling a woman she ought to use two strands of some thin yarn so it would be about the same thickness as the other yarn she'd brought. At last Adele returned to the front and looked out at her class. "Okay, ladies, it's hooks up." Adele held up her size L hook and waited until everyone had done the same, except me. I'd forgotten to bring anything but my purse.

Adele made a big fuss that it was lucky she'd brought extra supplies as she set me up. She demonstrated how to do the chain stitches and told the group how many to make. The room fell silent as six people moved their hooks through their yarns. I heard a little rustle in the back of the room but ignored it as I made my chains. Adele was just beginning to start the first real row, and she glanced over the crowd. I saw her eyes grow wide and her mouth fall open, and she took a step back.

Curious what she was reacting to, I looked behind me. My mouth fell open, too, when I saw Detective Heather standing against the back wall. I knew that she was a knitter, actually a very good knitter, but I didn't think she was here in that capacity. Not when I saw her badge show as the jacket of her blue suit opened. I also caught sight of her gun, but under the circumstances that seemed irrelevant.

Detective Heather walked down the center aisle and stopped right between Leonora Humphries and Adele.

"You're under arrest for the murder of K.D. Kirby," she said to Adele as she opened up her handcuffs.

I was down the aisle in a flash. "You can't do this," I said. "I made a deal with Barry, uh, I mean Detective Greenberg. No arresting her during the weekend."

Detective Heather flicked a lock of her blond bangs off to the side. "I don't know anything about that." She snapped the cuffs on Adele, who had begun to wail and was trying to reach out to me with her hands behind her back.

"Pink, do something," Adele said. Then she turned to her students. "There are pages with directions on the table. You'll have to finish them on your own." Leonora Humphries looked horrified, grabbed her things and left in a huff.

CHAPTER 19

"I CAN'T STAY," I SAID, RUSHING INTO THE SHEDD & Royal booth. "Detective Heather just arrested Adele." Dinah looked shocked but told me not to worry, she'd keep things going while I was gone. I grabbed my jacket and rushed out to the parking lot.

I never dial and drive, so I called Barry before I started the engine. "We had a deal," I said. "What happened?"

He seemed confused. "Heather arrested her?" I heard him blow out his breath. "I guess I didn't mention our agreement to her. I didn't think she'd do anything without talking to me." He tried to lighten the moment. "At least this time it's not you in handcuffs."

There was dead silence at my end and I heard him swallow. "I'll meet you at the station."

Detective Heather got to the West Valley Station before I did, not that it did her much good. As I got out of my car,

I saw her standing beside hers with the doors open. She looked frustrated and I quickly understood why. Adele was refusing to get out of the car.

"Hey, Molly, over here," Detective Heather said. "Tell her to get out of the car. She'll listen to you."

I almost said, "Are you kidding? Adele listen to me? She doesn't listen to anybody." But I figured that was counterproductive. I didn't know what to do, but I finally just started talking to Adele like I had to my boys in their younger days when they'd gotten into a mess. "Adele, it's okay," I said in my best calm voice. "It's all a mistake. You just need to go inside so we can straighten it out."

Adele didn't look like she was going to budge, but then she stuck her head out. "You promise?" she said in a plaintive voice.

She got out, and Detective Heather looped her arm in Adele's and took her inside. I waited until I saw Barry's Crown Vic pull into the parking lot.

"I'm sorry," he said as he joined me. Whatever calming effect I'd had on Adele had worn off, and she was making such a ruckus, I could hear her when I walked into the lobby. Barry went back into the cops-only area. A short time later, Adele came out with Detective Heather.

"Are the cuffs off my friend?" I said, trying to see Adele's hands. Adele held them out to show me that she was free.

"Barry convinced me we don't have enough to hold her—yet."

Adele threw herself in my arms. "I knew it. You called me your friend. That's almost the same as best friend, isn't it?" She looked at Detective Heather. "Actually, Molly and I are French toast sisters."

Detective Heather rolled her eyes. "That's not a ceremony I want to imagine." Adele was still holding on to me. She barely let go long enough for us to get in my car, then she latched right on again.

We returned to the show. The booth was a madhouse. In our absence Elise had come back with her husband in full Anthony costume. The bins of yarn were close to empty, and all of the thread we'd picked up had been sold or used for our free pin making. Dinah was taking away a tin with a few crumbs left in it and said that Bob had stopped by with a batch of Linzer Torte Cookie Bars to offer with our sales. Eduardo was on the front bench taking a selfie with a fan.

Rhoda grabbed me when I got to the booth. "Don't worry about a thing. We've all been doing everything just like you asked when you called. I went up to supervise the rest of Adele's class. Once they got past the drama, I helped them with Adele's pattern and made sure they all had copies to take with. I think they actually liked the excitement." She held up a list. "We've been giving out information about all the activities at the bookstore. These are the people interested in having crochet parties." The list had ten people, and I gave her a thank-you hug.

Sheila was trying to keep calm and teach two people how to crochet at once. "I want to make one of those," one of the women said, touching the soft shawl Sheila had wrapped around her shoulders. This one was made in shades of lavender with blues mixed in.

Adele was telling everyone how I'd come to her rescue and that was what best friends did. Somehow she hadn't focused on what Detective Heather and Barry had said about her reprieve being temporary.

The crowd in the aisle parted as Eric strode through. He

had that kind of effect. He was well over six feet with a barrel chest and super-erect posture. And this time he was in his motor cop uniform, though he'd taken the helmet off.

"Cutchykins, is it true? My mother said you were arrested." He stopped just outside the booth and Adele came out to meet him.

"It was all a mistake," Adele said and then waved her arm toward me. "Ask Pink about it. I was too dazed to understand what was going on."

Eric zeroed in on me. "She didn't kill that woman, did she? I know Adele is a very passionate woman." He left it hanging and looked to me hoping for reassurance. All I could do was tell him the truth about the hook and what Barry and Heather had agreed to.

"I can't believe that I'm saying this, since they are my cop brethren and sisteren, but you have to do something. I know how they operate. If they think she's the one, they won't look for anyone else."

Was there even such a word as *sisteren*? "I already have a whole list of suspects. That woman wasn't very popular," I said. His face immediately brightened, and he took my hands and squeezed them. "Adele always says you're her something or other sister. Thank you."

Adele had certainly blown a mere brunch out of proportion, but then that was Adele. One Sunday morning I had invited her over for French toast, and since then she'd proclaimed us French toast sisters. And continually told everybody about it.

There were still a few hours left while the marketplace was open, and I was determined to stay in the booth. Things calmed down immeasurably when Eduardo left. He promised to come back for the banquet and the evening program.

I was manning the front table when Ruby Cline came by. "There was so much commotion going on in this booth compared to that one." She pointed across the aisle to K.D.'s yarn store. They still had a big supply of yarn, and I noticed that Audrey Stewart was sitting inside knitting. There were a couple of women around her, but nothing like the crowd Eduardo had drawn. Mason was sitting on a chair next to her. He looked bored until our eyes met. I sent him a warm smile before turning my attention back to Ruby Cline. I had wanted to talk to her, and now she was here. This was my chance.

I'd learned from *The Average Joe's Guide to Criminal Investigation* that it was a good idea to start by asking things you already knew the answers to. Then right away you'd get a pretty good idea if somebody was being truthful.

"It's so sad about K.D.," I began. "I understand you knew her." I left it at that to see what she would say.

Ruby was about the same age as K.D., which put her in her early sixties, though to look at her, you'd never guess. Maybe it was true that the sixties had become the new forties. It wasn't so much her appearance as the way she was connected, relevant, in the middle of what was happening now. She was dressed in stylish black slacks with an amethyst-colored sweater over a white shirt with the cuffs, collar and tails showing. Her hair was reddish, blondish, brownish, no doubt a concoction of her hairdresser. The texture of her hair gave away that it was gray underneath the color, but the wavy style flattered her face. She wore diamond studs in her ears and a gold bangle on her wrist. I looked at her hands and saw only one ring. It was a white cameo set in a black background and worn on her middle finger.

Ruby took her time answering, pretending to be examining the crossed hooks that were blinking up at her. "What a fun idea," she said. I nodded and waited for her answer about K.D. "I'm sorry, you asked me something about K.D.?" She seemed puzzled, as if it was something so trivial she'd forgotten the question.

"I said I thought you two knew each other." Apparently Ruby had used the time to come up with an answer, because then she spoke readily.

"Of course, we knew each other. I own a yarn company and she has, I mean had, magazines about yarn and a store that sold our brand." She glanced around the area. "Have you heard if they have anyone under suspicion?"

"The police don't have anyone in custody," I said. "It was pretty crazy around here Thursday afternoon. Did you get a chance to have a moment alone with K.D.?"

Ruby flinched, though she tried to cover it up. "My grandson says that you're some kind of amateur sleuth. I assure you I had nothing to do with K.D.'s death."

I didn't say anything, but her comment didn't really mean a lot. Most killers don't go around admitting that they killed someone. And she had clearly lied by omission. She hadn't denied knowing K.D., but she certainly hadn't let on how well or for how long she'd known her, or that her old boyfriend had ended up as K.D.'s husband. She quickly changed the subject after that and wanted to know about the yarn from her company that we'd sold and if the thread had worked out.

"You can see for yourself." I stood aside and let her gaze back into the booth at the picked-over bins and hanging displays.

"It looks like you had a fire sale in here." She looked

around for a moment longer, as if she were thinking about saying something, but she must have decided not to because she wished me luck and left.

"What was that about?" Dinah asked, joining me at the entrance to the booth.

"I think Ruby Cline is worried about what I know. She asked about the thread. Paxton must have caved and told her about our trip up there. Maybe he mentioned that I'd seen the photos."

"I bet he didn't mention his wild driving," Dinah said, reining in her long red scarf.

I gave Dinah a quick recap of my afternoon, though thanks to Adele's histrionics, she knew most of it. "I don't know about you, but I need a coffee," I said. Dinah agreed, and we left Rhoda in charge while Adele recuperated from all the excitement.

The crowd was thinning out as the afternoon faded. We caught a glimpse outside through the windows in the corridor as someone exited the marketplace. The sky was turning into twilight.

"Thank heavens the snack bar has espresso drinks," I said, ordering a red eye. Dinah skipped her usual café au lait and went for the brew of the day. Then we gathered our drinks and headed for one of the tables in the area.

We'd no sooner sat down when CeeCee came by wrapped in the scent of roses and jasmine and stopped at our table.

"How could we have been in the same place all weekend and barely seen each other?" She looked at our drinks longingly. "I could use one of those and maybe a little something sweet to go with it." The fact that CeeCee was always concerned about her weight because she insisted the camera really did put on at least ten pounds didn't stop her from having a legendary sweet tooth. She told us to save her a chair and went on to the snack bar.

"It's been a long day," Dinah said, feeling the spikes in her short salt-and-pepper hair. "Even my hair is starting to droop. Remind me to re-gell it before the night's events."

I took a long drag on my drink, longing for the jolt of caffeine to recharge me. CeeCee rejoined us, carrying a coffee drink and a basket full of tiny, freshly made donuts. "I brought enough to share. In fact, do me a favor and dig in so I don't eat them all." She glanced toward the front. "I need a break. When I signed on for this weekend I had no idea how much work hanging out here, teaching that class and judging the entries in the crochet competition would be. And I certainly didn't expect Audrey Stewart to be here all weekend trying to be *the* celebrity of the place." CeeCee's eyes went skyward. "It's been quite a while since she was in a hit movie. If there hadn't been all that fuss when she was accused of shoplifting the knitting needles, no one would even realize she was once such a big celebrity." The round tables near us had attracted a lot of other shoppers taking a break. Most of them were working with yarn as they talked. CeeCee had a way of drawing attention to herself. I could never put my finger on it, but she always seemed to own the room. A number of the people looked our way, and I could see by their expressions that they recognized her. A moment later, one of them was standing next to our table.

"I'd be glad to sign an autograph and take a picture," CeeCee said brightly. She was definitely a trouper who rose to the occasion. All traces of the fatigue she'd just mentioned had vanished and she'd put on a happy smile. But everything changed when CeeCee saw who joined us as the photo was snapped, and her smile faded into a look of concern.

I recognized Julie by the butterfly on her hand. She was the woman I'd seen twice embarrassed by K.D. She was biting her lip and seemed nervous addressing CeeCee. "I was just wondering if the winners have been chosen in the competition."

"Dear, my lips are sealed on that for the moment. You'll find out tomorrow when everybody else does."

Julie didn't seem to want to let it go and did a final pitch for herself, reminding CeeCee that her jacket had really been meant for the knitting competition. CeeCee just smiled and nodded, and I realized it was my chance to ask Julie about K.D.

CeeCee gave me a dirty look when I invited Julie to join us. "It must be strange for you without K.D. here. You knew her pretty well didn't you?"

"I can't believe she's gone," Julie began. "She had such a presence." Julie became animated. "I've been part of the elite group at the yarn studio for a long time. Even though Thea Scott ran the store, K.D. usually made an appearance when our group was there."

I noticed that she talked as if she were a permanent part of the group and as if the other day hadn't happened. I wondered how to broach the subject of her basically being asked to leave. There was no subtle way, but I suddenly had an idea how to find out some other information.

"I know you were upset when K.D. refused to accept your entry in the knitting competition. Did you try to get her to reconsider?"

Julie slumped in her seat. "You have to understand.

There have been some changes in my life lately and I needed to find some work."

I didn't let on that Thea Scott had already told me about Julie's young children and about her husband losing his job.

"I got a position teaching knitting, and I sort of mentioned that I'd won a top prize for the last five years running." She turned to me. "I never got a credential as a master knitter, so being a competition winner gave me credibility. But when I wasn't even accepted in the knitting category this year—" She let it trail off. "Yes, I did try to talk to her."

"Then you went up to her suite?" I said.

Julie looked panicked. "Shush," she said, looking around. "Okay, I did go up there. But K.D. wouldn't even listen. I should have known. She is, or was, a hard woman. Look how she treats her own daughter."

"I thought Lacey handled her social media for her," I said. I noticed that CeeCee had edged away when Julie wasn't looking, but Dinah was all ears.

"We talked about it in the knitting circle. Lacey is in her thirties and riding in her mother's shadow. The social media thing is just like a bone K.D. threw her. I think Lacey thought she should have had the position Delvin Whittingham has. And as much as K.D. might have embarrassed me, it's nothing compared to what she did to Audrey Stewart. Thea wanted to let her pay for those needles and brush it under the rug. What's the difference if it was really a mistake or she took the needles?"

I was pretty sure that Julie wasn't going to go back to discussing her trip to K.D.'s suite since she looked horrified after she'd admitted that she had gone there. Dinah came to the rescue.

"I'm just curious," my friend said in a noninterrogating sort of tone, "when you were in K.D.'s suite, had the champagne been delivered?"

Julie looked mystified. Then she got it. "No, there was no champagne there."

"What about a crochet hook?" I said, still trying to pin down the time Adele's hook had arrived. Julie shook her head. "No champagne and no hook." She suddenly realized that CeeCee had left the table and any chance to plead her case was gone. She got up rather abruptly and left.

"And the plot thickens," Dinah said. "K.D. certainly didn't have a fan club."

"Sort of the opposite. She had a long list of people who weren't fans. And it keeps getting longer. You heard Julie. It doesn't even sound like there was a bond with her daughter. And she'd certainly backed Audrey Stewart into a corner. Who knows how far Audrey would go to stay out of jail. Mason hasn't said anything about it." I reminded Dinah of his attorney-client privilege. "But even with his skills, the way things are now I wonder if he would have been able to keep her out of jail. Not that she seems to have trusted him to take care of things." Dinah nodded. She knew that Audrey had shown up without Mason the morning after K.D. had died and actually worked everything out herself even though Mason would be the one to make sure that the yarn shop followed through and dropped the charges.

"I just don't get how Barry can still be so focused on it being Adele," I said. "We better get back." I got up and took our cups to the trash and we started to walk back. When we got to the front of the aisle and reached Rain's booth, I saw the long blue vest on the dress form and remembered the shawl I wanted to show Dinah. Her birthday might really be a long way off, but I was going to get it for her if she really liked it.

Rain was all smiles and a long way from how she'd seemed when we'd first met. "Business has been great," she said. "You're lucky I still have that shawl you admired in the color you wanted." She went to get the light gray shawl for Dinah. "And there's still tomorrow, though it's usually pretty quiet." Dinah tried on the shawl and modeled it for me. It seemed perfect for her.

"We better get it before it's gone." I looked at the thin group of garments on the racks now. Dinah put up a fight when I took out my credit card and said it was her birthday present—a very early birthday present. Rain had handed back my card and I was putting it away when the crowd along the front of the room thinned and I saw Barry come in and go in the direction of our booth.

Dinah saw him, too. "Maybe he rethought his deal."

"Or maybe he listened to me and he's still investigating," I said. Dinah knew I wanted to find out what was going on and urged me to go ahead, promising that she'd go back to the booth.

When I caught up with Barry, he had stopped against the wall at the front of the room. His suit and tie stood out. Even Mason had gone casual and was now wearing jeans and a sports jacket.

I skipped a greeting and got right down to business. "What are you doing here?"

His eyebrows shot up and his mouth had a hint of a smile. "That's quite a welcome." Typical Barry. He didn't answer my question, so I did it for him.

"You listened to me, didn't you, and you're still investigating."

Barry nodded. "Right, that's why I'm here." I didn't expect him to agree so readily. It felt fake and I knew it wasn't the truth, particularly when I saw how his gaze was locked on our booth. Then I began to understand what was going on.

"It's Adele," I said. "You're not going back on our deal, are you?"

He shook his head with a look of consternation. "I don't know why I ever agreed to that, but no, I'm not going back on it. I went out on a limb for you, er, Adele, and I don't want to look like an idiot if she suddenly takes off for Brazil."

"You're kidding, right? It's Adele. You can't really think she's guilty or taking off for parts unknown."

Barry looked directly at me. "My job is to look at the facts. Her hook was found at the murder scene. She was heard making threats, and she has no witnesses who can confirm where she was during the time the victim was killed. And now that we've tipped our hand, who knows what she'll do."

I blew out my breath, prepared to do battle with his facts. "How exactly have you figured out when K.D. was killed?"

"You know that I don't have to discuss this with you," he said. But he took out his notebook and flipped through the pages.

"We know she was alive when the champagne was delivered and for at least an hour after that, because according to Delvin Whittingham, she sent him some texts." I opened my mouth and he continued. "And yes, we checked his phone and hers. It was a little harder with hers because it was actually in the water with her. The time of death was some time after that but before you found her." He looked intently at me.

"Hmm," Barry said. "You didn't have a problem with Ms. Kirby, did you?" The little lift of his eyebrows made it clear he was joking.

"Have you talked to Ruby Cline?" I said.

He looked down the front aisle toward the imposing Cline Yarn International booth and nodded. "We talked to all of the vendors. There was nothing to imply that Ms. Cline was involved."

"How about this? She and K.D. Kirby were college friends, and I'm pretty sure K.D. stole Ruby's boyfriend and married him."

Barry stopped me. "I'm not even going to ask how you found all that out. I know what you're doing. It's really nice how you're sticking up for Adele."

"I'm just saying you should keep an open mind and keep investigating and not be so sure it's Adele."

"Really?" Barry said. I followed his gaze and almost choked. Adele had stepped out of the booth and seemed to be in the middle of a hissy fit. She picked up a ball of yarn with some knitting needles in it and threw it on the ground and then kicked it for good measure.

Oops.

"You know Adele. She's just a loose cannon," I said and he nodded.

"Exactly my thought," he said. "A loose cannon who could lose her cool and do something on the spur of the moment, like throw a hair dryer in a bubble bath. I hope you understand that I can't let it be personal. I have to do my job." He let down his cop demeanor. "That was always the problem with us. My job. The hours and the undependability." In order to hear each other over the noise we'd ended up standing very close together. Close enough that I could feel the heat coming off his body and smell the tell-tale fragrance of the lemon soap he used. He was so familiar and so distant at the same time. It felt very strange.

"There you are, Sunshine," Mason said, stopping next to me. He was all smiles, though I saw his expression darken when he looked at Barry.

Barry didn't wait for Mason to say anything and just explained he was there on official business.

"I was going for a coffee run," Mason said, putting his arm on my shoulder in a subtly possessive gesture. "Would either of you like one?"

"No, thank you," Barry said, straightening and stepping away. He took up his post a few feet down.

Mason didn't waste a moment talking about Barry but went right into how nice it was that we had a moment to-gether. "It's torture seeing you and not being able to spend time with you," he said. He glanced at his charge in the distance. Audrey Stewart was sitting alone knitting in the Knit Style booth. "I can't be gone long." He turned to me. "How's it going?"

I assumed he meant the investigation and started to talk about Adele being a suspect and how absurd it was. "There are so many other people it could be. Even your—"

Mason looked crushed and put up his hand to stop me. "Sunshine, say no more." He gave me a quick hug. "I can't wait until the situation is settled." And then he was gone.

CHAPTER 20

"ARE YOU CRAZY?" I SAID TO ADELE. I'D RUSHED back to the booth to try to do damage control and leaned down to pick up the abused ball of yarn. "You couldn't have done anything worse for yourself. There I was proclaiming your innocence to Barry and he looks over and sees you attacking some yarn and knitting needles."

Adele hung her head for a moment before she looked up with a big smile. "You were defending me. Thank you." She grabbed me in a bear hug that squeezed the air out of my lungs.

It appeared that even with her almost arrest, Adele still had no sense of how much trouble she was in. Her story was she'd never gone up to talk to K.D., that the hook had been planted and there was no way anyone could really believe she was guilty of anything.

"You do realize that innocent people are found guilty all

the time," I said. It seemed like that finally got to her. "Why were you throwing the yarn, anyway? It's hardly very professional."

Dinah had joined us and explained for Adele. "Leonora Humphries left a tote bag for her. There was a note in it saying that if Adele really cared about Eric, she would get out of his life. That there was a reason people who crocheted were called hookers and if Adele wanted to help herself, she should take up the real yarn craft of knitting like her fellow crocheter Rhoda. And to start Adele off on a new life, she'd included some yarn and needles along with a book called *The Average Joe's Guide to Knitting.*" Dinah took a breath and shrugged. "Adele didn't take it very well."

"I didn't know there was an *Average Joe's Guide* to anything beyond criminal investigation," I said. Dinah laughed.

Rhoda walked toward us, but when she got near Adele, she made a wide swath away from her and then spoke to her. "All I did was take a couple of knitting classes this weekend. It doesn't make me a traitor to our craft." She joined Dinah and me and opened her oversize tote to show the projects she'd started in the three classes she'd taken. The knitting needles clanked together and Adele flinched.

"What's wrong with being ambi-stitcheral?" She threw a hopeless nod at Adele before turning back to us. "I'm going home to change and pick up Hal. He wants to see those silver knitting needles. You know he works in jewelry, right? He's going to see if there's a way to make us some silver jeweled hooks." She looked back at Adele. "I hope you heard that. I'm trying to figure out a way for us to have fancy crochet hooks."

Adele looked a little dazed and rushed to join us. "I'm sorry for calling you a yarn traitor. It's just . . ." Adele began to cry. I'd never seen her cry. She could barely admit to having a vulnerable side. "I know Leonora has poisoned Eric's mind about me. He's the yin for my yang. Getting arrested was the final blow." We tried to console her and tell her we were sure she was wrong.

"He was supposed to come tonight," she said, "but he sent me a text that he had to cancel because he had to work." She struck a dramatic heartbroken pose. "It's just an excuse. I know it is."

"It will be okay. We'll all sit together at the banquet," I said.

"And I'll be the only one with an empty chair next to them. Dinah is coming with Commander, Rhoda is bringing her husband, and Elise for sure is bringing Logan. I heard Sheila even has a date. Eduardo's got his girlfriend. Everyone has someone," she said with a sad pout. Then she stared at me. "Wait a second, Pink, who are you coming with?"

"I'm going solo," I said. "Mason is on duty with Audrey." I mentioned how he'd just taken a few minutes away from her to do a coffee run. My late husband Charlie had worked in public relations, so I was familiar with the drill when it came to dealing with celebrities. No matter how exalted your position, theirs was higher, which meant sometimes you had to be an escort or even do gofer duty. "Mason has to protect her from herself, making sure she doesn't make some offhand comment about the knitting needles or maybe something else."

Adele's eyes widened. "You mean he thinks she's the one who threw the hair dryer in the tub?"

I shrugged. "He hasn't said it, but then he hasn't said anything about her. He can't. But I think he knows she really shoplifted the needles and that she might have killed K.D."

Adele seemed a little less woebegone when she heard I was dateless and was relieved to hear I had a suspect in mind. "You can leave if you want," I said to Dinah, Rhoda and Adele. "I'm staying in the booth until the marketplace closes. I brought my clothes with me."

"I did, too," Adele said. "Good, we can change together." I noticed that Dinah rolled her eyes at Adele's comment, then wished me luck before she and Rhoda left.

The crowd grew thinner and thinner as the afternoon wore on until finally the only people going by were other vendors or the support staff for the show. Mason waved and said he'd see me later as he followed Audrey to the door. All the while Barry wandered around the perimeter, keeping an eye on Adele.

I was glad to finally put the cloth covering over the booth and head upstairs, even if it was with Adele. The room showed signs of a lot of people using it as a pit stop over the weekend—some spare vampire parts, a receipt showing the entrelac knitting class Rhoda had taken and a black suitcase. I went to have a look at it, but Adele pulled it back. "It's personal," she said.

I decided I was never going to take a road trip with Adele. Sharing the room with her, even for that short time, made me crazy. The banquet was black tie optional, and I had definitely gone for the optional. A basic black dress and low heels were as far as I went. Adele wasn't satisfied and tried to pin crocheted flowers all over the bodice. We settled on one red mohair rose in the neckline center of the tank-style dress. I redid my makeup and jazzed it up by adding eye shadow and a lot of blush. I fluffed up my shoulder-length brown hair. It wasn't straight or curly—but it certainly had a mind of its own. I finished the look with a black mohair shawl that had some sparkle.

Adele had to give herself a facial and then use heat rollers on her hair before she got dressed. I was expecting some kind of over-the-top evening wear but was surprised to see a hanger with black pants and a black tunic. For Adele to forgo all color seemed very, very strange.

Since Adele seemed to be all over the room, I stepped out in the corridor to see if I could find a vending machine and get some bottled water. I glanced down the hall. At the end, the double doors of K.D.'s suite were still yellow-taped off. As I was looking at the doors, I was surprised to see a room service waiter pushing a cart that had appeared seemingly out of nowhere. He came toward me checking room numbers as he went.

I stopped him to ask about the vending machine and couldn't help but ask how he'd done the appearing out of nowhere act. He took me back down the hall and showed me the alcove that seemed to be an entry area for the suite. He pointed out the patterned wallpaper on the left. When I still didn't get it, he showed me a button that seemed to be part of the pattern. He pushed it and the wall slid open, exposing the service elevator.

"You aren't by chance the person who brought up the champagne. . . ." I didn't finish but instead pointed at the doors with the yellow tape. He swallowed so hard, I actually heard it, and then he gave me a small nod as an answer.

I crossed my fingers for luck. "Did you notice a large wooden hooklike thing and some yarn on the table?" I asked.

"You mean like a crochet hook?" he said, and my hopes

shot up. For a second anyway. "My girlfriend crochets. She keeps trying to get me to try. It's supposed to be good for your nerves, and ah, sexy." He leaned close. "She dragged me to that *Caught by a Kiss* movie, and Hugh Jackman sure has a way with a hook." He went on about the Anthony character and how he'd made it seem cool for guys to handle a hook. I finally had to stop him and get his mind back on the champagne delivery. "Let's see," he said, looking at the ceiling as he tried to think back. "The cops were more interested in what time I delivered it and if there was anyone else in the room. I said a woman with a knitted headband was just leaving when I got there." He went back to trying to conjure up the scene in his mind's eye.

"I remember pushing some magazines over on the coffee table before I set down the bucket and the glasses. And a hotel key. They call them keys, but they're really plastic cards. But that was it. No yarn or hook."

He'd started to push the cart down the hall, and I walked with him. "Did you see anyone loitering around the hall when you came out?" He shook his head and said the cops had asked the same question.

"I didn't know she was going to be murdered," he said, "so I was just trying to do my job and get out of there."

"Who has access to that elevator you showed me?"

"Guests aren't supposed to use it, but there's really nothing stopping them." He began to pick up speed. "I better get this delivered. Nobody likes lukewarm soup."

"I wouldn't want to get you in trouble," I said. "Thanks for answering my questions." He gave me a funny look.

"I get it, you're some kind of undercover investigator, right?"

"Yes, but way undercover, so if anyone asks you about me, you don't know anything."

He seemed to like the intrigue and promised that it was just between us. "Crocheters rule," he said as he rushed down the corridor.

I didn't really think he'd mention me or my questions to Barry or Detective Heather, but why take a chance. I glanced back the way we'd come, wondering about that service elevator and where it went. The room service waiter was way down the hall now and not paying any attention to me. I quickly went back to the elevator. If he hadn't pointed out it was there, I never would have seen it. Even so I had to feel for the button because it completely blended in with the floral wallpaper. It was a little creepy that there was no noise as the wall panel slid away and the elevator door opened.

Once I was inside, it was just like a regular elevator, though large enough to bring up furniture. I hit the ground floor button, and the elevator began its descent. It came to a silent stop and the door opened onto an industrial-looking corridor. As I walked into it, I smelled food and heard the clatter of noise from the kitchen. I was somewhere in the middle of the long hallway. Disoriented, with no idea what was where, I picked a direction. When I came to the end, I pushed through the doors and found I was right outside the entrance to the marketplace, which was completely deserted. I retraced my steps and then continued on to the other outlet of the corridor. This time it wasn't silent or empty. I was suddenly in the lobby, not far from the registration desk and the bank of elevators.

"Where did you come from?" Barry said, reaching out his arms to stop me before I backed over his feet. His voice startled me, and I flinched, wondering if he somehow knew I'd been snooping. When I recovered, I saw that he was leaning against a pillar near the bank of guest elevators.

I did what he did so much of the time. I answered his question with one of my own.

"What are you doing here?"

"What do you think I'm doing here?" he said. I shook my head with consternation and noticed there was just the slightest twinkle in his eyes. He knew what I was doing and was doing it back.

"It's not about Adele, is it?"

"What do you think?" This time it was kind of a question-statement combination.

"You don't seriously think she is going to try to take off for Switzerland?" I said.

His face said it all. He thought she might. "She's much more upset at Eric's mother," I said. "By the way, the reason she was manhandling that yarn was because it was a gift from Mrs. Humphries along with a note about how unsuitable she thinks Adele is for her son. I guess it's standard operating procedure for mothers to think someone isn't right for their sons. But maybe not to that extreme. I can just imagine what your mother would think about me."

Barry's face softened. "She would love you, particularly for the way you treat Jeffrey. And she would think you were way too good for me. She doesn't like me being a cop."

The elevator door opened, and Barry's attention went right to it as he watched it unload.

"Believe me, she's still upstairs. You know Adele. She never does anything halfway." I caught myself before I continued, realizing I was feeding right into his concerns.

"It doesn't bother you that Mason's work is requiring him to hang out with a young, hot actress?"

"How about young, hot suspect," I said, hoping to drop the idea into Barry's mind.

"Aha, so it does bother you." I realized he'd taken it the wrong way entirely and thought I was mentioning her possibility as a suspect because it did bother me. And if I tried to explain more, it would just reinforce what he thought.

As for if it really bothered me—no. My late husband had worked in public relations and dealt with many versions of Audrey Stewarts. I was used to it.

"Maybe his work is going to be a problem, too."

"It was more than your job," I said, quickly, then regretted it. It was pointless to discuss it.

Barry seemed surprised. "Then what was it?"

"How about how you just did things without consulting me?"

"I'm used to being in charge," he said.

"Exactly." I left it at that. This was getting way too personal. "I have to go." I switched the subject back to Adele. "You're not really going to sit outside her condo all night, are you?"

"I called in a favor and someone is taking over the night shift." I think he was as relieved as I was to be talking about Adele again. I rolled my eyes and turned to go.

"You look nice," Barry called after me.

CHAPTER 21

"PINK, WHERE HAVE YOU BEEN?" ADELE SAID WHEN I came back into the room. I doubted she really wanted to know and thought it was better to leave her in the dark about the fact that she was being watched. She was putting the finishing touches on her hair. She had tried to give her brown locks the tousled curl look.

She went to working on her makeup, muttering that when you were going to be on the stage, more was really more. Adele had a way of taking over the room, and it seemed very crowded.

"It looks like you'll be a while," I said, edging my way back to the door. "I'll meet you at the banquet."

Adele seemed disappointed. "I thought you could help me with some stuff, but never mind." She said it in a tone straight out of an old black-and-white melodramatic movie.

* * *

THE BANQUET WAS HELD IN A BALLROOM THAT
had been set up with a stage and a short catwalk. Black drapes
had been pulled along the side walls, and the center of the
large room was filled with a multitude of round tables with
white tablecloths and floral centerpieces. People had already
begun arriving. There was a table up front that had a big reserved sign, but beyond that it was open seating. I looked over
the tables for a familiar face. Dinah stood up at one near the
front and waved me over.

She had gone home to change and pick up Commander
Blaine. Even now none of us knew if his first name was
really a title, a nickname or the name he'd gotten at birth.
I suppose if they ever got married, we'd find out. He'd
taken the black tie suggestion seriously, and his traditional
black tuxedo made his thick shock of white hair seem even
brighter. Dinah had re-gelled her spiky hair and changed
into a silvery gray outfit. The shimmery fabric with a touch
of sequins caught the light and reflected on her face.

"You wore the shawl," I said, seeing the gray shawl I'd
gotten for her draped around the back of her chair.

"Thank you again," she said. "It looks like it's going to
be in the knit fashion show. Rain came by and asked if I'd
model it."

Commander looked over the other tables, which were
filling up with mostly women. His face brightened when he
saw Paxton Cline. "Good, another man." Paxton was sitting
with his grandmother. She seemed very contemporary,
wearing a black jacket with an aqua triangle shawl artfully
arranged into a scarf. I recognized the yarn as a silk blend
from their collection and thought it served as a nice adver-

tisement for Cline Yarn International. I wondered why she looked tense. Paxton had worn a sports jacket and slacks, probably the closest thing to formal he had.

"Hi, everybody," Rhoda said when she arrived at the table. "You finally get to meet Hal." The man with her gave a wave to us as she introduced each of us. He looked like he belonged with her. They were even dressed alike in plain dark suits. She sat down, but he went over to a long table set up below the stage that had the auction items on display.

"Hal works in the jewelry business," she said to everyone at the table. "When I told him about those fancy needles, he said maybe he could make up some hooks like them."

Elise was the next arrival with her husband in tow. There was still a trace of the sparkly stuff he'd had on his face when he was dressed as Anthony. Elise was bubbling about all the vampire kits she'd sold.

"There's Sheila," Dinah said. "And look who she's with."

"You're right," I said, standing up and waving to get their attention. We'd all known that Sheila had been interested in her boss practically from the day she started working in the lifestyle store near the bookstore. But this was the first time they'd gone anywhere together. Nicholas had a self-effacing charm, and no one ever guessed he was the author of the Anthony books.

Sheila was beaming but was so nervous when she reached the table, she knocked over her wineglass when she went to sit down. Luckily it was empty and no damage done. Nicholas knew some of us and introduced himself to the rest. We quickly found out that it wasn't exactly a date. He'd come to see the fashion show with the idea of acquiring some one-of-a-kind pieces for his store.

Eduardo's arrival caused quite a stir. He was tall, incredibly good-looking and wearing a black leather tuxedo. His girl-friend was nothing like I expected. It was pretty clear that he had all the plumage in their relationship.

"Where's Adele?" Rhoda asked, scanning the room.

"She'll be here," I said.

Meanwhile the reserved table was filling up. CeeCee waved to us as she stopped at the special table. She'd come alone and was perfectly dressed in a stylish maize-colored silk suit. She was waving to the crowd as well, and several people came up and took photos with her. CeeCee never complained about those kinds of interruptions. She liked the attention. Delvin took one of the seats near her. His version of a tuxedo was priceless—tails over black jeans and a white T-shirt. And his hat, a top hat, of course. Kimberly Wang Diaz came in and grabbed a chair where she could see the crowd. Since she was getting an award, she'd dressed to the nines. It had been a smart move on K.D.'s part to give an award to the newscaster. It was a way to guarantee the event would make the late news.

Lacey Kirby created a stir when she reached the reserved table. All the smiles faded for a moment as she received supportive pats from her tablemates. I could only assume that they were making comments about her mother and how sad it was that she wasn't there.

Audrey Stewart made her way through the room to the front. She'd gone for simple elegance. Mason was a few steps behind. I watched him scanning the crowd until he saw me. His whole face lit up and I felt myself smile. They sat down at the reserved table as well.

Commander seemed relieved that there were even more men in attendance now, though I was noticing that it seemed like only our group had brought dates.

Thea Scott stopped at the reserved table, but I saw Delvin shaking his head and pointing off toward the rest of the tables. I guessed being the manager of the Knit Style Studio wasn't enough to garner a seat there. If Mother Humphries was in the crowd, she was certainly staying far away from us.

"Can I talk to you for a minute?" Paxton came up behind me, leaning close and speaking in a low voice. I nodded and got up. Our table was on the edge of the front row, next to the dark curtain that had been pulled along the side wall. Paxton led me to the back corner of the room.

His bland looks were gathered up in worry. "What is it? Is something wrong?" I said.

"Gran is upset with me," he began. "I didn't mean to, but I ended up telling her that you'd gone with me to get the thread. I kind of mentioned that you have investigated some murders and solved some cases for the cops. She got all upset when she realized you'd seen the photographs in her office. There wasn't any bad feeling between Gran and K.D. Kirby. They'd been talking a lot recently. Gran said that K.D. even invited her up for a glass of champagne."

"So your grandmother did go up to K.D.'s suite," I said.

He looked horrified when he realized he'd just made things worse, and he struggled to fix what he'd done. "She was just up there for a few minutes. She didn't even finish the champagne. She brought the glass back to the booth with her. My grandmother would never kill somebody. She's a nice person."

Something Barry had said once echoed in my head. Nice people could be killers given the right circumstances. Like maybe having married your boyfriend.

Paxton pleaded with me not to mention the photographs or the champagne to the cops. "I saw that detective hanging around outside."

I didn't have to be Hercule Poirot to figure out that Ruby Cline had lied to the cops. When I got back to the table, Dinah wanted to know what was going on. She slipped into the empty seat next to me and I filled her in.

"The thing is Ruby Cline could have motive. Paxton said she has a memory like an elephant and doesn't let go of things. She could have been carrying a grudge against K.D. for stealing her boyfriend. Maybe something set it off, like K.D. was going to take something else of hers. Ruby had means. Well, anybody who came in the room did. The hair dryer was there all along. And now it appears she had opportunity. If she had a glass of champagne it had to be after the waiter was there."

Dinah's eyes widened as I talked. "Now it makes sense. The waiter mentioned leaving glasses, yet only one glass was there when I found K.D. How convenient that she took the glass with her fingerprints all over it with her. Remember we saw the man in the suit in her booth? I bet he's a lawyer and she was getting advice from him." A server came by and started delivering the salads. "I have to talk to Barry and tell him about the champagne glass. Maybe it will get his mind off Adele."

"And here she comes," Dinah said as we both looked toward the back of the room. "What's going on with the ninja outfit?" Even though I'd seen the black pants and tunic hanging in the room, somehow I'd expected her to add something with color, but she hadn't. And then I saw she was pulling something, the small black suitcase. She seemed preoccupied as she looked around the room before heading to the side and almost blending in with the dark curtain as she made her way to our table. She left the suitcase in the folds of the curtain and then put on a false smile as she walked up to us.

I glanced back at the doors and saw that Barry had just come in and taken up a position at the back of the room where he could see everything that was going on. Was it my imagination or was his gaze trained on the suitcase? Then he glanced in my direction, and even at this far distance I could swear he had an I-told-you-so look on his face.

"Sit next to me," I said to Adele, as Dinah got up and went back to her seat. I must have sounded a little too animated, because Adele gave me a funny look.

But her expression changed to one of gratitude as she sat down. "It's really nice of you, Pink, trying to make it not so obvious that Eric didn't come." Something was definitely up. Adele was being too subdued. She seemed almost nervous.

I was too keyed up to eat. Not that anyone noticed. A bunch of conversations started up at our table, though I barely heard what was going on, other than it seemed all the men were relieved to have one another and not to have to talk about yarn.

By the time the plates were cleared and the pieces of flourless chocolate cake were being distributed, Delvin had gone up on the stage. He began with some comments about K.D. and how this banquet had always been the high point of the weekend for her. He did a few minutes on what a legend she was and then tried to lift the spirits of the audience by telling them how successful the show had been.

"While you're enjoying your dessert and coffee, we're going to start off the program with our prime fashion show. You will note that this is the crème de la crème of the designs from our attendees." Rain came by and got Dinah, pointing her toward the dark curtains at the front that marked off the backstage area.

"And we're lucky to have Kimberly Wang Diaz to do the commentary for our wonderful knit fashion show." She joined Delvin on the stage. The microphone was off to the side, leaving the catwalk area clear for the models.

I expected some kind of angry noises about knitting from Adele, but she was strangely pleasant. She even asked Rhoda's husband if he thought he really could make something like the silver needles for crochet. Adele's good behavior was making me very, very nervous. First the plain clothes, which certainly looked like blend-in-the-crowd traveling clothes along with the suitcase, and now this acting out of character. She was up to something. I shuddered to think that maybe Barry was right.

"About those needles—" Hal started to say, but he was interrupted as the fashion show began with Dinah as the first model. Our whole table applauded, even Adele. While Dinah did the whole twirling and turning model thing, Kimberly Wang Diaz read the description of what Dinah was wearing. As I listened I understood why Rain wanted Dinah to model the shawl. It wasn't so much a description as a sales pitch, reminding people that there was just one more day to shop her booth.

I looked over at Rain. She was still dressed in the knitted jacket and slacks she'd worn all day. But then the jacket was the sample of the ones she had for sale. She was on the edge of her seat as the newscaster read the script, and she mouthed the words along with her. She really beamed when she heard the applause.

As I looked around the room, I noticed something disturbing. Ruby Cline and her grandson had left. I was barely aware of the rest of the fashion show, wondering if there was something I should do about their departure. When I focused on the stage again, Lacey Kirby had joined Kimberly.

"The auction was one of my mother's favorite parts of the show. She loved delivering a big check to whatever charity she'd chosen that year," Lacey said and named the charity her mother had chosen for the current year before encouraging everyone to bid generously in memory of her mother. She called Audrey to the front, whose job was to hold up the auctioned items.

I saw Mason take out his phone and answer it. He glanced toward the front of the room and apparently thought it was safe to leave his client because he headed to the back and then went outside.

I was only half paying attention, still thinking about Ruby Cline. However, when Dinah returned to the table, I did zone back in and told her what a great model she was. She showed off the gift of some wooden knitting needles that was her prize for taking part in the fashion show. Adele barely reacted to the enemy tools.

"I feel kind of funny about it now," Dinah said. "I hope people don't think I was pushing them to buy her pieces." I assured her it didn't really matter.

Several items were auctioned off, and then I heard Lacey mention the silver knitting needles with the diamond accents. Maybe it was because those needles were keeping Mason and me apart, but I'd grown to really dislike them.

"Things with a story always seem to have more value," Lacey began. "And this complete set of knitting needles has a big one." She paused as a murmur went through the crowd. "In case any of you haven't seen them," Lacey said, giving a nod to Audrey who held them up as the audience strained to look at them. The needles were famous or maybe infamous thanks to all the news coverage they'd gotten. I doubted there was one person who hadn't gone to look at them.

"They're valued at $3,500, but there's no reason they can't go for more. Remember, the money is going to charity." She asked for an opening bid of $50.

Before the words were out of her mouth, someone had bid and then someone topped it. The bidding was fast and furious and in no time had reached $3,500. Rhoda and her husband seemed to be deep in conversation, then she nudged him, but he shook his head. Rhoda raised her hand.

"We have $3,600 from the lady at the front table," Lacey said. Rhoda looked horrified, as did her husband. She stood and put both of her hands up this time.

"Wait a second," Rhoda said. "I wasn't bidding on the needles. There's something about them. I wasn't sure if I should bring it up, but I'll have a guilty conscience if I don't." She mentioned that her husband worked in jewelry and had looked at the needles. Then, seeming frustrated, she turned to him. "You tell them, Hal."

Hal got up with an uncomfortable smile. He moved to the position just below the bottom of the catwalk, and someone handed him a microphone. "The description of the set of knitting needles says they are sterling silver with diamond accents and gives a value for them. But it's all incorrect. They aren't sterling, just silver plate, and the stones on the end—they're cubic zirconiums." He paused while the audience reacted. "And the value, it's more like $500." He turned to Lacey and apologized. "Right is right and I couldn't let it slide. Not when I knew."

A bunch of conversations had started up, and Audrey looked aghast as she took the microphone from him.

"Are you kidding? You mean I did all this and they're fake? All that fuss K.D. made, insisting on pressing charges so I would actually go to jail?"

Julie jumped up. "Tell me about it. K.D. embarrassed me in front of everybody because I brought some other yarn into her store. And then she accused me of trying to enter the same sweater I entered in the knitting contest last year."

I had forgotten all about Julie. She seemed all fired up until the woman next to her made her sit down.

"I know what you mean," Audrey said. "If only K.D. Kirby had listened to reason to begin with I never would have—"

Delvin grabbed the microphone back and got up on the stage. "I'm sure K.D. had no idea the needles were only silver plate. The person who dealt with everything in the store was Thea Scott."

Lacey was next to him now, and she pointed her finger accusingly at the store manager, who had gotten up and stepped away from her table. "You had to know the needles were only silver plate and the stones fake."

Thea shook her head in annoyance and turned back. "Why couldn't K.D. have let me handle it from the beginning? I thought we should just accept payment for the stolen needles and drop it." She glared at Audrey Stewart. "I thought everything was going to be okay when K.D. was out of the picture. But you couldn't just pay for the needles, could you? You had to put them in the auction."

"You knew all along they were silver plate, didn't you?" Audrey said in an accusing manner. "You were the one who tried to steal them from the auction display."

All the while, Thea had begun to step backward. She looked at Lacey. "I just want you to know that your mother wanted the store to be so high-class, but she didn't pay very well. She insisted that I act like I was on the same level with our customers. But I couldn't afford their designer jeans and fancy hairstyles on what she paid me. They had purses that cost thousands of dollars. The first time I sold the silver plate needles it was a mistake, but when nobody noticed I kept on doing it." By now she'd reached the back of the room, but Barry was standing in front of the exit.

At that moment, the door opened, pushing Barry to the side as Mason came back into the room. Before anyone could react, Thea had slipped out. But probably not for long. Barry was already on his phone. I guessed a cop would snag her before she left the building.

Mason seemed surprised to find everyone looking at him. "What's going on?"

CHAPTER 22

UNDER THE CIRCUMSTANCES, THE NEEDLES WERE removed from the auction. But the whole episode acted like some hot sauce to what had been a sleepy affair. There were a lot of questions about the other items and then a lot of heavy bidding. I seemed to be the only one to realize that it sounded like Audrey was pretty close to confessing that she'd killed K.D. Well, maybe not close, exactly, but it could have been the next thing she was going to say when Delvin grabbed the microphone.

The auction ended and the award ceremony began, though I'm not sure if giving out one award counted as a ceremony. Lacey read something her mother had written about Kimberly Wang Diaz and how for years she had covered the yarn show with a feature story that helped inspire the public to take up knitting. That and the newscaster's flowery thank-you were all caught by her cameraman.

The award was a bronzed ball of yarn with a pair of knitting needles stuck into it. There was a break in the program, and I went back to talk to Barry. First I asked him about Thea, and he confirmed what I'd thought—she was being questioned as we spoke. Then I got down to what I really wanted to talk about.

"I have a question for you," I said. I saw his eyes roll back and forth.

"What is it?" he asked.

"Do you know how many champagne glasses the waiter left?" Barry took out his notebook and started flipping through it.

"I seemed to have missed that," he said, his mouth twisting in annoyance. "But I'm guessing you know."

"There were two," I said. "And how many were at the crime scene?" He didn't bother with the notebook but just looked me in the eye.

"Obviously you know there was just one." He blew out his breath. "Could we not play twenty questions? Just tell me what you know."

"If I do, you have to promise not to snap on the cuffs and arrest me for investigating," I said.

"It's all about making deals with you now. First I had to promise not to arrest Adele and now not to arrest you." He seemed to be mulling over my offer, but I was pretty sure it was all for show. "Okay, I won't arrest you, so go ahead and tell me everything," he said finally.

I told him about Ruby Cline and the champagne glass, but it fell apart when he said it was probably wiped clean of prints by now and useless as evidence if she even still had it. I brought up how both Audrey Stewart and Thea Scott both had motives connected with the silver needles.

"Nice try," he said. "They all had motives, but where's the evidence? We need something like a crochet hook at the murder scene."

I headed back to my seat just as Delvin returned to the microphone and began making announcements about the next day's schedule. As I got closer, something seemed off. Then I realized there was an empty seat beside mine. Where was Adele? I looked around the whole room and didn't see her. If the black curtain hadn't fluttered I would have missed her altogether. She and her suitcase were practically lost in the dark folds. She was moving toward the front of the huge room. And then I saw her destination. The red exit sign was almost hidden by the impromptu stage. Barry was right. She was going to take off.

I was much closer and quickly followed her. I was sure Barry had seen her empty chair, too. I didn't look back but figured he was probably somewhere behind me planning to nab her and then gloat. I'd almost caught up with her and reached out to grab on to her, but all I got was a handful of her tunic. I tugged hard and she fell backward into her suitcase, which in turn fell into me, and we went over like three dominos just as Barry got there.

"So where were you going, Brazil, Switzerland, someplace else far away?" I said, trying to crawl away from the suitcase.

Adele rolled over and sat up. "What are you talking about?" I pointed to the suitcase. For the first time Barry's presence registered to her. "What's he doing here?"

Barry crouched down to untangle us. "Is there something you want to tell me, Adele?" Barry said in his understanding cop voice.

Adele looked at me. "All I did was stand up for crochet. They only offered a few classes and they let us give free crochet lessons, but that was going to be it, unless I did something."

I began to get an uncomfortable feeling in the pit of my stomach. Was Adele about to confess? Just at that moment Mason joined our little group. He'd heard the tail end of what Adele was saying. "You might not want to say anything more," he said, ever acting as a lawyer.

And Adele being Adele didn't take his advice.

"I did what I had to do. I told them I would single-handedly do a crochet fashion show." She unzipped the suitcase, and inside it was packed with items she'd made. Now the black clothes made sense. They were just a backdrop.

Mason chuckled and shook his head with amused disbelief as he helped me up. He took over damage control and spoke to the roomful of people who were all staring in our direction. "Just a little accident over here. But it looks like everyone is fine."

Barry tried to help Adele up, but she insisted on doing it herself. I thought he might leave after that, but he went back to his position by the door. He still didn't believe her.

Delvin seemed a little discombobulated when after a slight delay with some explaining, Adele handed him a CD and told him to play it. "Okay, then, we have another fashion show," he said. "From the Tarzana Hookers."

Once I understood what was really going on, I'd told the rest of our table and everyone had volunteered to model one of the pieces Adele had brought. Even Eduardo picked out a granny square scarf, which made an interesting look with his leather tuxedo.

When the evening finally broke up, quite a few people came by our table and made assorted comments including how they never realized how nice crochet was, how we seemed like a really lively bunch and how we had added a little excitement to the evening.

Adele took all the items and put them back in the suitcase. I couldn't quite tell, but it did seem like there were some other clothes items underneath. I didn't get much of a chance to see what they were, because Adele zipped up the suitcase and, in an annoyed huff, left. When I looked at the door, Barry was gone, too.

"You don't really think she was planning to take off and she made up that whole thing about the fashion show?" Dinah said as we all walked outside.

"No, it couldn't be," I said. "At least I don't think so."

I WAS ON MY WAY TO THE GREENMOBILE WHEN Mason caught up with me. He had lost his work look, taken off his tie and put on a warm smile.

"Audrey went home," he said with a discreet sigh of relief. "I still can't talk, but I thought maybe we could spend some time together." His dark eyes were warm. "After all the almosts we've had, I guess I'd like to make sure it was real this time." He stayed by my car as I opened the door. Around us the parking lot was emptying, and I saw his black Mercedes sedan was parked nearby.

"I'm pretty exhausted," I said. He tried to hide it, but I saw his expression fall. "But some company would be nice," I added quickly.

"Great, I'll follow you home," he said, back to his upbeat self. He waited until I got in and headed for his car.

As I drove home, I started to feel nervous anticipation.

So far it had just been phone calls and stolen looks over the weekend. This would be the first time we would be up close and personal.

But it was Mason, I reminded myself. Mason who'd rescued me a number of times, helped me solve some murders. Supportive, fun Mason. No pressure to be anything but a casual couple. No strings or titles to our relationship. Not like Barry, who had been pushing for us to get married. It was what I'd always said I wanted. Then I had a dark feeling. Just like I kept saying I wanted to try flying solo and live alone. A warning bell went off in my head. The definition of anything with Mason was probably best defined as "whatever." Friends with benefits, casual hookups and then we'd go our separate ways. Sure, Mason had said *love you* at the end of our calls, but it could just be an automatic way of saying good-bye to whichever woman he was involved with.

I thought about Dinah and Commander Blaine. They did a lot of things together and still had their space. But underneath it all was an understanding, a commitment of sorts.

"I don't want just some kind of arrangement," I said out loud. "What have I gotten myself into?" My shoulders slumped as I realized I should have thought this all out before.

I pulled into my driveway, still deep in thought. Mason's black Mercedes pulled up right behind me. He was out of his car and walking up to me before I'd even cut the motor.

As soon as I unlocked the door, he opened it with a flourish and showed me a bottle of champagne. "I've been carrying this around in my car since I got back."

We walked across the backyard together. We'd both fallen silent, and was it my imagination or did he seem a little hesitant, too? When we got to the back door, we both stopped and faced each other at the same time.

"There's something I need to talk to you about," Mason said in a serious tone.

"Funny, I was going to say the same thing to you." I was holding my key. Whatever warmth there had been during the day was gone, and there was a brittle, sharp feeling to the cold. The sweatshirt I'd found in my car and put on over my black dress offered little warmth and I shivered. "We can talk about it inside."

I opened the door and expected the usual greeting committee of Cosmo and the cats and was surprised to see someone else in the mix. A little gray scruffy-looking terrier mix was with them. He pushed through to the front and put his paws on my knee like he was welcoming a long-lost friend.

"Who are you?" I said, looking past him into my kitchen. The lights were on and I heard voices. Mason shut the door behind him and then took the lead as if to protect me from whoever was there. I found it hard to believe someone was robbing my house and had brought the cute little dog along.

I caught up with Mason and we both peeked out of the kitchen into the living room. The first thing I noticed was the pile of boxes and assorted stuff in the entrance hall. My two sons were in the living room talking, well, maybe it was more like arguing. Seeing it wasn't really an intruder, Mason slipped behind me and I walked into the large, high-ceilinged room.

"Who's going to explain?" I asked, gesturing toward the boxes, not to mention the little gray dog who'd become my shadow.

Peter, my dark-haired older son, who was an ambitious television agent, spoke first. "Is it true that someone died at that yarn show you went to?" I nodded and my son shook his head with disapproval. "What is it with you and murder?"

"That's beside the point right now. What's going on?"

"I helped Samuel move his things, but I didn't think he should come back here." Peter had been trying to get me to sell the house and downsize since Charlie died, and having his brother living here complicated matters.

I looked at my younger son. His sandy hair was pulled back into a small ponytail. When he looked up, I could see the heartbreak in his eyes. "Nell and I broke up."

Peter was out of Samuel's line of sight, and his eyes went skyward with disbelief. Judging from his expression, I was guessing Nell broke up with Samuel. The gray dog moved in even closer until he was almost sitting on my foot.

"That's Felix," Samuel said. "Nell and I found him in the street. She made me take him with me." It was then that it registered that I wasn't alone. Not that it was a problem. They both liked Mason. Peter had actually been the one who introduced us and had been pushing for him all along. Samuel liked him, too. Samuel worked as barista at a coffee joint, but his real dream was to be a musician. Mason had helped him get a number of gigs and had the ability to be supportive without being bossy or overstepping.

"What's going on?" Peter looked from me to Mason and took in that we were both dressed up and it was late. It was easy to make a lot of assumptions. I didn't answer but led Mason back into the kitchen.

"We need to talk before I say anything to them," I said.

"Right," he said, and we went to the farthest part of the kitchen. Mason was still holding the champagne bottle but now put it down, saying he'd planned to bean a robber with it. We both let out a nervous titter of laughter.

"There's something I need to say," he began. A feeling of doom hit my stomach. What kind of bomb was he going to drop? Give me the parameters to our casual relationship? Or maybe he was going to make it clear I shouldn't expect to make any claim on him. He'd taken my hand and actually looked nervous. He began to speak without looking at me.

"I know what I said before. No strings, casual relationship, no expectations, no road to anything but a good time. And I understand that is what you want." He paused and looked at the floor. He was usually so self-assured, this seemed very strange.

"I know that's what you want," he said. "But I just can't do it."

I started to pull away, realizing he'd reconsidered now that he'd had time to think. "I get it. The timing is just off. You snooze you lose," I said, trying to lighten the moment.

I heard him chuckle, and when I looked at him, he was grinning and his eyes were warm. "I'm not doing a very good job of explaining. What I'm trying to say is I don't want that kind of relationship. I want something more. I want strings."

I froze and our eyes met. "You should see yourself," he said, still holding on to my hand. "You have that deer in the headlights sort of look. I don't know exactly how far this is going to go. I guess what I'm trying to say is I think we need to belong to each other." He let out a big sigh of relief. "There, I said it. If it doesn't work for you, we can part as friends."

I started to laugh. It was relief, exhaustion and too much time spent thinking about murder. "You should only know what I was going to say," I began. "It was pretty much the same thing." I mentioned how I had claimed to want the house to myself, and the whole trying my own wings thing. "And when I finally got it, I hated it. I realized the whole thing about a casual relationship, two ships passing in the night, wasn't really what I wanted after all. What you described sounds perfect."

We hugged each other and it evolved into a kiss, which was short-lived because I realized the little gray dog had just peed on my foot.

When Mason saw why I'd let go, he started to laugh. "Oh, how I've missed all this." He glanced toward the living room and the sounds of my sons arguing. "It doesn't seem like the time to tell them about us. It sounds like you're needed in there. Can I call you later?"

I nodded and we lingered by the door prolonging the moment, then Mason opened the door to go. "Love you, Sunshine."

"Me, too."

Well, at least I didn't think it was just his way of saying good-bye anymore.

It was back to reality now. I went into the living room. Peter wasn't happy with Samuel's decision, but I appreciated that he helped his brother move anyway. My older son was getting ready to leave when I came back into the room. I walked him to the door as he gave me a laundry list of what I should do, which started with only letting Samuel crash there for a defined amount of time.

Samuel was slumped on the soft leather couch. Whoever thinks it is only girls who are upset over breakups is wrong. I sat down next to Samuel. "Do you want to talk about it?" I said.

He shook his head and then let it hang. I asked him if he was hungry, but all he was interested in was a cup of tea.

I think it was less the tea and more the sympathy that went with it. I made us a couple of cups of gold rush tea I'd gotten for the holidays. It had a wonderful fruity aroma, not that Samuel noticed. I wanted to say something to make him feel better, but I didn't think those words existed.

"Thank you," he said at last. He didn't elaborate, but I knew it was for being there. He grabbed one of the boxes and went to his old room.

I was sorry about his breakup, but I was so glad to have all this life back in the house. Even the little gray dog.

I took Felix to the back door and let him out in the yard, hoping to discourage him from having another accident, then I headed across the house for a nice hot bath.

I poured in some bath salts and started to fill the tub. I had just gotten in when the phone rang. I got out, leaving a puddle on the floor.

"Is everything under control?" Mason asked. When he heard he'd gotten me out of the tub he apologized, though I barely heard it thanks to a flurry of barking coming through the phone.

"What's with Spike?" I said, picturing the toy fox terrier pestering Mason.

Mason's tone lightened. "It seems I came home with a souvenir of the little gray dog's hair on my pant leg and Spike is indignant. It doesn't help that he's been alone too much this weekend." Spike's barking evolved into some kind of happy whimpering as Mason talked to the dog and probably gave him a bunch of affection.

"Now that there's peace again, let me get to the real reason I called. I had a thought," he said. "What if we both take a couple of days off and drive down around to Coronado. Now that Samuel is staying at your place, he can hold the fort down and we could just leave on the spur of the moment when the yarn show is over. No baggage, except of course Spike. We'd buy what we need on the road?"

I had to admit that it sounded wonderful. "But I can't leave until things are settled for Adele. Unless something happens, Barry is going to arrest her on Monday."

"I'm betting you make something happen before then," Mason said.

"It's not so easy. Barry is sure it's Adele, and I'd have to have real evidence to point at someone else."

"I'm sorry I can't help you, but . . ." He let his voice trail off. Then he seemed to reconsider. "I suppose if you didn't ask me anything about her and I didn't mention my client, we could talk about it." I heard him let out his breath. "That doesn't sound like it would be much help. I'm sorry to have let you down."

"That's okay. I think I'd feel a lot worse if you broke your trust with your client and told me a bunch of stuff."

The TV was on in the background, and a familiar voice got my attention. "Turn on Channel 3," I said. "This is too weird." When I looked at the screen there was Kimberly Wang Diaz doing a feature story that had shots from the whole weekend, starting with an interview with K.D. I could see it had been done in the suite. They were sitting in the living room with the coffee table between them. I looked for Adele's hook, but it wasn't there. Nor was the champagne. All I really saw were two hotel keys on the coffee table.

"That's odd," I said before telling him about my conversation with the room service waiter. "He said there was one key on the table when he delivered the champagne." The more I thought about it, the more it made sense. "Think about this: There were two keys to start with. Someone must have come to the room and taken one of the keys with them. And then let themselves back in while she was in the tub. It wasn't a big secret about her ritual. Even I knew."

I stopped for a moment as the TV droned on and Kimberly's report continued. I saw that she was on the vendor floor. I strained, trying to see if she was going to pass our booth, but she just went along the front area. The little gray dog had come in to join me and jumped on the bed.

"That sounds like a way for someone to have opportunity, but who?" Mason said.

"Just knowing who wouldn't be enough. I'd have to have some real evidence, too."

Kimberly's segment ended at the banquet. Of course, she mentioned the drama with the silver knitting needles and that Thea had been detained. But the big focus was on Kimberly getting her award, and then the weather report came on with all their charts and pictures of storm clouds.

"But I have every confidence you will find the guilty party and the evidence. I have so much faith in you that I'm going to go ahead and book the reservations. Audrey's not going to be at the show tomorrow. Sorry I can't go into details why."

He didn't have to. I could figure it out. Any worries about charges against her had evaporated when the real value of the needles came out.

"And another thing," Mason said. "I think it is time to update your phone. That BlackBerry is practically an antique. I sent you a bunch of text messages while I was babysitting my client and I never got a response from you."

"Huh?" I said, taking out the squarish smartphone. I found the text messages he'd sent hidden somewhere and apologized. I stared at the phone a little longer as Mason told me to go finish my bath.

The idea of taking off on an impromptu trip with Mason sounded romantic and exciting. I went back into the bathroom, but the water had grown cold and I gave up on the bath idea. I would just put on some body cream and call it a night. With the stopper up, the water began to drain from the tub. A paper towel took care of what was left of the puddle I'd made when I got out of the tub. I opened the jar of body cream and began to slather it on my arms. The fragrance stirred a memory, and something Mason had said went through my mind. Felix walked in to see what was going on. I looked down at the scruffy gray dog. "Thanks to you I might just have figured out the whole thing."

CHAPTER 23

BY MORNING I HAD A PLAN. I THOUGHT OF CALLING Dinah and asking for her help as a backup, but it had been a late night for her and she'd done so much for me all weekend. Besides, I was sure that I'd be in and out without being seen. Then I'd let Barry know.

I rushed through my morning preparations and went to the greenmobile. The dim light due to the low-hanging clouds made it seem even earlier, and the moisture in the air absorbed all the sound. It looked like everybody else was still asleep as I started my trek across the Valley to the hotel. It was way too early for even the vendors, and the parking lot was almost empty. I was relieved to see the delivery truck just pulling up. I'd counted on him as my means of getting into the marketplace before it opened for the vendors.

I waited until he loaded up a dolly with supplies, and then as he started toward the entrance of the convention center, I followed him. The corridor was deserted, but the lights were on. I watched as someone from the hotel unlocked the door for him and then walked away. So much for the added security they'd promised, but then it was the last day and the auction was done.

It was no problem for me to slip inside the marketplace. Most of the lights were still off, and I stepped into the shadows, tracking the squeak of the dolly as the delivery guy made his way to the back of the huge room.

Mason's words had reminded me of something I'd read in *The Average Joe's Guide to Criminal Investigation*. Criminals left evidence of their presence behind, but they also took evidence of the crime scene with them.

In the dim light, the booths shrouded in tarps looked almost ghostly. My heart was thudding against my chest as I waited for the deliveryman to leave the supplies at the snack bar. I listened as the dolly squeaked its way toward the exit. There was the whoosh of the door opening and closing and then heavy silence. I didn't really need to be stealth anymore, but I still crept along the front of the aisles. The stage area with its black curtains appeared like a big void.

I had my fingers crossed that I would be right and the evidence would be there. I stopped at my destination and checked the area again to make sure I was alone. Taking a deep breath, I peeled back the tarp and took out my flashlight.

In this semidarkness, the dress forms appeared sinister, like torsos that had lost their heads. I flipped on the small flashlight and shined it on each one. I stopped the light when I got to the dress form wearing the long vest. And then my heart fell. It was blue, and I was looking for the gray one.

Of course, Rain had switched out the sample, which only reconfirmed that I was right. I glanced around the small space. Obviously, she must have realized what had suddenly hit me the night before.

It's a funny thing about our sense of smell. It's so connected to memory. Who can smell suntan lotion and not think back to a day at the beach? That's what happened when I caught a whiff of my body cream the night before. The heavy scent of coconut suddenly evoked memories, though not as nice as a day at the beach.

I hadn't noticed the tropical scent when I'd found K.D., but then the shock of seeing her in the tub must have masked it, to my conscious mind, at least. But when I smelled the body cream the scene had immediately flashed in my mind. Then came the image of Rain as she picked up the dress form she'd left in front of our booth. I'd had trouble remembering her name, and something made me think of the beach and I had called her Sand. But now I knew it was that tropical scent heavy with coconut clinging to the long gray vest she was wearing. And I was sure I knew how it got there.

When I'd seen the puddle next to my own tub, I'd been reminded that I'd seen water on the floor in K.D.'s suite. It must have splashed out when the hair dryer went in. And it also must have splashed on the killer's clothes, leaving them with a souvenir just the way the gray dog's hair had gone home on Mason's pant leg.

I was saying "killer" in my mind, but I knew it was Rain. I had never even considered her a suspect. She'd offered up an alibi without even being asked. The waiter had seen her leave the room when he was on the way in to deliver the champagne. And Delvin had heard from K.D.

after that about changing Rain's booth around. So it had seemed that K.D. was alive and well for quite a while after Rain had left the suite.

Only after Mason had brought up sending me texts at the show had I realized something. I had been thinking all along that K.D. had talked to Delvin about changing the booth, and then I remembered someone had mentioned text messages. Anybody could have been anywhere when they sent a text message from K.D.'s phone, and then thrown the phone in the tub with her.

And it occurred to me that Rain could have lifted one of the hotel keys during her first visit and then used it to come and go at will. The service elevator would have made it simple to do without being seen.

But all my figuring was worthless unless I could give some real evidence to Barry, like the vest so they could match up the residue of bath oil on it to the special blend that K.D. used. Obviously, Rain had figured out that I'd noticed the scent on the vest and stopped using it as a sample. But what had she done with it? I glanced around at the racks of knitted items. She wouldn't have put it there because the scent would still be evident.

The table at the back had a heavy covering that went down to the floor, and I remembered her stowing her belongings back there when I'd stopped by her booth. Could she have stowed something else as well?

I was almost afraid to look. Afraid that I would find nothing. Images of Adele being arrested for real floated through my mind. I was certain a jury would never find her guilty, but then who knew for sure. I took a deep breath and got ready to bite the bullet and look. The covering was heavy and it slipped from my hand the first time. The second time I held it tight and leaned down, training the flashlight in the dark space. All I saw was the dark carpet. I was about to admit defeat and leave but ran the flashlight over the carpet one last time. I saw a smidge of yellow piping.

I got down on my knees and reached all the way to the back. My hand felt something cool and plastic. When I pulled it out, I saw the yellow piping was on an opaque garment bag. I stood up and set it down on the table and began to lower the zipper. I'd barely gotten it halfway down when the scent of the tropics laden with coconut blasted my senses.

The last thing I wanted to do was move the evidence. I reached for my phone to call Barry. The stress of the search and the excitement of the find had made me lose touch with my surroundings, and I barely noticed that something had brushed against my hair. When the something touched my neck, it got my attention and I instinctively reached for it. Why was there a double strand of yarn around my neck? My instinct was to tug it loose, but when I tried, it only got tighter.

"Drop the phone," Rain said from behind me.

I hesitated and the yarn tightened even more. I felt it cut into my skin, and I coughed in response before I dropped my phone.

She reached around and grabbed the garment bag. She started grumbling that I couldn't have left well enough alone. "I thought I'd get this out of here now, when nobody's paying any attention." I didn't know if she was talking to me or just mumbling to herself.

She seemed at a loss for what to do. I took the opportunity to try and squirm away, but every time I moved the yarn got tighter. By now I had figured out that she'd dropped a yarn noose over my head. I could feel that it was already making a mark on my skin. I have been in some tough spots, but this was right up there. One good tug from her and I'd be a goner.

Stall, I told myself, trying to keep myself from panicking. "Why did you do it?" I said.

Rain seemed uncomfortable with the question at first. "I don't have to tell you anything," she said in an angry voice. Then I heard her let out her breath. "Why not?"

"How about this. I've had a booth in the marketplace since the show started. K.D. appreciated my loyalty and always gave me that prime spot you were in, and gave it to me at a discount. She knew how much I depended on the money I made from my sales at the show. This time it was even worse. I owe the wrong kind of people a lot of money. I have a problem with bingo." Her voice sounded panicky. She didn't loosen the noose, but she didn't tighten it, either. "I needed to sell out everything I brought. You saw what a prime spot does for you. The people come there first before they've spent everything somewhere else."

She was behind me, and I couldn't see her expression, which made it impossible to see if her speech was distracting her enough so I could make some kind of move. "I was sure there had to be a mistake when you were in my spot, and then to be given a location way off in the corner where nobody would have seen my things? I was sure there was no way that K.D. had done it deliberately."

Now her voice erupted in anger as she continued. "But it wasn't a mistake. She said everything was different now. No more discounts and the cost for the spaces had actually gone up without any notice. For what I paid, the only spot I could have was that horrible one. And if I wanted her to change my location, I'd have to pay the new full price for it." Rain stopped for a moment as if she were still having trouble believing it. "I tried to reason with her, but she got all haughty and said she'd done me a favor even letting me stay in the show all these years when all the other vendors only sold yarn and supplies. She criticized me for using a knitting machine to make my pieces. And then she told me to take it or leave it, no negotiating. When I balked, she asked me to leave. She said she was expecting someone."

Rain had gotten to the end of her speech, so I prodded her to continue. "So, you swiped the key when you left," I said. There was silence for a moment, but then she mumbled a yes and explained coming back when K.D. was in the bath. I could tell she wasn't pulling the yarn as tightly, and it released a tiny bit.

I heard the sound of the door opening and then some voices, and I looked up. Since it was mostly dark in there, all I could make out was there were three figures.

"Bob, it was so nice of you to bring more of these Linzer Torte Cookie Bars for our booth. Though I don't know why you have to pick up the other tin right now," Adele said. Her diction was strange, as though she was making a point to somebody. Her voice changed, and it sounded like she had turned and was talking to someone behind her. "This isn't what it seems. I was too distraught to go home, so I stayed in the mini suite we took for the weekend. It wasn't to rendezvous with Bob. He was just meeting me there so I could bring him down here." Then she made an annoyed sound. "I don't know why you're still following me."

Someone flipped on the lights, and Adele, Bob and Barry all froze in surprise when they saw me.

"Oh, you're here," Adele said in surprise. "Pink, tell him to stop following me." She obviously didn't realize the predicament I was in. Barry, ever the detective, noted Rain standing behind me and seemed to be trying to size up the situation. His eyes narrowed, and he had a wary expression as he took a step toward me. Rain responded by pulling on the noose, and I coughed again. I tried to raise my hands to the yarn, but she saw them and commanded me to put them down as she gave the yarn another yank.

"Stay where you are, or she dies right now," Rain said in a fierce voice.

Adele and Bob still seemed confused, but Barry's gaze went right to the band of yarn around my neck, and he immediately understood the risk.

"I'm sure we can work something out," he said to her in his trained calm voice.

Rain was having none of it and commanded me to walk toward the door. "Don't try anything or I give this a tug and it's lights out for her. This yarn has a wire core and won't break, either."

I had no choice but to walk to the door, trying to match my steps with hers, so she wouldn't pull the yarn any tighter. I heard the rustle of the garment bag and realized she was taking it with her.

Even though they hadn't heard our conversation, Adele picked up that Rain was the one who'd killed K.D. and then tried to frame her. In typical Adele fashion, she brought it up.

"See, I told you, it wasn't me," Adele said to Barry. Then she turned her attention on Rain. "Why did you take my hook?"

Adele had the ability to annoy people, and her comment seemed to set off Rain. I felt my captor stop walking, and I did, too. "I figured it would be better if I pointed the finger at somebody. And you were such an unpleasant jerk when I asked to leave my dress form in front of your booth, which was supposed to be my spot, I figured you had it coming," Rain said in an angry tone. I could tell by the sound of Rain's voice that she had turned to face Adele and for that second was distracted. It was now or never if I was going to make a move.

One possibility had floated through my mind. I'd only have one chance. Slowly, I started to raise my hands, hoping it wouldn't register. Then I took my shot.

"Hey, there," Rain yelled, seeing me doing something. She went to tug hard on the noose yarn and suddenly went flying backward and landed on her butt with only a handful of yarn.

Before Barry could make a move, Adele flew at Rain and sat on her. "You ruined everything for me. You stole my hook and made my boyfriend's mother think I was a murderer and now he's gone. He was the yin for my yang."

I couldn't wait to tell Dinah that she had saved my life. The pendant with the hidden cutting edges hung on the chain around my neck. In that moment when Rain looked away, I was able to grab it and drag it across my restraint. The yarn with the wire core might not have broken, but it still could be cut, though I'd nicked my neck in the process. But it hardly seemed important, all things considered.

Barry let Adele handle the situation for the moment as he looked at my neck. "You're bleeding," he said in a worried tone.

CHAPTER 24

BARRY INSISTED ON CALLING THE PARAMEDICS, but it was definitely overkill. They let me go after applying a little antiseptic and a small bandage. The place was flooded with cops, which was also overkill. Once Rain was in handcuffs, she didn't put up a fight. Although Adele didn't let up on her until she was taken away. It figured, Adele's fussing had less to do with K.D.'s actual death than her being framed for it.

"How about you tell me what you know," Barry said. "I mean everything you know. And all spoken in statements." He didn't have to worry. After all I'd just been through I wasn't up for playing a dueling game of answering each other with questions. I explained the evidence in the garment bag to Barry and what I had figured out. Barry wrote it all down, and when he shut his notebook I expected some kind of comment about how I was in trouble for investigating.

"Good job," Barry said half under his breath. "Except you almost got yourself strangled in the process." He said that part a lot louder.

Once Rain's booth had been covered with tarps and surrounded with yellow tape and then blocked off by a series of the curtained partitions, the cops filed out, taking the evidence with them.

Bob, the barista from the bookstore, stood around taking in the scene. He'd only expected to drop off the tin of Linzer Torte Cookie Bars, pick up the tin from the other day and be on his way. The rest of this was all extra. The way Bob was watching all the details, I knew it was going to end up somewhere in the alien love story screenplay he was working on between handing out shots of espresso. He seemed almost disappointed when Barry took him to get the cookie tin and then walked him to the exit.

Barry had arrested Rain based on what she'd been trying to do to me. But once they looked over the vest and found that the strong scented residue matched K.D.'s special bath oil, she was charged with second degree murder, since it was hard to prove she'd premeditated it. As for what she'd tried to do to me, she was only charged with some kind of assault because the D.A. had a hard time thinking of yarn as a murder weapon.

Barry finally got ready to leave. He looked exhausted from spending the night in one of the uncomfortable chairs in the alcove in front of K.D.'s suite so he could watch Adele's comings and goings in the mini suite. There were shadows under his eyes and dark stubble on his chin.

"I hope you can go home and get some sleep," I said.

Barry let out a tired sigh. "For a few hours anyway.

Jeffrey's got a performance in the afternoon. I'm sure he'd love to see you in the audience. I have plenty of tickets," he added with a laugh.

I gestured toward the marketplace. "I'm tied up here all day, but tell him to break a leg."

"Will do," he said. Just before he turned to go, he hesitated. "See, I knew following Adele was a good idea." Before I could respond he was on his way to the exit.

Surprisingly, the marketplace opened almost on time, and it was my job to tell Delvin and Lacey what had happened.

Delvin seemed almost disappointed it had turned out to be Rain. "I guess it had nothing to do with the big announcement K.D. was going to make. And now I suppose we'll never know what it was about."

Lacey was more subdued. "I'm just glad it's settled. It was hard to grieve when I knew I was a suspect." She took out her phone and began to compose a tweet.

"Remember to put 'allegedly' before anything you say Rain did," I said.

She nodded solemnly. "Right. We don't want to do anything that could help her get off." They went toward the stage to start off the day's program, and I finally headed to our booth.

Kimberly Wang Diaz and her cameraman arrived, apparently having heard about Rain being arrested. I managed to avoid her, but Adele volunteered to give her an eyewitness account.

The Cline Yarn International booth was open for business, but only Paxton was working it. I stopped by to tell him about Rain. He seemed to want to tell me something, but every time he started to say anything, he stopped himself.

The crowd was thinner than the day before, but all of the Hookers showed up. Dinah was thrilled to hear how I'd been able to use the pendant to get myself free. Adele was still pouty about Eric bailing when she came into the booth but told anyone who would listen that she'd played an integral part in saving me and nabbing the killer.

Elise came with Logan in his full Anthony getup, hoping to move the last of her vampire crochet kits. Sheila was anxious to sell the kits she still had for her muted colored pieces. Rhoda apologized for the fuss Hal had caused by figuring out that the knitting needles weren't sterling silver, but she said he was already working on making some special hooks up for us. Eduardo wore the pirate outfit again and sat on the bench with some steel hooks and crochet thread ready to give lessons on Irish crochet.

We'd retired the pin making business and just concentrated on trying to move the yarn and supplies we had left. Bob's Linzer Torte Cookie Bars were a huge hit again, and I wished he'd stayed to see it.

I wasn't surprised that Thea Scott was no longer running the Knit Style booth across the way after her admission about substituting the needles. The cops had talked to her, and she'd given up the whole story. According to Lacey Kirby, who had taken over running the booth, Thea even admitted that she'd been the one who had tried to steal the needles from the auction so that no one would realize they were fakes.

But I was stunned when Audrey Stewart came in. Mason had said she wasn't going to be here. I'd been waiting to call him and tell him about the whole Rain situation, but Audrey's arrival pushed the issue. Feeling like a tattletale, I took out my BlackBerry and found a quiet corner.

Mason's voice brightened when he heard it was me and even more when he heard what I had to say. "We can go ahead with our plans. Adele is off the hook," I said before giving him the full rundown. "That was the good news. The bad news is Audrey Stewart just came in and it looks like she's headed for the stage."

"Not my problem," he said. "She called this morning. I was never so happy to be fired by a client." He went back to our plans and reconfirmed the time he'd pick me up. "I can't wait," he said.

"Me, either." He didn't seem to want to end the call, but I had to go.

"Love you," he said.

"Me, too," I responded.

When I'd put my phone away, I heard Audrey's voice coming over the sound system and stepped out of the booth to see what she was up to.

"I wanted to come clean about the knitting needles," she said, looking over the gathered group. "You see, it was really a cry for help. I'd been forgotten. No work was coming my way. The honest truth is, I saw other celebrities, some very minor ones, shoplift or do something crazy and they were all over the media. And all that publicity got them a lot of attention and suddenly they were hot again." She sighed. "Now I see what I did was wrong. I know now I need help and I'm going to get it. And I want to beg your forgiveness."

I noticed that Kimberly Wang Diaz and her cameraman were in the audience getting it all. CeeCee had joined me. "She's certainly laying it on thick. What is it with these young celebrities? In the old days, people looked for publicity through positive acts. Now, it's do bad things and ask for forgiveness to get attention. I suppose we should be grateful she didn't release a sex tape." Audrey got applause from the audience and blew them all thank-you kisses before she exited the stage.

CeeCee and Delvin took her place to announce the winners of the design contests. I recognized the butterfly on Julie's hand as I saw that her fingers were crossed as she pushed past me. Delvin read the knit winners first and then CeeCee listed hers. Julie's name wasn't among them, and I saw her pushing through the crowd to get away.

"There's one more award to give out," CeeCee said. "Delvin and I talked it over and we decided there should also be an award for a piece that combined knitting and crochet. We're calling it the Bi-Stitcheral Award, and it goes to Julie Johnson."

There was a whoop as Julie turned back and rushed to the stage. With the awards given out, CeeCee and Delvin left the stage. I was going to get back to work, but Ruby Cline and the man in the suit I'd seen earlier in the weekend moved along the edge of the crowd and went up on the stage. Delvin seemed surprised to say the least and stopped to watch.

Ruby took the microphone and they walked out to the end of the catwalk. I saw that Paxton had joined the assembled group. The first thing the head of Cline Yarn International did was to introduce herself. The man with her wasn't a potential mate she'd met online, as Paxton had thought, but was her attorney. "With everything that has happened this weekend, I had to make sure all my documents had been signed and it was okay to go ahead and make this announcement," she said. "K.D. was supposed to be up here, too." Ruby paused and bowed her head sadly. "We were going to do it jointly."

Lacey was standing next to Delvin now and both seemed to be holding their breath. "K.D. and I were college friends, though we had a falling-out that lasted way too long. It's not important now, but it was over a man. Recently we got together and mended fences. All was forgiven when it turned out he'd left both of us." Ruby apologized for the personal stuff and got back to the point. They were both in the yarn business, and since K.D. was looking to scale back and Ruby was looking to do more, they decided to become partners. Or sort of partners. Ruby now owned a controlling interest in the new enterprise. K.D. had wanted to be the face of the yarn show this last time, though changes had already been made as to how the show would be run and the spaces were priced.

It turned out that blood was thicker than yarn and K.D.'s plan was to have Lacey take over the magazines with Delvin acting as her right-hand man. The look on his face made it clear that he wasn't happy with it. The Knit Style Yarn Studio would now become the Cline Yarn International Studio and would feature all kinds of classes and special events. As an aside, Ruby mentioned she would not be pressing any charges against Thea Scott. Instead they were working out a repayment plan. Any customers who'd bought the needles would be given a refund.

"And finally, I had insisted on a change to the show," Ruby said. "For all these years, K.D. had made it for knitters only, but I said we had to include crocheters. Not only is it a very worthy yarn craft, but as a yarn merchant I'm particularly fond of crocheters, since their craft uses more yarn than knitters."

There was a smattering of laughter at the comment and one very loud cheer. I didn't have to turn to know it came from Adele.

At least now I knew why Paxton had acted so strange that morning. He must have known what his grandmother was going to say.

As Ruby finished, Lacey took the stage. "I appreciate the confidence my mother had in me, but in fairness, I think Delvin and I should run things together." She held her arm out toward him, and he joined her onstage. They hugged and an "aww" went through the crowd.

And then it was back to business as usual. Everyone left the stage but Delvin, and he announced a demonstration of knitting with beads.

So it seemed that everything was settled and I went back to our booth. The crowd was a little thicker now, and business was brisk. Eduardo was finishing a crochet lesson when he called to Adele, "I think you're being paged."

We all stopped and listened. "Will Adele Abrams please come to the stage area," the disembodied voice said.

Adele was out of the booth in a flash, and I followed along behind her, curious about what was going on. When I got to the stage area, I shook my head with disbelief. Two lines of uniformed police officers walked in and took up a position next to the catwalk. They put their arms together and created an archway, and I saw that Eric Humphries, in his full motor uniform, stood at the end. His mother was near him and looked horrified as someone dropped a trail of rose petals under the arch. Adele was speechless as she stood near the beginning of the row of officers, and Eric had to gesture for her to walk through. When she got to the end, he went down on one knee, and I thought his mother was going to faint.

He had a loud cop voice so it was easy to hear what he said. "Adele, you have brought color to my life. You are an exciting and dangerous woman. Will you marry me?" Actually he only got "Will you" out before she started saying yes. Everyone applauded, including the cops, who had lowered their arms. That was when I saw that one of them was Barry. I'd never seen him in his uniform before.

He came over to me when the group broke up. "Eric called me after I left here. It was the least I could do after treating Adele like a suspect all weekend." He shrugged sheepishly. Then he looked at me intently. "Is your neck okay? Is everything else okay? You're happy with Mason?"

I glanced up at him and our eyes met. "You were the one to step away, remember? You even told me how good Mason and I were for each other."

"I didn't say you had to listen," he muttered. Then he was looking at his watch and saying he had to hurry to get to Jeffrey's show.

After that it was all pretty much over. The crowd thinned to nothing and the marketplace finally closed. Mr. Royal came to pack up the booth.

"You did good," he said with a happy smile as he saw how little merchandise was left. Not only had we sold lots of books, tools and yarn, but we'd collected a long list of people interested in the crochet parties. There were other lists of people who wanted to join some of the bookstore groups. We'd given out tons of cards that listed our location and all the things we offered.

CeeCee stopped by before she left. Her eyes were shining.

"That reporter from Channel 3 did an interview with me. It turns out she's a big fan of the Anthony movie, and she said on camera she thought the Oscar buzz was real and that I'd get a nomination when they're announced in a couple of weeks."

Adele took down the banner and threw it away. She looked at the crochet logo that had caused so much trouble. "I'm going to give this to Ruby Cline for her store. She's somebody who will appreciate it."

As I was helping Mr. Royal put the leftovers back into the plastic bins, my phone rang. It was Mason telling me all the final details were taken care of. He'd talked to my son about the trip and he'd been glad to take care of everything while we were gone. "See you soon," he said. "We're going to have a wonderful time."

They were rolling away all the curtain-covered partitions as I got ready to go, and the space had gone from being a bazaar of yarn shops to just a big, empty room. Adele hugged me before she left. "Thank you for everything. I want you to be my maid of honor," she said. "I can't wait to design the dresses."

Dinah knew I was waiting for Mason. "Have fun," she said with a devilish smile. She was off to a line dancing event at the senior center that Commander had organized.

And then I was standing in front of the hotel waiting. I shivered from the chilly air and the anticipation of what was to come.

I heard a siren in the distance, and then it grew louder, and when I looked toward the street, I saw a rescue ambulance fly past. A moment later a small fire truck went by as well. It was drowned out by the thwack of a helicopter as it flew low over the hotel. I heard more sirens and went to the end of the curved driveway to look up the side street. Still with their lights flashing, the equipment had stopped barely a block away. I strained my eyes to see what had happened. The headlights of the fire truck illuminated a tangle of cars. I leaned closer to get a better view, and my breath caught as I saw the familiar black Mercedes on its side. And then I began to run.

Dinah's Granny Square Pins

Supplies: Size 3 (2.10 mm) steel hook
                     1 ball of DMC Cebelia, 50 grams 100%
                     Crochet Cotton (enough to make several pins)
                     8 small pearls or beads
                     Needle or piece of thin wire to get beads onto
                          crochet thread
                     Small safety pin

Note: At the yarn show, Dinah gave out small safety pins to attach
the finished pin with. But you can coat the finished granny square
with fabric stiffener and attach a pin back to it.

Finished Size: Approximately 1¾ inches square
Stitches Used: Chain (ch), slip stitch (sl st), double crochet (dc)

Use needle or wire to string beads onto the crochet thread.
Chain 6 and join with a slip stitch to form a ring.

Round 1: Ch 3 (counts as first dc), move bead up, 2 dc, ch 1,* dc, move bead up, 2dc, ch 1 * repeat from * twice more; attach with sl st to top of the beginning ch 3.

Round 2: Ch 3 (counts as first dc), turn work, 2 dc, ch 1, 3 dc (first corner made), ch 1; * 3 dc, ch 1 3 dc (next corner made) ch 1 * repeat from * twice more; attach with sl st to the top of the beginning ch 3.

Round 3: Ch 3 (counts as first dc), turn work, move bead up, 2 dc, ch 1, 3 dc, ch 1, 3 dc (first corner made), ch 1; * dc, move bead up, 2 dc, ch 1, 3 dc, ch 1, 3 dc (next corner made), ch 1; repeat from * twice more; attach with sl st to the top of the beginning chain 3. Fasten off and weave in ends.

Adele's Stash Buster Wrap

Supplies: Size L (8.00 mm) hook or size needed to obtain
gauge

Approximately 400 yards of assorted bulky
weight yarn. If you're using lighter-weight
yarn, you can use a double strand.

Tapestry needle

Large kilt pin or other shawl pin

Finished Size: Approximately 52 inches × 16 inches

Stitches Used: Chain (ch), single crochet (sc), double
crochet (dc)

Gauge: 8 double crochet stitches = 4 inches
2 double crochet rows = 2 inches

Note: You might want to decide in advance in what order you'd
like to add the new yarn.

Ch 100 loosely

Row 1: Sc in second chain from hook and across. 99 stitches made.

Row 2: Ch 3 (counts as first dc) and turn work. Dc across.

Row 3: Repeat row 2.

Row 4: Repeat row 2.

Row 5: Ch 1 and turn work, sc across.

Repeat rows 2–5 until the work is approximately 16 inches, ending with a row 5 row. Add new yarn as other runs out.

Fasten off and weave in ends with tapestry needle.

To wear, overlap the ends and hold in place with a kilt pin or shawl pin.

Bob's Oatmeal Power Squares

3 cups rolled oats
1 cup organic brown sugar, packed
2 teaspoons ground cinnamon
2 teaspoons nonaluminum baking powder
1 teaspoon salt
2 large eggs
1 cup milk
2 teaspoons vanilla extract
½ cup butter, melted
¾ cup mixed raisins, dried cranberries, dried cherries,
    dried blueberries (or dried fruit of your choice)
1 cup chopped walnuts
Paper baking cups

Preheat oven to 350 degrees. Generously grease a 9 × 13 pan.

In a large bowl combine oats, brown sugar, cinnamon, baking powder and salt.

In a separate bowl beat the eggs. Mix in milk, vanilla and melted butter. Add to the oat mixture and blend. Sprinkle in the dried fruit and chopped walnuts.

Spread in the greased pan. Bake for 40 minutes. Cool completely before cutting into squares. Put into paper baking cups to serve.

Makes about 24 squares.

Bob's Linzer Torte Cookie Bars

1½ cups flour
1½ cups powdered sugar
1½ cup ground walnuts
¾ cup softened butter cut into pieces
1 teaspoon ground cinnamon
1 cup raspberry preserves

Preheat oven to 375 degrees. Grease a 10 × 15 pan.

In a large bowl mix flour, powdered sugar, walnuts and cinnamon. Cut in the butter using a pastry blender until the mixture is crumbly.

Spread ⅔ of the crumbly mixture in the pan and press down. Spread the raspberry preserves on the crust. Sprinkle the rest of the crumbly mixture on top and pat down gently.

Bake for approximately 20–25 minutes until golden brown. Cool completely before cutting into bars.

Makes about 42 bars.